Crossroads Magic

Dixie Jo Jarchow

Published by Wintergreen Books, 2024.

CROSSROADS MAGIC

First edition. July 8, 2024.

ISBN: 979-8227636362

Written by Dixie Jo Jarchow.

Also by Dixie Jo Jarchow

The Hunt for Mel's Gold
Hades' Redemption
Huntress Moon
The Gingerbread Man
Walking In the Graveyard
Crossroads Magic

Watch for more at dixiejojarchow.com.

I'd like to thank all my beta readers: Tom, Jules, Maggie and Mike. Also the Oshkosh Area Writers Club for their support.

Chapter One

Nothing says midwestern Thanksgiving like a green jello mold. Liv Hermes placed the plate with the shiny, vibrating mound on the table. Lumps of pineapple, horseradish and diced cucumbers swam in a murky sea of lime jello. The long, heavy table, filled elbow to elbow with her family, utilized all the leaves but still overflowed onto a separate card table for kids, crammed into the corner. A collective groan rose.

The Lake House had plenty of room for everyone at the big table in the dining room. So why was the entire family crammed into her sibling's bursting house here in Minnesota? Not to mention Liv was sleeping on the floor. At the Lake House, everyone would have had accommodations, at least a couch. She longed to stretch her aching back and hear the pops of each vertebra as it released.

Liv frowned. She was the oldest of the four siblings and stood at the head of the big table, vibrating jello on a plate before her. On her right was James, who she got along best with in the family. The only one she got along with. The rest of her siblings were in somewhat of a truce with her, at best. Not open combat, but more of a cold war where barbs were thrust under their breath, but no punches were exchanged. When they were younger, there'd been some punches thrown and hair pulled but they were too mature for that now.

"Come on, it's tradition!" Said Liv. It represented the way their family used to be under their parents' watchful eye.

"Can we skip the jello next year? It's the grossest and no one eats it," one of the kids said.

"You mean you aren't looking forward to the red version at Christmas?" Asked the child's mother.

"It doesn't taste bad," said Liv. "And it's part of the Thanksgiving and Christmas traditions of the Hermes family." No one would have uttered a peep if her mother presented the jello. Liv felt like an outsider in her own family.

"Let's vote," said James.

"We will not be here for Christmas, but I'd vote 'no' if we were staying," said one of the wives. "Our family is going to Acapulco!" She presented the announcement like it was a gift.

A cheer came from the table except for Liv, who ground her teeth.

"We were going to meet at the Lake House. All of us," she said. "That was the plan."

Her sister said, "I vote for Acapulco."

"There's room in our rental. Everyone can come," said Philip. His wife sent him a look which he entirely missed. "We rented a house for a week. Cost us a mint. If everyone wants to come and split it, that'd be great."

"Is that a per person split or per family?" James asked.

"Per family," said the wife. They had three children and James had two children.

"Let's do it. We've got money from dad's and mom's estate. Here we come, Acapulco!" Said her sister.

"The whole idea of me having the Lake House as my inheritance was that we use it for family events," said Liv. "I don't have the money to just run off for a couple of weeks." Her two brothers and sister had agreed to split the money left when their mother and father died and she would keep the immense Lake House for family gatherings. No one wanted to sell the memories the Lake House held, plus they wanted the money more than the memories. To Liv, everything good was tied to the house in her own idealized version of history.

"Acapulco! Acapulco!" The kids chanted. Hard to argue with the frigid temps frosting the windows outside. Flakes swirled and blew apart like the pieces of her family.

Philip's wife got out a sheet of paper and a calculator to figure the cost per family for the Acapulco trip. "Everyone pays for their own airfare." She smirked.

"Because you already locked in a great fare for her family," said Liv's sister.

Liv watched the green jello shake as different people moved to sit down at the table.

"Are you in, Liv?" Asked James.

"When is she ever part of this family?" Asked her sister.

Liv sucked in a breath and her bravado crumbled. She towered over the family whether they stood or were seated. She was tall and thin, while everyone else in the Hermes clan had dark hair and eyes and was short and heavyset. What really set her apart was the bright, pale hair. James called it Lutheran Blonde. Liv wore it long and it hung in a straight sheath of white past her shoulders.

"I think I'll pass. If I was going to go somewhere, it wouldn't be Acapulco."

"Where would it be?" Asked James.

"I don't know," she said, after a long pause. Had anyone ever asked her what she wanted before?

"They have great sunscreen now, if you're worried about burning," he said. Liv's skin was paper white, unlike her olive-skinned siblings.

Where would she go if she could go anywhere? Her mind was blank and unwilling to speculate.

Liv spent her days writing grants in a small office without a window. It used to be a closet but corporate made it an office instead of giving her a bump in pay. It was ideal work for an introvert who loved to generate paper in orderly sections and fill out blanks and be left alone.

"Liv, are you in there?" Her sister snapped her fingers in front of Liv's face.

"Ewww, who went heavy on the horseradish in the jello?" Asked her other brother.

"I used mom's old recipe!" Liv shouted at him. "Next time *you* make the jello."

"No one even likes the stupid jello. No jello next year," he decreed. "Who's with me?"

Raucous yells filled the table. The youngsters took it up without even knowing what they were yelling about and banged their tiny little fists on the card table. The plates and silverware chattered with each hit.

Liv wanted to scream back, but the air wouldn't come out of her lungs. She picked up the offending plate of jello. It slid from side to side on the plate. It was hard to balance and Liv hesitated, her intention unclear. Liv spent her whole morning in her sister in law's kitchen, creating this masterpiece of lime and horseradish, for these ungrateful jerks.

"To heck with this." Liv heaved the plate of jello at the middle of the table. It bounced off the turkey intact and rolled down the table, knocking into tableware and bouncing onto the baby's tray. There was a collective gasp as the baby opened and closed her mouth, gnawing on the green blob.

Dead silence. Then pandemonium as everyone tried to speak at once. The baby's mother, pried the jello away from her child with one swift yank and swiped her finger through baby Jane's outraged mouth.

Baby Jane grabbed a tiny handful of green goo off the front of her high chair and popped it in her mouth.

"*She* likes mom's jello!" Liv yelled over the noise and left the room. Her long legs flew up the stairs to her room and she began to pack.

She heard someone on the stairs. James, the peacemaker, she bet. Every family had one.

"Sis, are you okay?"

"I'm fine," she said.

"You're packing," said James.

"Yeah, I'm going back to the Lake House. The house that we all agreed I should take as part of my inheritance so you could get more cash. The house that we agreed we would meet at for holidays. The house that is crushing me with repairs already, big and small. And all I wanted was to have family gatherings there." Liv began to cry. "That poor baby. Her mother is never going to forgive me."

"Baby Jane loved the jello," countered James.

More steps on the stairs. "Here comes retribution and guilt," said James. "Leave the tears on your cheeks."

Filling the doorway, her other brother put a hand on each side of the door frame. "Do you even care that baby Jane might have suffocated? I will never come to that stupid Lake House. You wanted it, you can rot in it." His wrath showed in the way his heavy jowls shook as he pronounced his judgment.

He looked for the door to slam but it opened the other way. So, instead he stomped down the stairs.

James shook his head and imitated the jowls shaking. Liv smothered her giggles until James started laughing. Her belly hurt but it was good to laugh so hard with her brother.

"A pompous jerk, as usual," said James.

"I really should apologize. Do I look like I've been laughing about a baby smothered in green jello?"

"No, but you can't keep a straight face. You know you'll laugh. Keep it short."

"I'll smooth it over and all will be well."

James shook his head. "I don't think things will ever be the same. Next you'll be seeing Elves and fairies again."

"Never again," said Liv, her voice low. "You can engrave that on my tombstone. And in the mealtime, I never want that brought up again." The remark about her seeing fairies evoked a horrible misunderstanding that had pretty much wrecked her young life. Her family never forgave and never forgot. It was constantly brought up that she'd seen a fairy in the garden.

"You're a real jerk for bringing that up right now."

"What are brothers for?"

Liv started unpacking. She would apologize and make this right. Family was important to her. Her mood sank as she descended each step back to the dining room.

Liv stood at the doorway. Everyone turned to watch her. She took her seat at the head of table, opposite baby Jane who sported a change of clothing and wet hair.

"I'm sorry I threw the jello."

A soft chant started of "jello, jello." It was quickly hushed by the parents. Everyone waited expectantly but that was all Liv had to offer.

"I just thought we would be meeting more often at the Lake House. That was the whole reason for keeping it: so the family could gather there. I may as well sell it." Liv played her trump card.

"Let's not go over this old fight again," said her brother. Protests murmured and eyes rolled. No one wanted to lose the house. Their whole lives had been lived there.

"You all love the idea of the Lake House and gatherings but it's a fantasy for you, like Santa Claus. Not real."

A collective gasp startled her. She'd forgotten the children, most under ten, who still believed in St. Nick and his abundant gifts.

The little ones burst into tears, one after another. The older children fought it with trembling lips but the pull of the other children's tears made them cry too.

"What is wrong with you?" Her brother Philip snapped. "You have no heart at all."

Liv said, "Sorry" and left to finish packing her bags. No one came up the stairs to talk her out of it this time.

Chapter Two

Liv scrolled through the internet while sitting on the overstuffed blue couch. It faced the panoramic wall of glass windows that provided spectacular images of Lake Michigan in the throes of November. Angry black seas tipped with white against a pearl gray sky. Usually those images soothed Liv but today, they just reminded her of winter and high heating bills along with it. A brisk chilling wind made its way through the old windows and she pulled her sweater closer. The Thanksgiving parade marched past on the tv with the sound off.

Her big reveal of the evening? Taking the house as her portion of the inheritance had been a bad bargain. No one wanted to dump it but the upkeep was going to slowly suffocate Liv like a beloved boa constrictor. She considered selling it but discounted the idea almost immediately. She could never sell this house that her dad had built for the family so long ago. Too many memories in these walls. Walls that needed repainting, she noticed.

Maybe rent it out? The thought of other people in her house was distasteful. And she'd seen some of the videos where people trashed the rentals. It would be heartbreaking.

Liv watched a video of an aurora on her meditation app. So relaxing the way it shimmered and moved across the sky. An ad popped up on her feed for glass dome hotels in Iceland. How did the algorithm know? For every person scrolling right now, and there had to be millions, the internet sent ads that touched on something they were interested in. Kind of scary.

Those glass igloos were gorgeous against the white snow and inky sky as the aurora danced above. It would never work; Liv was perpetually cold. She should go somewhere. Liv had some savings in her "fix the roof" fund. She knew she'd be bitter with envy that everyone was warming their toes in the sand while she huddled in front of the fire, waiting for the inevitable flood of photos.

Another ad for Iceland popped up. Liv clicked it away before she could consider it. The mountains were amazing and the waterfalls. Wow. Work had been bugging her to take her three weeks of vacation. Maybe she would.

Was there anywhere she wanted to go? She didn't have her heart set on Iceland. She pulled on her wool socks and snuggled under a throw. Tropical spots would fry her pale skin. No fun to spend the whole time bathed in sunblock and coverups. Would anywhere make her family jealous and wait for *her* photos?

None of her family had been to Iceland whereas several had gone to Europe. Was her passport ready? Ireland might be fun but Liv didn't want to go anywhere there was the possibility she would be involved in violence. She didn't trust her luck. That left out whole swaths of the earth. Australia and New Zealand had magnificent scenery but also the top eleven venomous snakes and spiders.

A random factoid came up in her scrolling: Iceland didn't have snakes. Was it true? All signs pointed to Iceland. Iceland, it was. Liv sighed.

Plan in place, she scrolled for a great flight price and whooped when she got it. Everyone apparently left Iceland when winter came. Accommodations were more difficult and she settled for joining onto a small tour group that already had rooms reserved in several youth hostels. Liv planned her itinerary around them and other points of interest near them.

Next, she notified work. None of the schools she worked with were in session over the holidays so getting the info she needed for grants right now was always tough.

Should she rent the Lake House out? The money would help with replacing the money she used on the trip.

"Let's throw caution to the wind!" Liv found an agency to list it and filled out the online form. She took some pictures and sent them off, hoping it wasn't a scam. All of her stuff was pretty much in one room. Her parents had died in February and she blushed, thinking her stuff was still in boxes awaiting unpacking. Should she get a camera to watch the people who might rent it? The cameras were reasonably priced but did she want to spend her vacation monitoring her home?

Time to make her To-Do lists. Northern Lights, Christmas in Reykjavik, the Blue Lagoon, whale watching, driving the Ring Road. Looking at the list of activities, Liv could easily fill three weeks.

Work flew by and Liv smiled every day as she completed mundane tasks like stopping her mail and hiring someone to shovel in case of snow. She had talked to James several times but he hadn't mentioned Acapulco so she had avoided mentioning Iceland.

Liv was at the airport with her two small bags, when she summoned the courage to call James.

"I'm going to Iceland for the holidays."

"Iceland? I couldn't even find that on a map. I thought you couldn't afford to go anywhere." The accusation in his voice made Liv's heart ache just a little. James sounded like the rest of her family.

"I took it out of the roof fund. Plus I rented out the Lake House through an agency to make some money. I'm at the airport right now, waiting to board."

"The airport? Was this an impulsive move or did you plan it? The Acapulco thing didn't work out for us anyway. I was going to call you to see if you wanted company for a couple of weeks at the Lake House since we aren't going anywhere. I'm sorry for not letting you know earlier, I just assumed you would be there."

"Oh," Liv deflated and her shoulders dropped. "I'm sorry I won't be there. What happened?"

"There was a fight over whether baby Jane counted as a share. It got really nasty with the wives."

"Let me guess, They didn't think she should count since she didn't need a seat on the flight."

"Got it in one."

"At least the jello didn't cause any permanent damage," said Liv.

"Ha, don't think you're out of the woods yet, sis. It was brought up during the fight."

"The jello? You've got to be kidding. That was almost three weeks ago!"

"And it will never be forgotten: the jello and the outing of Santa. You've scarred children for life."

"I was hoping the Battle of Acapulco would supplant me as the Bad Angel of Christmas."

"Philip's family is still going. Now she's bitching about how expensive it will be to rent the whole house when they only have two adults and three kids. Serves her right."

"Wasn't she kind of mad when Philip first brought up the idea?"

"Yeah, that's what is so crazy. First, she didn't want anyone along and now, it's vital when she realized how much money she could save. She's certifiable. When they find out you went on a trip by yourself without consulting them, they're going to be pissed, especially the wives. There's supposed to be a category one tropical storm slash hurricane the week they are there. Wouldn't it serve them right?"

"That's an evil thought," but Liv smiled into the phone.

"Who are these people living in our house?"

"Now it's 'Our House'? I don't know who they are, only that the management group has vetted them and taken a deposit." Her flight was called over the speaker and Liv's breath caught. It was really happening. "Listen, they called my flight. I have to go."

"Text me when you get there," said James

"No, it might be expensive. I'll email. Love you. Sorry for traumatizing your kids."

"I think they already forgot. No lasting trauma. No harm done to our household. Just the shattered dreams of parents trying to keep up the magic a little longer. I'm sure they would have heard the news at daycare anyway."

"I'm sorry it had to be me."

"You were already in the well anyway for throwing the jello at the baby."

"I did not throw the jello at the baby. It just happened."

"I've retold that story at least eight times at work. It's already a classic and your aim gets better each time."

Chapter Three

Liv's muscles were tightly coiled as she found her seat in the spacious plane. What was she thinking, going to Iceland? The Lake House needed work and the money she used for this stupid revenge trip could have and should have been used to fix the roof. She would have driven home now except that a family had rented the Lake House. She could have had a cozy Lake House Christmas with James and his family except for this impetuous mistake.

She ate the snacks she packed before the plane even took off. She popped the calming gummy, closed her eyes and stepped quickly into strange, vivid dreams. Witches chased her, throwing spells to prove there was really magic. Fairies with sharp teeth grappled with her, tearing at her clothes. She re-lived when she'd seen a Fairy in their garden and ran to tell her mother and father. She was six and her credibility wasn't the greatest, but she stuck to her belief that she'd seen a Fairy for the next four years. She'd lived through the vicious teasing and daily taunting of her family as well as schoolmates and teachers. Had she really seen one or had she dreamed it? To this day, it wasn't clear in her mind. The chemical odor of the plane stung her nostrils.

Mature Liv knew there wasn't any magic in the world, no Fairies, Fae or Witches. Liv knew it in her heart and in the most secret parts of herself. She believed in facts, figures and charts, things she could count and verify. She had the soul of an accountant.

Liv woke when the plane bounced lightly onto the tarmac. Her stomach clenched as the last residue of the gummy moved out of her system, leaving her groggy and disoriented. The airport was deserted, except for her fellow passengers and she hoisted her backpack and headed to the taxi area. She was scheduled to meet up with a tour to go to the hostel and then Glymur Waterfall after that. Hostels were booked for the three night sightseeing tour so she just had to get to the meeting in the morning of the tour and get on the van.

For her first travel experience in a long time, Liv thought a woman-only tour would work the best for her. Maybe she would make a friend or two, although the introvert inside mocked her. She'd be lucky if she talked to anyone. She grabbed the shuttle van along with others who were going to the hostel. Some of them had to be her tour group and she watched them with interest.

An older couple holding hands took the front but the rest were women. Women mostly older than she was, some with white hair. They looked like they could be lively, if prodded. She wasn't much of a prodder though. They spoke quietly among themselves and had definitely read the tour book about dressing warmly. They resembled the Amish with their long skirts, capes and sturdy shoes. One lady had a muff which went out of fashion in the 30s. Liv thought she would keep an eye out for one on the trip.

It was almost an hour ride through the darkness to the hostel. Liv could smell the water of the fjord on her left and occasionally glimpse it when the moon allowed. On the right was a mostly flat land with hillocks covered in moss and small bushes. Everything had a smattering of snow on it, Not the huge winter landscape she'd been warned about. To someone from Wisconsin, this was nothing.

The van jolted to a stop and Liv piled out with the group. She grabbed her key from the front desk clerk and escaped to her room. Liv took a single which was more expensive than rooming with someone but she wasn't quite up to bunking with a stranger right now. There was a nice desk, a bed and a long couch with storage.

Traveling made her feel like a sheen of soot covered her. The bathroom was a community one and Liv took her bag and showered quickly. The less time naked, the better. Liv stifled a huge yawn and plugged in her phone. Their tour started at nine tomorrow morning.

The breakfast bar was included with her stay and she resolved not to miss it. A polite knock tapped on her door.

"Who is it?" She asked through the door.

"Minerva. You don't know me but the hostel is out of space. Can I stay in this room just for tonight?"

"Hold on." Liv called the front desk and heard a recorded message that the inn was full.

She cracked open the door and saw a short woman with dark red hair and wild eyebrows that reached out from her face like tentacles. She wore the black dress and sturdy shoes of everyone else in her group. "Are you part of the tour group tomorrow?" Liv asked.

"Yes, our whole group is going on the tour."

"Well, come on in. I'm tagging along with that group too. The single woman crew, right?"

"Yes, that's us, except we had some cancellations at the last minute and added an older couple to make the trip more reasonable. They seem pretty harmless. Thanks for taking me in. I was going to sleep on the floor of one of the other's rooms but it is so damned cold."

Liv's feet were so frigid they stuck to the floor. "What kind of group are you?"

"Oh, just like-minded women traveling together." She slid off her dark long skirt and overcloak and laid them on the spare chair. Minerva dug into the thick white comforter that laid on the couch. Liv noticed the abundance of dark hair on Minerva's legs. Taking women's lib a bit too far, in her opinion. Who was she to talk? She hadn't even brought a shaver with her. Space was an expensive item on an international trip. Plus, her hair on her legs, as everywhere, was thin and almost white. She didn't need to shave most of the time. Her lack of love life certainly didn't warrant it.

"You almost look like Amish or nuns. You're all dressed in dark long skirts and the long black cape kind of thing and the sturdy dark shoes."

Minerva laughed. "I guess we do. We aren't Amish and definitely not nuns!" Still chuckling, Minerva pulled the heavy comforter over her head and went to sleep.

Liv's alarm went off the next morning and she yawned, cracking her jaw. Minerva's wild dark hair lay spread across her pillow but it was all that was visible of her. Liv grabbed her clothes which she had laid out and her bathroom kit and opened the door as quietly as she could. At least Minerva hadn't snored.

"Yikes!" Liv found another dark clad woman outside her door, just about to knock.

"Sorry, I'm here to wake Minerva. I'm Gale," she said. She was taller than Minerva and not as thin. A solid, middle aged brick of a woman with steel gray hair, cut short like a helmet. She wore glasses with sparkles on the sides.

Not knowing what else to do, Liv held out her hand. Gale frowned, her lips pursed tightly.

"Go ahead and wake her. I have my key," Liv gritted her teeth, slightly offended that her hand had been refused but went on to take her shower and wash it from her mind. When she came out, Minerva was gone and the couch was remade as if she had never been there. Liv checked her room safe and closet and was pleased her instincts about the woman had been correct. Nothing was missing. She headed down to the breakfast buffet.

Minerva waved to her from her table of darklings and Liv smiled and waved back. Ravens was a more accurate description of what they looked like. They were certainly solemn as they picked at their food. Liv went through the breakfast line and by the time she was through, Minerva had cleared a space for her to sit with them.

"This is ..."

"I'm Liv Hermes. I'm part of your tour group."

"Liv graciously allowed me to bunk in her spare bed last night. We had a tour member cancel so we're pleased you could jump in and help us defray the costs. Here's a copy of our itinerary."

"Thanks for the itinerary, I have a copy." Liv accepted one anyway to make sure they matched.

"Today we're going to the Glymur Waterfall. It's the second tallest in Iceland. It used to be the highest but recently another higher waterfall was found off a glacier, so it fell to number two," said Minerva. "It's remote and no one visits it anymore, even though they can't get to the one on the glacier."

Liv smiled at the excitement in Minerva's voice. She was much more interested in the Northern Lights and the access to the hot springs. She wouldn't mind seeing a dormant volcanic rift or some mountains. A small, sturdy shuttle pulled up during breakfast. Liv got in line near the end with Minerva clinging to her side.

When they sat down together, Liv started scribbling furiously.

"What are you writing?" Asked Minerva.

"Trying to remember everyone's name from breakfast," Liv said.

"Gale is the tall one. Not as tall as you but tall in our group. Banya wasn't sitting with us. Bea was on your right."

Liv scribbled a rough description of each. Bea was easy because she was the oldest and seemed in charge. Gale was taller but Banya, she couldn't place. She hoped she could sort them out by the end of the trip. Minerva had red hair and wild eyebrows. The two elderly people got on the bus. They looked very similar to each other.

"Do you know the couple's name?" Asked Liv, wanting to complete her roster.

"No, I don't recall. Like you, they are filling out the tour to keep the price down."

Liv would make a point to meet them as soon as they got to the waterfall.

"Have you heard of Wicca?" Minerva leaned her head together with Liv as they sat together in the small van. It was a eight-seater plus the driver. When all their luggage had been piled in the back, the van was stuffed.

"Is that witches and stuff?"

"More like having a deep relationship with mother nature. We're all Wiccan from the same coven. Wicca is a pagan, earth-centered practice. We're Esbats, which means our goddess works through the cycles of the Moon." Minerva actually held her breath waiting for a response from Liv.

"Well, that's cool that you all travel together," was the best, most supportive thing she could come up with. Magic in all its manifestations was a taboo topic for Liv.

"This is our first, you know, major trip. We're going to do a sacred ceremony at the Glymur. It's an intensely serious thing. I'd invite you but it's very, you know, private and sacred. We go out into the plateau overlooking the river and...."

"No problem," Liv held up her hands. She didn't want to be privy to any sort of fake magic stuff. "I am going to go on the lower Waterfall Trail. I just hope it's passable in the winter. The guide book advises against it but it doesn't look like there's been much snow here." Liv frowned.

"There should be no problem with either trail right now. Did you wear hiking boots?" Asked Bea.

"Yes and I'm from Wisconsin. We get anywhere from 50 to 100 inches."

"Wow. We've got to make the most of our five hours of sunlight, right?" Said Minerva to no one in particular. Liv thought the advertised sunlight thing was overrated. It was gloomy and overcast. A thin covering of snow topped the hillocks and filled the crevices making for a checkerboard effect. The whole world seemed black and white, with green mosses peaking through here and there.

The van driver introduced himself as Galen and gave a running commentary on the intercom as they drove through the desolate country. Occasionally an Icelandic pony raised its head to monitor their progress. Steam escaped from the ground everywhere she looked. The thin tendrils filtered through the ground and disappeared into the gray sky.

"This barely counts as our quotient of sunlight," said Minerva.

"I think this might be as good as we get. I read there are gnats or mites that can swarm and make it hard to breathe," said Gale.

"Gale, right? They wouldn't be alive in the winter, would they?" Asked Liv.

"This isn't much of a winter," said Gale.

"What do you do, back home?" Asked Liv.

"I live in England. I'm a lab tech for a water testing company. We try to keep our personal life separate from our spiritual life."

"How do you guys get together?" Liv was fascinated.

"We have an online private chat room where we meet on a regular basis and do our rituals. Each meeting has an agenda and runs according to Robert's Rules."

"Robert's Rules?"

"It's a parliamentary procedure. All very proper."

"I love your accent," said Liv.

"We can pick out you Americans from the first word," said Gale.

"Or our shoes, right?"

"If they wear gym shoes, right. Your boots look quality," Gale said.

"They are comfortable. I thought we'd be doing a lot of walking," said Liv.

The van turned into a side road. The ground was tan to dark gray where it showed through the snow. The gravel parking lot sloped down and two trailheads were visible at the edge.

The van driver pulled a sweater on and announced, "It's going to be a lot cooler on the plateau trail, those who are going that way should dress accordingly. It's also cold on the canyon waterfall trail." Which, by elimination, meant it was cold everywhere but on the bus, Liv thought.

The four Esbats huddled together around a map. Liv stood alone with her stuffed green backpack. The two elderly people were together off to the side.

"We four are going up the plateau trail. We are going to perform a ritual and we would appreciate some privacy," Bea said. Minerva carried a small backpack and the other two stood with them.

"You aren't going with them?" The van driver asked her.

"No, I'm not part of their group," said Liv.

"We'll be fine. We have studied the map," said Gale.

"Ho ho, this area is tricky. The map might not do you any good if the Elves don't like you. It's a true story about this waterfall, you know," said Galen.

"Pfft!" Bea waved her hand at him dismissively. "We'll stay on the path. Are there wild animals here?"

"No, worse, angry Elves. If they don't want you on their waterfall, they'll move the trail or confuse you so you can't find your way. The walk to the Falls on the right is generally safe. No one ever got hurt there unless they did something stupid." Galen looked at Liv. "Stay on the trail and don't do anything stupid."

"What about people who come here without a guide? There must be hundreds of them every year," said Bea.

"Not so many since it is now the second highest waterfall. Plus, the Elves and Forest folk were acting up a few years back. It's better to just avoid Glymur right now, believe me. It's off the Ring Road so less publicized." At their blank looks, he added, "The Ring Road is the road that goes around the whole of the island. Most take the lower path. The high path? Some of them come back and some of them don't." He shrugged.

"We'll take full responsibility for ourselves," Bea told him.

The van driver threw up his hands and said, "It's very dangerous in winter. I won't wait for you."

"You won't have to," she retorted.

The Esbats moved off following Bea. Their trail was open for about a hundred feet but then quickly disappeared around a bend. Liv and the van driver watched the landscape swallow them.

"I hope the waterfall Elves like them. The women are pagan, so the chances are decent. You can go on by yourself to the lower Waterfall Trail. No Elves there, usually. Turn around before the first bridge and come back. You'll see that there's a cord across the river but no log. I advise you that it is dangerous, not just because of the slippery ground. I'm going to wait here three hours, no longer. The weather looks like it might change and I want to be drinking hot cocoa by then."

Liv was shocked he openly discussed something like Elves. It made her want to slink and hide, anticipating an avalanche of ridicule. It would have been that way back home. She smiled and walked away. Liv approached the elderly pair. They wore nearly identical clothing: sturdy, well worn boots, dark pants tucked into them. The ensemble was topped by heavy sweaters with turtlenecks underneath. They each had a bottle of water clipped on their belt and a foldable hat. Only the colors of the sweaters differed.

"Are you guys going on the trail? I'm Liv by the way."

"We are the Volks, Jin and Jane. We'll go as far as the river with you," Jin said. They were thin and frail looking, with pale wisps of white hair that showed pink scalps. Liv worried about them on a serious trail.

"I'm not sure it's safe to go farther," said Liv.

"Don't cross the river, the log isn't there right now," said Jane parroting the van driver's warning.

Liv smiled. They were worried about her. They should be worried about a fall for themselves. She turned and took a deep breath and headed down the trail. The trail started out wide and relatively smooth. Her heart was pounding as she made the first turn and slid out of sight of the van driver. All that stuff about angry Elves unsettled her. The trail became rockier until Liv started questioning her choice. The path led sharply upward. What if she twisted an ankle? Her pace slowed when she realized she was leaving the Volks behind. She hurried back to check on them.

"Don't worry about us, dear. We'll just putter along. We're going to look at the river and then we'll wait for you," said Jin.

"We don't want to trespass where we're not wanted," said Jane. Jin patted her hand which was tucked into his elbow.

"Don't worry, my dear. We'll be fine," Jin reassured her.

At least they had someone to go for help if one of them did fall. Liv felt better that they were going to wait for her. If one of them did fall, she could rescue them. The river was fast and narrow, bits of it covered with snow and ice. It might be tricky for an elder to continue on the trail. "I won't be gone long." Liv turned and climbed the narrow trail.

"Lovely," Liv breathed out. "Nothing sinister could live here. It's too gorgeous."

She'd been foolish to let the van driver spook her about the area. It was a special treat to be alone in this ancient place. Gray green moss hugged the rocks that rose in towering cliffs, making them seem soft and welcoming. The water of the Botnsa River flowed strongly, even in December. Liv couldn't see the falls but the mountains and valleys spread before her. The sound of breaking glass came to her and she realized it was the unique sound of these falls echoing off the high, narrow canyon walls.

The trail appeared to be a dead-end but as she got closer to the spot, the trail took an abrupt left turn into a cave.

Liv hesitated but only for a moment. The cave wasn't dark although the low ceiling made her duck. She could see there were two exits but they were so close, either one would work. The cave was much cooler and damper inside the rock. Liv lost her footing in the wet gravel once but soon the cave opened up into a glorious view of the river again. The multiple openings alleviated her dread of closed spaces.

The air and light made Liv realize she'd been holding tension in her shoulders and back. She rolled her shoulders and swung her arms from the waist. It was a little scary that the van driver, Galen, thought it was unsafe and she was by herself. Liv took a glance back at the cave, remembering the slippery rocks. This was probably as safe as it was to go, but something urged Liv on.

The trail was steep as she traversed down to the river's edge. Someone had built wooden log steps into the trail and Liv was grateful for them. A large snowflake meandered past her face. The van driver had been worried about a change in the weather.

Up ahead on the trail was the bridge. An inch thick cable was strung across the river. There wasn't any log. Water burbled along at times covered by a thin layer of snow. It formed a delightful counterpoint to the sound of the falls farther up the river.

Liv imagined the rocks under the water would be slick. Her boots would get wet. She looked down and frowned. The Volks had warned her not to cross the river. So had Galen, their van driver. Wet feet the rest of the day and possibly the trip? Who knew how fast her new boots would dry. Her boots were water proofed but Liv didn't put much stock in how long the chemical spray she'd used could hold out. The stream of water was too wide to jump and flowed pure and clear as it rushed along. Ice and a smattering of snow made it impossible to tell what was solid and what was merely slick rock.

The gurgle as the water jumped over the rocks was amazing. The van driver told her Glymur was dangerous in the winter but the four witches insisted this was crucial to their reason for the trip to Iceland. Something about a ceremony they were performing.

Liv looked up at the cliffs on either side of the river to see if she could catch a glimpse of her tour mates but the cliffs rose vertically and towered over her and it was impossible to see. She made the final turn to look at the river crossing. Liv, ever cautious, decided against getting her boots wet.

At the other side of the river, a small man with one foot in the water, struggled to free his foot from under a rock. He cursed vividly in several languages.

Chapter Four

As Liv approached, she expected the man to get bigger from her perspective but the man stayed small. Was he a dwarf or a midget? He had a cap on his head so it was impossible for her to tell if his head was large or not.

"Can I help you?" She called.

The man paused in his tirade, turned his head to look at Liv and squeaked. "Get away. I didn't do anything."

"I'm sure you didn't. Can I help you free your foot?"

He studied her for a moment. "Yeah, help me if you dare. I thought you were one of those things with your white hair and being so scrawny."

"A ghost? Nope." Liv smiled. One of her frequent and hated nicknames was 'Ghost.' Liv pulled on the cable. It was tight. To heck with the wet boots. The man was in trouble. Liv decided the bits of snow probably had rocks under them. It took a moment for the water to get into her boot once she stepped onto the first rock. When it did, eeeyah it was cold. She fairly flew across the river to escape the frigid water.

The dwarf's foot was wedged under a large round boulder. Half of the boulder was submerged in the river. His foot must be numb after being trapped.

Liv examined the rocks and decided which one would be the key to freeing the man. She wrapped both hands around the rock but it wouldn't budge. It was too slippery to get a good hold on. Liv looked around and found a sturdy stick and made a crude lever to help lift the rock.

"Ready? Now." She groaned and the rock finally moved a tiny bit. She could feel the rough wood of the branch scraping her hands. She wished she'd worn her gloves.

The dwarf groaned and slid his foot back out of the hole. He stood up and kicked the rock. Letting out a howl when his foot made contact with it.

Liv laughed. It just bubbled up and came out. And she was sorry about it because the little man started cursing her and ran lightly across the remaining rocks, crossing the last two without even touching the cable. He scurried down the trail. His gait was odd but he moved quickly in almost a skip. He threw something back at her. A magnificent throw for such a small creature. It landed right at the edge of the water in front of Liv.

"You're a right arse wipe," he yelled back at her in accented English.

"He moves fast for a little guy," muttered Liv. "And what is this?" She moved to the edge of the water and picked up a small silver locket with a red stone in the middle. A heavy silver chain held it and Liv admired the workmanship. Ruins were etched around the setting that held the red stone and Liv wondered what they meant.

The locket tingled in her hands and the vibration moved until it seemed like electricity shot through all her limbs. Liv yelped and dropped the locket but instead of falling to the ground, it fell into her coat pocket. The stinging faded and Liv wondered if she'd imagined it.

"You're welcome," she yelled.

The forest echoed back at her: "Arse wipe."

Chapter Five

Liv held the cable to make her way back over the river. It was frigid and her fingers were numb. At least if she fell in, it wasn't too deep here. She kept the other hand out for balance and chose her stepping stones carefully. Her boots were already wet so about halfway through, she walked through the water holding onto the cable, without regard for whether her pants got soaked. Liv hit a brisk pace and rounded the trail to where she could see the Volks couple. They waved when they saw her and tut-tutted over her wet pants and boots.

The pants were a brand that was supposed to shed water easily, but she was shivering by the time she walked up to the Volks. Jane put a hand around her waist and Liv noticed the pants were almost dry. Maybe the super fabric just needed a minute.

"Jump up and down a few times, it will help dry your socks and boots," Jin told her. She looked around but no one was watching. Liv jumped a few times. Jin held onto her hand. She did feel warmer. Her feet and hands were almost toasty. Old folks knew stuff. Liv smiled at them and the three walked together back to the van. Liv felt something in her pocket.

"I helped a dwarf who had his foot stuck and he gave me this," she held out the amulet. Jin and Jane both took a step away from her, their mouths open. "What's the matter?"

The couple looked at each other and smiled. "You accepted it," said Jane.

"He threw it at me, but yes, I picked it up. More to see what it was than accepting it," said Liv. "What's wrong?"

"Nothing. You just have to be careful in Iceland. Some gifts are burdens, not gifts," Jin told her.

The van driver looked up as they came around the final curve of the trail. He was leaning against the bumper and crossed his legs.

Galen shook his head and smiled when he saw her. Flakes were coming down fast now.

"Are we late?" Liv asked. She hurried up to the van but slowed when she saw no one was in it yet.

"No, but you're the only one who isn't. No hide nor hair of them pagan gals. And look at this weather coming in. I warned them," said Galen.

"There are still a few minutes left. I'm sure they'll be along." Liv pulled out the amulet from her pocket and examined it. The vibration started in her fingers again. Was she allergic to the metal? Was it radioactive?

"What have you got there?" Galen leaned in to see.

"I helped this little guy who was stuck on the bridge and he threw this at me and called me an arse wipe." Liv held it out, but the van driver backed away as if it was on fire.

"I can't be touching that shite! It's magical, I can see the shimmer from here. That must have been a magical being you helped. He begifted you with a powerful amulet for helping him."

Liv laughed. "There's no such thing as magic. And if he was a magical being, I'm a monkey's uncle. He was swearing the whole time and very unpleasant."

"That's how dwarves are! You're lucky you didn't run afoul of an Elf. Those are nasty things! Compared to them, dwarves are pleasant as peas and pies on Thursday."

"I helped him. I didn't run afoul of anyone. And I doubt he would have thrown it at me if it was a magical item."

"Don't be showing that to anyone. It's valuable and you don't know these people you're with as well as you think."

"I don't know them at all."

Liv slid the amulet back into a pocket over her chest that zipped shut. The prickling in her fingers stopped. Her chest warmed and she was grateful for the heat. The temperature had dropped in the short time she'd been hiking. Her feet began chaffing in her boots from the hike. She should have broken them in better.

"Where are the ladies? Now, they really are late," said Liv.

"Well, that's that. Get on the van. I've got to go report this."

"Should we go look for them? How far could they have gotten with those stubby little legs?" Asked Liv.

"You can stay if you like. These parts get ugly when it's dark. This is one of the old waterfalls, ancient with sinister power you wouldn't believe. No, better come with me. They'll send a recovery squad if the ladies don't show up tomorrow. Powerful witches, mages and things I don't even want to think about, will go in, during the twilight and ask for them back. Our mission is to notify the powers that be so the rescue can begin."

Galen jumped into the van and Liv noticed how white the skies had become with the beginning of the snow, leaving few points of reference. How would the Esbat ladies find their way out?

What were her choices? She could stay and wait in the snowstorm for the Esbat witches. Alone? Galen was already starting the van. The Volks had settled in their seats.

She spared one last look down the higher path and moved into the bus.

The guilt began in earnest. "I barely knew them. I don't even know their last names."

"And I wouldn't say a word about the amulet, if you're questioned. That will only raise suspicion that you had something to do with all this," said Galen.

"Who is going to be suspicious of me? I didn't do anything."

"The Inquiry Board. We don't often lose tourists, but when we do, they have to investigate. They're the ones who will authorize the Rescue, if there is one."

"Why wouldn't they send a rescue? Those were nice people from what little I know about them." Liv flushed with indignation and began to rise.

"These people who think they are magical, come to our home and perform their shoddy little rites on the land of my ancestors. Something goes wrong and we're supposed to be all giddy about their mishap. I went to the Grand Canyon once. All these warning signs and railings. I bet they lose more people there than we do in Iceland. You're a tourist here at your own risk and no one will warn you twice!" He drove up the black rock drive away from the trail and followed the main road to another turnoff. Through the growing snow, Liz saw a light gray house that sat calmly against the black lava landscape and snow.

"There's nothing you can do for them now," said Jin. Jane patted Liv's shoulder.

"Here, I'll let you off at the hostel and then I'll do the paperwork to start the wheels in motion." Galen stopped and motioned her out with a shooing action of his arm. He dumped Volk's luggage on the ground. She was grateful she only had the backpack but now she had to carry the older people's luggage.

He threw more suitcases on the ground and helped the Volks couple out. They were welded together, arms linked, and kept their heads down against the storm. Liv picked up their bags and tried to hurry them out of the wind and biting snow.

The van was moving, spinning its tires. Liv watched the dirty white van hurtle down the road until it disappeared into the snow. She sighed and walked into the hostel. There were so many windows and skylights that the space reminded her of a cathedral. It was a dull gray outside but there were so many reflecting surfaces in the building, it seemed bright and cheery. She wouldn't have known it was a hostel except for the large professional sign in front that proclaimed it. It looked like a large, converted single family home, almost a lodge.

Liv dropped the bags and moved out of the hallway. The Volks collapsed on a small bench, still huddled.

"Where is the rest of your group?" The man at the front desk tried to look around Liv, but he was short and didn't get up out of his chair. His pale hair was plastered in a comb-over on his shiny head. He wore a plaid shirt with a leather apron. Liv guessed him to be about 70 years of age and he probably had been born in the building.

"I wasn't with the four ladies. I basically booked as an add-on to fill out the tour as did Mr. and Mrs. Volks. The ladies went on a different hike today onto the high trail while I went on the lower path at Glymur. The Volks stayed by the river. It really wasn't good for hiking. I mean, the van driver warned us but the Esbat group, the four ladies who are missing, insisted. I'm not sure what happened to them today. Galen, the van driver, said he was going to take care of it. I'm not sure where he went. I still need a room though, as do Mr. and Mrs. Volks."

"Of course. We have a lovely room for you. I hope the ladies find their way here not too late, to not wake everyone up. Didn't they take a tour guide into the canyon with them? Glymur isn't a place you want to fool around in."

"No, they had some ceremony they wanted to do privately. I'll be happy to be woken up as long as they are ok."

"You think something went wrong with them? In Glymur?" The male innkeeper had a deep crease between his eyebrows. Liv watched it open and close as his facial expression changed from inquisitive to wary. "No one would doubt you."

"I have no idea. I'm going to bed. What time is breakfast?"

"It's all on a sign in the large room. Breakfast is from 8-930. Enjoy your stay. The waterfall does not always treat strangers kindly, although you look like you know what you're about," he added quickly with a tiny bow or was it a nod? "There's a legend of an old man who went there to gather eggs. He got stuck in just such a storm as this. He spent the winter with an Elf Lady and got her with child. He went back to his people and refused to acknowledge the boy as his. The Elf turned him into a whale and he exploded." The innkeeper made a motion with his hand to represent the explosion. "They have found whale bones in the lake." He nodded at Liv, like they shared a secret and pointed her to the large staircase in the middle of the entry. A sign on the wall said "Hostel Accommodations."

Liv found the luggage bags in the common room. She barely glanced at the other luggage but wondered if she should look at the name tags. Although she planned on being there for two and a half weeks, she had packed sparingly so it all fit in one neat large backpack. Her coat was for travel and it had 27 separate pockets and could hold everything from her phone to pens and pencils. It cost a mint, but allowed Liv to travel with just the backpack. The hostels all claimed to have laundry facilities and she meant to use them, when possible.

Should she open the Esbats' suitcases and look for any clues? What if she got caught pawing through someone's stuff? Liv nixed the idea and got ready for bed. Perhaps everything would be sorted out in the morning.

The room was small but semi private with a door and a shared bathroom. The bedroom had the requisite safe, desk, lamp, chair and small couch. Liv opened the safe and put the amulet into it and spun the dial. The piece of jewelry gave her a disquieting feeling and she would sleep better without it on her person. She stowed her backpack in the closet and laid down. No one woke her and she slept well enough in the tiny room although she could hear the storm screaming all night.

She ate breakfast while a young female attendant, maybe in her early teens, watched Liv from the doorway. The indentation between the girl's eyebrows looked just like the inn-keeper's so she guessed they were related although her eyebrows had been plucked to a thin line. The girl's dark blue eyes were rimmed with black makeup and seemed to jump out of her face. Under her bored scrutiny, Liv found chewing awkward, forced. The girl's hair was naturally blond but had been darkened by some kind of thick paste. It looked dry and brittle. The girl's cell phone rang and she turned away, her shoulder length bob swinging side to side.

Liv went to the front desk and asked if anyone had left a message for her. Neither the van driver nor anyone in the tour group had left word. On the plus side, the much feared inquisition hadn't contacted her either.

Liv pulled out her agenda. "I am supposed to have a tour of the Ring Road."

"No one travels today, even one such as you. Look outside," the innkeeper told her, nodding towards the window. He looked like he hadn't moved from his wooden chair behind the desk since yesterday. Liv noticed a nameplate that said "Your host: the Siggurdsson family." Liv went to the front window of the converted house and saw white. Initially, the light streaming in through all the windows blinded her but after a minute, she could discern vicious gusts of wind driving the snow past the window. She couldn't even see the road. Liv thrust her hands into the pockets of her hoodie. Her hand touched something warm. The amulet! Liv frowned. She put it in the safe in her room last night. She was sure of it. Liv opened the pocket of her hoodie. She looked down without touching it and there it was. The pale metal gleamed again the deep red stone.

Was it safe in her pocket? Probably not since she didn't remember putting it there. Liv slipped it around her neck for safety. She could feel the heavy chain, pulsating under her shirt, against her heart. Her phone buzzed a text and she took it out.

"You're the talk of the town, sis. J"

Did she want the juicy details of what a bad sister she was? Naw. She closed her eyes and said a prayer that the women would find a path out of the Glymur area. Minerva with the wild hair, Gale who 'towered' over the rest at 5'6" and Bea, the boss, with white hair. She couldn't remember the last woman. It was something unusual. She'd have to check her notes.

Liv's chest cracked like she'd broken five ribs. It burned and her skin sizzled where the amulet touched her. Liv gasped and pressed her hands to her chest but it didn't stop the fiery pain that coursed through her veins. Liv bent over and she could hear the innkeeper speaking to her but couldn't understand the words. He put one heavy hand on her back, patting her as if she was choking. It made her straighten up in an attempt to tell him she needed an ambulance.

A high thin scream burst from his lips when he saw her chest. He removed his hand and bowed to her as he stumbled away and disappeared behind his desk.

The vicious pain slid from her. She was sore everywhere but at least she could breathe. Jin was holding one of her hands and Jane the other. They were both smiling at her. Where had they come from?

"There, the worst part is over now," said Jane, patting her hand. Jin led her to a small bench and helped her sit down. Liv's legs were rubbery and there was still a smoldering fire inside her chest.

"I'm sorry, my Lady. I had no idea you were one of the Light Folks. I apologize for touching you," said the innkeeper from behind the desk.

"Light Folk? What are they?" Liv asked.

He stared at her, his eyes wide. "Oh, I get it. I won't say a word." A thin sheen of sweat covered his forehead and upper lip. He disappeared into the back, behind the curtain, where he lived with his daughter.

His daughter, the teenaged girl with the swinging Goth hair, was pushed out from the back and executed an awkward curtsy before she fled back to the private area of the inn.

"I've never been curtsied to before." Liv rubbed her chest but the amulet was gone. The amulet, or where it had been, formed raised ridges on her skin above her left breast. She was branded! She looked down at the carpet to see if it had fallen off of her. Where was the amulet?

"The amulet is inside you now," said Jin gently.

The innkeeper came out again with both hands clasped in front of him and his eyes on the floor. "Your friends came out of the forest. Some of them, anyway. They'll be bringing them over when the snow stops." He retreated with another small bow and disappeared.

"Some of them? And when is the snow expected to stop?" Liv called after him. The girl brought out a steaming cup of hot chocolate for her and did a little better on the curtsy this time. The cup chattered on the saucer as her hands shook. She set it down on the table.

"This storm is expected to stop sometime tonight, unless you wish it to be different," the girl murmured without any eye contact. Liv sat on the comfortable couch and watched the storm. Jin and Jane hovered nearby.

"I wish this storm would dissipate. I'd like to know what happened to the four ladies." The hot chocolate was thick and creamy, warming her throat and relaxing her. Her chest squeezed in pain and she couldn't believe it was from the hot drink. The amulet? Was she having a heart attack? Stroke?

The sensation of the amulet digging into her chest, burrowing itself nearer her heart, frightened her when she thought about it. Heart attack, my grandma's butt, she thought. Then, just as violent and sudden as the pain had come, it was gone. She recovered quickly and couldn't even believe she'd been in crippling pain a moment before. Liv should have checked out the medical care when she was booking her tour. What if she had to go into the hospital? At least James knew where she was. As little as they seemed to care about lost tourists, how much less concern would there be about a sick one? Liv looked out the window and started. The snow was gone and the sky was clear. Liv sat down again to drink her cocoa.

A farm truck rumbled by, so beat up that Liv wondered that it was still in working order. It turned into the hostel and Liv watched as the Esbats appeared out of the back. Not four of them but three. Hard to pick them out individually when they all dressed in their dark cloaks and long skirts. She saw Minerva's reddish hair and Bea's white hair and who was the third? Gale, the 'tall' one.

"Where is the other one? The fourth one?" Liv turned around so she could see them limp in. They had bruises on their faces and hands and their clothing was ripped in places. Banya was missing! That was the name of the fourth woman.

Chapter Six

The three Esbat witches trudged in the door to the community room. Bea, Gale and Minerva moved like spent zombies. They headed towards the staircase without acknowledging Liv.

"What happened to you guys? You were there at the waterfall and then you weren't." Liv jumped from her seat at the sight of them. Bea, the leader, shook her head and waved Liv off. They looked beat or maybe beaten described it better. Their hair was burned at the ends and the skin that was exposed was bruised darkly. Their wet clothing hung limply and had rips as if something had used its claws on them. Their eyes were red, rimmed with black as if the delicate under eye skin was bruised.

Liv followed them to the staircase and watched them go upstairs. What the heck had happened to them?

Liv sat down with her cocoa, hoping she would hear through the grapevine what had happened. What an adventure on her second day in Iceland. Plus the amulet in her chest. Can't forget that. Liv touched her chest, feeling the raised brand. She vowed to start a travel log. "Dear diary," she thought.

Would her Ring Road tour be back on once the snow was done? The drive was supposed to be spectacular. Someone else would be driving and she could focus on relaxing. Liv heard the showers from upstairs and hoped the ladies would come back down to talk after freshening up.

She pulled out her phone and emailed James, "Lost my tour group in a snowstorm. Three out of four were found. Hope to find the fourth soon. They profess to be witches! A dwarf threw a magic amulet at me. Having a lovely time. All is well." He would laugh at her sarcasm. She left out the amulet embedding itself in her chest but wondered idly if it would show up on the X-ray at the airport like things did on the smuggler shows.

The storm snuck back in while she had her head down emailing and was roaring along at gale force as if nothing had interrupted it. The van driver, Galen, came in and sat down for some coffee, dripping clumps of snow on the floor. Liv brought her cocoa over and sat down.

"So what happened? I only saw three come back. Is anyone out looking for the fourth little witch?" Asked Liv.

"They straggled out to the trailhead, those three you saw. They had the burn marks and the smell of Hades on them. That's the mark of meeting a demon." He shook his head. "I was parked there waiting out the storm. With these huge winter storms from the Arctic, they often come with a break after the initial blow. The women dragged themselves out to the trailhead and I helped them into the truck. They didn't say much. What can you say? They went in looking for trouble. You can't expect to walk around unscathed after being so audacious."

He looked up as the innkeeper entered the room. Liv caught him making some sign to the man out of the corner of her eye. Was it the sign of the Cross?

"Well, thanks for the coffee, but I have to get home." He stood and tipped his cap in a small bow.

"But it's snowing again," said Liv.

"Aye and now it's in the right direction to guide me home. I live next farm over," he said and went out into the storm to the van.

Well it was good to know the storm had a predictable path. The girl, Lilly, came and curtsied to her again, eyes down. "We moved your bag to a separate room. The group you were with is already asleep and we didn't want you to be bothered with them."

"Thank you! Hey wait!" The girl did one quick bounce of a curtsy and retreated out of sight. Liv realized she wouldn't get any answers and went up to check out her new room. More of a suite, it had a lovely sitting room with a large window that showed a view of the storm and a separate bedroom and private bath. Liv took a couple of pictures.

She laid down on the soft bed and the scent of lavender surrounded her. Did they scent the sheets? It was lovely. Liv drifted off into a dream that was vivid and realistic. Liv usually didn't remember her dreams but this one was a doozy. She dreamed of a group of nordic people who looked like her: tall, thin and almost colorless. There were three men wearing shining armor and one woman, the leader, in a thick plush robe of white fur. The leader spoke to her without moving her lips.

"Welcome. You have chosen to wield the Amulet of the Cruor. It will be your mission to protect us. Train hard to find the secrets of the Amulet. You have access to an amazing array of power if you can control it. We thank you for taking up the mantle of power for our people, Elf Warrior." And then she and the soldiers faded into nothing.

Liv opened her eyes. Had she been sleeping or was it a hallucination? The woman seemed so alive, so real. The message, she discounted completely. Magic? How stupid was that? Liv scratched at the brand on her chest. She could barely feel it now but she knew it was there. The skin was reddened and slightly raised. She wished she'd taken a picture of the amulet before it burned its way into her body.

Did this dream really mean anything? Was she really in charge of fighting for an entire race? Nothing in her life as a grant researcher had adequately prepared her for this.

Liv took her phone and headed down to the common room. Maybe she could find her own answers. First she googled "Cruor" and got coagulated blood. eww. Next she looked for Iceland legends.

Huldufólk or Hidden folk were Elves, dwarves and fairies that lived among the forests and fjords. Elves were tall, thin and fair. They were magical and could disappear into the landscape at will.

The short man she saved at the bridge didn't fit the bill as he was short, dark and foul mouthed. He fit the dwarf image she had in her mind. Fairies? They were delicate and small, as she remembered. They mostly cared for flowers, the link said.

Why would a dwarf throw something valuable at her? She found her answer in a chat room about Hidden Folks. One of the topics in the forums was Gifts from the Other Realm. The little people can't abide owing someone a blood debt so he had to give her something. Maybe it was the only thing he had on him? But, she didn't think he was an Elf so did the rules apply?

Liv asked the chat room why he would have an Elven protection amulet?

"The dwarves and fairies HATE the Elves. He was probably keeping it from anyone who could become the Elvish protector. He got in a bind when he didn't have anything to give you of value and had to throw it at you, hoping you left it there." Mithor, the Wise, said in the chat room.

"Without a protector, the Elves will be at a major disadvantage against the Dark Mage in the upcoming Battle." Elinor the Fair chimed in.

"When is this battle? How does the protector learn how to wield the amulet?" Asked Liv, the Ordinary.

The chat room remained silent and Liv logged off with thanks.

At least she knew a little more about this mystical amulet. Not that she believed a bit of it. Liv was definitely a hedger though. Just in case it was real, she wanted to learn as much as she could. How could she test it?

She went downstairs and pulled open the door. Liv squinted at the wind and went out into the storm. She fought the wind for the door and barely won. The ice scraped against the rock front of the inn. She hadn't thought the intensity could get much worse but she was wrong. It was hard to keep her footing and the wind snatched at her breath. Her coat whipped around her knees. Liv put her hand on her amulet scar and formally wished for Banya's return to the inn. She went back in when the wind began to howl.

The innkeeper brought her a Brandy and a piece of dark chocolate which she accepted with grace. Was this the cure-all for everything? Not that she was complaining. She sat down to watch the storm out of the window. Jane and Jin waved at her from across the room. The comforting warmth of the chocolate and Brandy spread from her stomach outward and Liv could barely keep her eyes from closing. What was it about this place that sapped her energy? Working in a small office for years had robbed her of any muscle tone she ever had. When she got back home, Liv vowed to start an exercise program.

The door banged open and Galen walked in carrying the last Esbat, Banya. She looked tiny in his arms. Liv jumped up to help. Part of the storm came in with them and Galen laid the woman on the couch nearest the door and shut the door. Her chest rose slightly.

"She is still alive! Help!" Called Liv.

"She staggered out of the storm into the road, almost ran into the van. I don't know how she got here from the forest without transport," said Galen.

Liv held the woman's cold hand. "Are you ok, Banya?" Banya's eyes were red and inflamed. She'd bitten through her bottom lip and blood stained her chin. She glared at Liv.

She looked more angry than hurt and shoved Liv's hand from hers.

"I didn't want to come. I couldn't help myself. I wish I'd died out there."

"Where were you, Banya? The others all made it back," said Liv.

"The others are all sheep. They're only worthy as things to sacrifice. I never knew there was so much power! The Dark Mage is everything. He expelled the others except Minerva. She's the only one who showed any aptitude at all. I didn't show any for the higher magicks! I was left wandering in the forest. I wasn't even worthy to sacrifice. I've done what had to be done. At least Minerva tried to touch the power. I think it broke her."

"You smell like them. Watch yourself, Liv. You have no idea of the forces out there. Take your little tour. Soak your body for an hour in the Blue Lagoon water and go home, where it's safe." Liv smoothed Banya's brow. Banya cried out in pain and licked her lips. "Whispers in the wild say you picked up an amulet."

Liv stared at Banya without answering.

"I hope you did. I'm looking forward to him ripping it out of you."

The innkeeper looked at Banya and pulled out a phone. He turned away and spoke in another language, possibly Icelandic. "I've called for transport. She needs more help than we can give her. Glymur can be cruel to those who don't belong."

Bea came into the room and stood in the doorway looking at Banya, tears rolling down her face. "I wish we'd never come here." She came forward and held Banya's bruised hand and whispered to her.

"What happened to you in the Glymur canyon?" Asked Liv.

Bea answered. "Horrible things. I can't even remember most of it. We got turned around right away and our compass didn't work anymore. We tried to summon something. Something else came. I've never been so terrified in my life. It tried us on like we were pieces of clothing. Most of us broke under the horrible pain. The degradation. Whatever that thing was, it liked Minerva. We left when we were discarded. When it couldn't take anything more from us, we were cast out. We tried to stay together but Banya got lost on the way out in the storm."

"Then, we heard a voice, saw a bright light and went to it. I thought we were dying but it led us back to the trail. Thank goodness it saved us. We might have endured that torment forever," said Bea.

Tears flowed down her cheeks and Liv patted her shoulder, watched her flinch from the slight contact.

Liv went to her room. The more she could distance herself from the Esbats, the better. Bea freaked her out and Banya more so. When she dreamed this time though, it was of their drawn, pale faces as they came in. Their red tinted eyes, burnt hair and the odd bruising on their faces.

Chapter Seven

Liv gazed out her window into the storm until a vehicle came to take Banya to the hospital. Liv cried when she saw them carry Banya and put her in the SUV. She looked so damaged. Liv was exhausted but it was too early to retire.

Time for a list to help her organize her thoughts. Whenever minutiae threatened to overwhelm her, Liv turned to her lists. A source of pride for her and ridicule from others.

She had definitely seen the little person on the bridge. Was he a dwarf or a gnome or just height challenged?

She had a dream where the Elves told her absolutely nothing about the amulet. It was a dream and reminded her of her "fairy" issues when she was little.

The weird reaction of Galen, the van driver, Jin and Jane and the innkeeper to the amulet. Wouldn't anyone be weirded out if they found a piece of jewelry in a foreign land?

The return of the battered and broken Banya when Liv wished for it. Could be a coincidence. So far, she had nothing concrete except a raised circle on her chest. Maybe it was just a rash. Liv rubbed it idly. But where had the amulet gone? Liv could barely feel the soft raised ridges, but they were there. And that was the only real evidence from all the strangeness.

Google didn't reveal anything new or, more probably, she didn't know where to look. Liv's stomach rumbled. Being a make-believe warrior was hard work. Liv went down to find some dinner. She hoped they had something since she wasn't scheduled to be here tonight. The Esbats weren't scheduled for a meal here either. She increased her speed.

She turned into the common room and found they had all preceded her. They were sipping warm broth from cups.

Liv sat at a small round table by herself but within listening distance of the Esbats.

"Just hard tack and cheese, My Lady," Lilly curtsied and placed a plate in front of her.

"So why do you rate a curtsy?" Asked Bea. Half of her face was green from an emerging bruise and several of her fingers were taped together.

Liv smiled and shrugged. The hardtack was delicious, flat bread toasted to a deep brown. The cheese was sharp and had a lovely tang to it. European eating at its best. Lilly brought a dark red wine that paired wonderfully with the cheese and bread. After enjoying her meal, the girl brought coffee, rich and black.

"Well you really rate the service," said Bea. "I heard you got upgraded to a suite, too."

"They were probably trying to help you all recuperate by getting me out of the common room. The benefits of NOT getting lost."

"We aren't going to continue on with the rest of the tour. Just so you know. As soon as Banya gets released, we'll catch a flight. Maybe even if she doesn't get released right away. I know I'm ready to go home."

"Sorry to hear that. I'm looking forward to this storm being over and seeing some Northern Lights and mudpots."

"I, for one, have had enough of Iceland, and witches and Elves for that matter. I may go back to the Catholic church when I get home. I haven't really decided. I just know we have to get out of here as soon as possible," said Bea. "No one has told us anything about Banya. She looked awful."

Should Liv say congrats they were leaving or sorry about Banya? She sent a short wish out to the universe that Banya would come back. "Enjoy your trip home," was the best she could sincerely say. Inwardly, she scoffed at anyone who dabbled in magic. It just wasn't logical. Eventually, science caught up with the phenomenon and explained what occurred.

Liv had her fill of socialization today and it was getting dark. The raging storm of snow had an ominous gray cast to it. The innkeeper came up to her, his hands clasped in front of him.

"What's the forecast for tomorrow?" Liv asked.

He shrugged. "We don't even try to predict the weather here. With the Arctic Sea on the north border, anything can happen. Most weather models don't waste their time to include us unless one of the volcanoes is erupting and screwing up air travel."

"I hope the Ring Road tour can go tomorrow," said Liv.

"There's a lot of magic in the air tonight. Who knows what will happen, if you want it badly enough?" He walked swiftly away and Liv was left to wonder. Could she feel any magic tonight? The dream Elves told her she needed to protect them from the Dark Mage. If there was magic, a huge "if" for Liv, how would she access it? And her wish for Banya to come back hadn't happened. Banya hadn't made it back from the hospital. That wish hadn't had the bone wrenching pain in her chest that the other wish had. Was she asking half-heartedly?

The physics of the universe did not support her wishes being more important than anyone else's wishes. It was bull and she knew it. She went up to her suite after a long last look at the snow.

"Wake up, you idiot!"

Someone was shaking her and Liv struggled out of a deep sleep and dragged herself from the warm comforter. Banya would not stop shaking her. Banya? What was she doing back? Banya's face sported an ugly bruise on her forehead and one of her eyes was bloody and swollen.

"Stop shaking me! You're scrambling my brain. Hey, you got out of the medical facility. Good on you." Liv smiled at the woman who just looked exasperated. In addition to being battered and bruised like the rest of the Esbats, her leg was stiff under her long skirt, and she limped as if she had injured it. Her arm was in a sling. There was a faint smell about her that Liv didn't like: burnt skunk spray? Whatever she'd rolled in was powerful.

"Get up. Get dressed or get naked if that helps you move faster. Tonight is ripe for magic. Even the idiot innkeeper can feel it and you're napping away the precious hours. How will you save anyone laying there like this?" Banya asked.

"Who do I have to save? Looks like everyone is accounted for now that you've returned."

"Get up! You've got the power, you need to train to access it. So far it's been ice cream and cookies but he's coming and you aren't in any shape to challenge him."

"Who is this guy? Everyone seems to know about him but me. And why do I have to wander alone in the wilderness? Who is going to teach me? This is not the magic I dreamed of." Liv turned around to put some pants on and when she turned back to speak to Banya, the woman was gone.

Liv dropped onto the bed and then checked her watch. Was the goat cheese giving her weird dreams? This is not the magic she dreamed of? As far as Liv knew, she didn't dream of magic, except the stupid Elves. She dealt with numbers and percentages and achievement graphs. That was the first time she'd thought about work the whole vacation. At least that was a success.

Liv couldn't go back to sleep even though it was 4 am. Too much energy in the air. Banya or Phantom Banya had been right about that. Whether it was magic or not was up for debate. Liv went into the sitting room of the suite and picked up a book that was on the small reading table with the lamp. Had it been there before? She thought not. The title was in Icelandic cursive and incomprehensible but the interior pages were partially English. It looked like it had been sewn together by hand.

The pages showed something about rituals. There were diagrams of blank faced people in circles and standing at points on a star. They all wore hoods and long robes with rope belts. She tried to decipher what they were doing and what the expected result was supposed to be. Liv had no idea where this was going.

Was Banya really alive or was Phantom Banya gone to heaven or hell, whatever, yelling at her but not helping?

"This is a nice suite," Banya limped out of the bathroom area. Was she just using the bathroom? Ghosts didn't use the facilities, as far as Liv knew.

"Do you think I'm in danger if I continue with my trip? So much weird stuff has happened," said Liv.

"You need to stay. I don't think you'll be allowed to leave, at this point," Banya said, touching the books on the bookshelf. "Don't bother reading the book." She pointed to the book in Liv's hands. "You won't get it. _We_ didn't get it and we read all the books AND believed. Didn't save us."

Liv believed that Banya was dead and she was hallucinating. Too much Brandy? She was arguing with a ghost. Who used the bathroom.

"Yada yada nada. You still don't get it." Banya shook her head.

"So help me," said Liv.

"Not my place. Besides, you picked up the amulet. Now you're involved whether you want to be or not."

"So tell me how not to end up like you guys; all beat up and half dead."

Banya confronted her, turning her by the shoulder so they were face to face. "You don't deserve this gift! You're ungrateful, not to mention totally unsuitable. Who chose you anyway?" She was waving her good arm and limping around Liv.

"You don't deserve it!" Banya screamed, working herself into a frenzy. Banya thrust her fist into Liv's chest. Her hand disappeared into Liv. The burning spread out like tendrils, squeezing Liv's heart. The pain was like a sharp stick, forcing its way into her chest.

"No, you can't take it," said Liv. She gasped and her heart beat as if it would explode. She put both hands on her chest, struggling to pull out Banya's hand.

"But you don't want it. Give it to me. I deserve this." Banya beat at Liv, trying to pull out her hand.

Liv gritted her teeth and wrapped her hands around Banya's and pulled the woman's fist out of her chest. Banya screamed and writhed. She ended up on the floor, curled into a ball.

"I'm going to go to the bathroom and look at my chest. I want you gone when I come back out." Liv slammed the door of the bathroom, hoping her point was made. She opened her shirt and her chest where the amulet was, glowed ragged red like a burn wound against her alabaster skin.

Liv stormed out of the bathroom, ready to do battle now that she knew her chest was still intact. Banya was gone. Liv remembered she had told her to leave but was surprised she had. Was the woman a ghost or real? If she was real, how could she put her hand into Liv's chest? If she was a ghost, well, what the heck? Ghosts didn't exist. Magic didn't exist and life was a series of coincidences, neatly explained by science. That explanation was getting tougher to swallow.

No way was she getting back to sleep now. She finished dressing and slipped into her shoes and headed down to the common room. The Esbats were seated around the long table with candles lit. They were all in their dark cloaks, talking quietly. Liv counted three of them but no Banya. When they noticed Liv, they joined hands and began to chant.

Liv gasped. Their covert looks told her she was the reason for their chanting.

Bea stood up and said, "Begone, evil."

"I am not evil. Shouldn't you be packing for going home tomorrow?

"We never got a chance to unpack, sadly."

"So I just continue the tour alone? " Liv paused. Did she want to travel with these hard luck babes? Or did she want to be alone for the next ten days? She hoped Mr. and Mrs. Volk would continue. It was hard to choose which was worse. If the witch wannabees went home, she wouldn't be in a combative relationship with people who thought her evil. Maybe she could pretend none of this ever happened.

"We don't care what you do, We have to save ourselves."
"Why do you think you're still in danger?" Asked Liv.
Looks were exchanged. Throats were cleared. Another of
the Esbats spoke up.

"Several of us heard or got the impression that the waterfall didn't want to let us go."

"When you came out the first time, it was because I wished you to come back," Liv couldn't believe she was saying that. It sounded like someone else's voice coming from her. Did she really believe it? Couldn't argue with the slightly raised brand burning in her chest. Something had happened and ignited within her when she wished the Esbats to return.

"You think you 'wished' us back?" Asked Bea.

"Maybe. Something happened when the amulet burned me. Here's the scar."

The Esbats crowded around to look at her chest. "So tell us what happened," said Gale.

"I helped a little person, possibly a gnome or dwarf, and he threw this necklace at me. I put it on and it dissolved into my skin. When I wished for you to return, you did. I'm not saying it's magic but something happened. And I'm not evil."

"This would be so much easier if you *were* evil," said Bea. "We found a spell to eradicate evil. We're still heading home and nothing will stop us. Maybe you should wait in your room while we do our spell."

"Have you heard anything about Banya?" Asked Liv.

The Esbats exchanged looks. "We haven't heard anything," said Gale.

Lilly came out with a tray. "I can take your breakfast to your rooms, if you like."

"That will be fine. Not that I have a lot of choice." Liv went up to her room, making sure that Banya wasn't hiding somewhere first. The innkeeper had gone all out again with eggs, bacon, and some kind of yogurt. There was also a pot of freshly brewed coffee. This must be what royalty felt like: half the people chanting for your destruction and the other half poaching your eggs.

Chapter Eight

"They clearly don't want you here," Phantom Banya sat on her bed and moved the book Liv had been glancing through, putting it behind the thick curtains. Snow still drove across the entire window and Banya tried a couple of times to close the heavy drapes but they didn't move.

"Why aren't you down chanting with your friends?" Asked Liv.

"They are boring. Though they are right, about some things." Banya moved until she was directly in front of Liv.

"OK, what are they right about?"

"Minerva doesn't want you here. If she can hurt the Esbats she will, although them going home isn't going to help their situation. Minerva's powerful. She can follow them anywhere."

"I thought Minerva was one of you. How can I get rid of Minerva? Just by wishing?"

"You're an idiot. Wishing means nothing. You don't deserve the gifts you've been given."

"And you do, I suppose?"

"Let me have them. Give them to me freely and you'll be free of all the pain and problems. Go on with your tour and go home to your family. The power will be safe with me." Banya fell to her knees in front of Liv.

"First, I'd like to know more about it before I toss it away like so much trash and second, my family doesn't like me right now. They're probably chanting around the Thanksgiving leftovers about me." Banya faded and Liv decided to write to James about what was going on.

"Dear James, You'll probably think I'm nuts but this trip has been a real head trip." Liv decided to keep it vague in case the family wanted her declared crazy. "Some of the women on my tour group got lost in the canyon. There was a horrible storm, unlike anything

I've ever experienced. They are at the top of the world here and the weather is a real force. Anyway, they found most of them the next day but one straggled in later, worse for wear. They may all go home so I might be a solo traveler. The room is gorgeous and the inn is feeding us during the storm. Love you, Liv"

Touching base is good. Keeps you grounded, she thought. Where's that book that ghost Banya was trying to hide? Liv pulled it from behind the curtain and reclined on the bed. As before, some of it was in English and some another language, perhaps Icelandic. She examined each picture and read whatever words she could.

The first image looked like one of the monks finding something. Maybe the amulet, but it wasn't very clear what it was. Lightning reached down from the sky and touched the thing in the monk's hand, that was pretty clear. The monk held the thing over his head and the other monks knelt down. So the amulet was powerful, only she didn't know how to use it. Liv turned the pages to the next drawing. It showed the aurora, she thought, moving across the sky. A bonfire with the other monks holding hands around the fire.

In the next image, which faced the campfire one, the guy with the jewel, held his hands pointing at an approaching army. Lightning and fire were depicted as coming from his fingertips and the thing, whatever it was, was in him. Just like the amulet was in her. Liv rubbed the ridges on her chest absently. It looked like the dark army was streaming out of the ground like ants. Liv flipped the next page but there weren't any pictures of whether the monks won or the army of darkness. Liv preferred Hallmark movies where you knew the ending from the first kiss.

Liv might be able to produce fire and lightning from her fingertips. Also the aurora seemed significant. She thought the aurora must still happen even through the storm. It was a lot higher in the atmosphere than the storm and separate, she reasoned.

Liv reached out and the beginning of fire touched her fingertips. She closed her eyes and stretched out to the aurora in the heavens beyond.

Her hands had to fight through the massive snow in the atmosphere first but she took a deep breath and pushed her way through. The aurora beyond the snow glowed. She could see it in her mind. It rippled and bent to her hands. The room became a rainbow of shimmering light arcing over the high ceiling. It moved at her thought and she made it dance just for her. The fire leaped up to join it and Liv let it go, afraid the room would catch on fire. She knew she couldn't control it yet, but joy filled her.

Liv had always wanted to fit in. She was a white haired, pale freak in her family. She suspected she thought differently and was fundamentally a different type of person at her core than her brothers and sister. Liv loved them on one plane. Hadn't she taken the house as a sacrifice to preserve the family?

When she opened her eyes, her hands were full of snow which dropped as it melted in her warm hands. What was an aurora anyway? She found it on her phone.

The aurora was energized particles like a charged gas or plasma. Examples of plasma include fire, lighting, electricity and magnetic fields.

Could her affinity or whatever the amulet gave her, be for plasma? It was a hypothesis but how to check it? Liv didn't want to see the Phantom Banya, with her burnt hair and black eyes, ever, ever again.

Liv looked out her window and could actually see things other than snow. Maybe it was going to be over soon and she could continue on with her tour. Liv debated taking the book with her. That Banya would come back and maybe succeed in taking the book, cemented her resolve to take the book with her. She put her jacket on and slipped the small book into an inner pocket with her phone.

Liv went back to brave the Esbats. She had every right to be in the common room, but they were huddled in the entrance to the private part of the lodge watching a small television.

"What's up?" Liv asked the black clothed backs of the short women.

"The volcanoes are erupting," said Bea.

"Which one?" Liv asked.

"All of them."

Liv peered in at the small screen. A map of Iceland was overlaid with red slashes where the magma burst through the thin skin of the earth.

"They canceled our flight. All flights have been canceled because of the thick ash. I guess we're staying for a few days anyway."

"Hope you're happy," said Gale as they went to their private common room.

"Not sure, really," said Liv. Was she supposed to be friends with this sorry lot who wished her ill?

Liv moved to the bigger window in the front room. The snow was definitely lessening but she could see the dark ash against the white backdrop of the storm. The exposed sky looked dark and angry with the soot and the reflection of lava in the sky. Everything was on fire.

Liv reached out as much as she knew how, to the plasma. Was lava considered plasma?

Nothing happened either inside her or outside. Plasma Girl. What would Plasma Girl do, locked in a snow-bound inn with a group of Wicca who wanted her dead? Luckily they were too chicken to do anything about it. She would watch her back anyway. She wasn't sure what that group was capable of. Minerva especially looked crisped around the edges. Although she hadn't spoken, Minerva turned and glared at her.

The innkeeper stepped into the room. "Oh, hello. Did you need anything?"

"No, is there any update on the weather or the volcano? I know the Esbats were hoping to catch the next plane out of here."

"All flights are canceled. All tours are canceled until further notice."

"I want to see the eruption."

"That, I can arrange!" He seemed energized when he could do something for her. "Lilly can take you. She's a little in awe of you." He hurried off and Liv could only smile. She would have time to grill Lilly later today. She went up and got her room in order and got her bag. Just in case she had to leave in a hurry.

By the time she got down to the vehicle, the snow had stopped. A random flurry chased by Liv's face, followed by a gust of ash.

Lilly curtsied and went out the door to the rough service vehicle that looked vaguely military. Liv's butt hit the seat, Lilly popped the clutch and the huge machine rolled backwards and then leaped forward, grinding up the hill outside the inn.

Liv started to be concerned when the smoke got thicker.

"Don't worry," said Lilly. "We're going to turn into the wind soon." As if to prove her word, she yanked the wheel in a sharp maneuver that made Liv happy that she had eaten lightly. The air cleared up miraculously and Liv could see again. They were climbing again and she could see the whole of the valley laid out before her. Spouts of smoke dotted the valley below her and it was light enough she could see flashes of red and yellow coming through the crust like water through cracked mud. Everywhere she looked was on fire.

A tingle ran through her arms up to her chest. Lilly stopped the truck and Liv opened the door and stumbled out onto the black lava rocks and fell to her knees. Her hands and arms were on fire, pulsing with energy. Liv screamed as the pulsing forced her chest to open and accept the fire. When her hands hit the ground, it began to pulse in time to the energy. The hard lava rose up slowly and jerked back down. Pieces broke off and floated as the ground rose and fell.

. A blinding pain to her head knocked her to the ground unconscious.

****

"If we wanted to kill her, now is the time," said a soft voice that probably belonged to Lilly.

"Not you too," mumbled Liv. She wondered if Lilly still had the shovel or rock she'd hit Liv with.

From her humble life of sitting in a room at work creating the illusion of school achievement from hard data, now everyone wanted her dead: her family, the Esbats, and the Innkeepers. Was there any group left who wished her well?

"Is she awake?" Asked Lilly in her soft voice. "Her eyes moved."

"No, she's concussed. I don't think we ought to do anything bad to her. She's here because the Elves chose her. What do you think will happen to the people who hurt the Elf Warrior? Nothing good, I can tell you," the Innkeeper said.

"But they would be dead too," said Lilly.

"No, they would have plenty of time for slow and terrifying retribution for the people who destroyed their chance. Leave her be. If she dies on her own, it's not our fault."

"Those witches want her dead. Maybe they will do the work for us," Lilly said.

"No. I don't want such a cursed thing happening under my roof. Disaster could spill over on us just like that," he snapped his fingers and the sound hurt her brain. Hurt wasn't the right word. The sound pressed in on her temple slightly so she felt it but it didn't really hurt. Liv expected it to hurt.

Light moved across her face and Liv held herself motionless. If they were back to kill her, she was ready to leap up and draw whatever plasma she could to defend herself, or hit them with the book, but nothing happened.

"She looks as inconsequential as a piece of blank paper." Liv recognized Gale's voice. They weren't whispering so they didn't expect her to be awake any time soon.

"Maybe she'll die," said Bea.

"Better hope not. From what Minerva said, this pale slip of milk is our last hope for breaking free of the dark one. I thought going home would sever the hooks he has in us," said Gale.

"Minerva made it pretty clear that we're the first troops to fall in this war of theirs," Bea's voice said. "I'm still not sure which side I want to root for."

"Let's see: eternal slavery on one side and loss of magic on the other. Not a tough choice," said Gale.

"I like to view it more as unlimited power versus who-cares-about-Elves?" Said Bea.

"I don't trust that side. You can smell the corruption of their spirit. I just want to connect with something that values the planet, not the male-oriented religious experience I grew up with," said Gale. How many people were there in her room? Liv wanted to open her eyes but it was better that they not know she was aware. How come everyone knew more about being the Elf Warrior than she did?

The light moved across her face again and the Esbats left. Liv checked her pocket to make sure the book was still there. She focused on the book and asked it, "How do I use this power? I may need to fight for my life and those of the Elves soon. I need help."

Liv waited and then watched the light recede on the ceiling. When it was a dark twilight, she tried to sit up. Her head felt like a broken egg. She took her hands and held them on either side of her temples and pressed gently.

Jin and Jane slipped into her room. Jane took one of her hands and Jin smoothed his hands on her temple.

Liv pushed herself up until she could sit. The pain disappeared! There was pressure that one might perceive as pain but not the kind of pain that made you squint. The fading light helped.

"Thank you," Liv said. Jin smiled and he and Jane left the room.

A moment later, a quiet knock and the door opened and Lilly slid in with a tray.

"Do I need to worry about you poisoning me?"

"No, milady. I only hit you with the shovel because you were making the ground shake and I was scared."

"It's okay, Lilly. the pain has gone away."

The girl drew back from her and dropped the shaking tray on the small reading table. She fled the room. Liv smelled the coffee, inhaling the lovely deep aroma. Was her sense of smell enhanced? She could definitely see better in the darkness of the room or maybe she was just adjusted to it.

Liv sipped the coffee and pulled the magic book out of her coat pocket. She slipped out of her coat. She probably wasn't going on any unexpected adventures tonight, at least she hoped not. Although her pain was gone, a weariness seeped into her body. Try as she might, her eyes began to close and she locked her door and crept back to bed.

She dreamed that the Elves had come again and examined her. They held hands and chanted around her as she laid in bed, asleep. One of the Elves, the head woman leading the chants, put one slim white hand over her chest and spoke in low, melodic tones for several minutes. Liv felt the weariness and pain float away. Her spirit was lifted and a feeling of well-being suffused her.

"Teach me how to use this power, Lady," Liv said.

"I cannot. Your experience is unique and I have not had the same experience. All I can tell you is that an entire race is counting on you. Anthor will help."

"No pressure," said Liv in her mind. "It's just all our lives on the line." Liv would have rolled her eyes except they were closed.

"I am sorry. All we have is our regular magic. Your magic is stronger and comes from an elemental source."

"The plasma: I figured that out. How do I summon it when I need it?"

"Anthor will help you."

"Who or what is Anthor?"

The Lady Elf shrugged her elegant shoulders. "He should be there already. Time is different for us. I don't know. I'm so sorry." Then, she and the other Elves bowed slightly and faded out of Liv's dream.

Her eyes snapped open. She felt great: no headache and her body didn't have any ache or pains. Time to get to work. She went down to find the innkeeper.

"I need the keys to the truck."

"Maybe it's not so good an idea for you to be driving right now," he said.

"I'm cured of the concussion and I have a mission from the Lady." Liv held out her hand imperially, demanding the keys. The innkeeper did a short bow and dropped them in her hand. It was twilight here but it seemed like it was always twilight. Liv found the lights for the truck and turned them on for safety. Her vision seemed enhanced but maybe not everyone's was.

The air smelled burned and the ash was thicker than it had been earlier. Liv pulled up the collar of her shirt till it covered her nose and drove to where she thought Lilly had stopped before. The glowing lava and the lights of the city seemed to be in the same aspect as before. Liv stopped, set the brake and then jumped out.

This time would be different. She chose a vent, a small one, nearest to her and tried to block all the others out. They glowed like red wounds on the earth. She took a deep breath and put one hand on her chest about where the mark of the amulet was and placed the other on the ground. Liv focused on bringing up just a slender tendril of power and directing it towards a nearby wooden pole, silhouetted against the gray sky.

At first, nothing. Then, her brand began to heat up, warming her hand. The pain started, just a burst of agony in her chest but instead of fighting against it, Liv opened herself to it. Welcoming the power into her vessel.

It took many tries and finally, when Liv was about to give up, the trail of magma jumped and the pole burst into flame.

"Yes! Score one for the Elf Warrior." Sweat ran off her body and Liv pushed her damp hair back off her face and watched the large pole burn with the tar inside it flashing flames of red. She really couldn't leave this thing burning even with lava and smoke everywhere, it was irresponsible.

Liv thrust her hand to the ground and pulled energy back into her brand. She imagined the energy coming back like she was pulling on a heavy rope. Hand over hand she dragged the energy back and was pleased to see the pole extinguish until it was merely a dull glowing red.

Energy sapped, Liv sat on the ground and caught her breath. God forbid she have to sustain this power for more than a single thrust. Maybe it was like a muscle where she had to use it to strengthen it. Tomorrow would be soon enough to practice again. Tonight she needed a bath and food. Liv headed back to the inn with renewed purpose.

Chapter Nine

Liv woke in darkness the next morning, confused. She'd had dreams she was at home in the Lake House with her whole family around her. It hadn't been a happy dream. All of her family looked exactly the same: short, dark and angry. Liv was tall, thin and very light, almost see through. She tried to make everyone happy but nothing worked. She woke up frustrated. It was a mirror of her real life with her family. What was she going to do about that? Another problem for another day.

Liv imagined coming home to the big empty house, conserving energy by taping off rooms with plastic to avoid cooling and heating them. Keeping the house at fifty four degrees F to save on bills. Did any of that bring her joy? The day to day problems almost outweighed the vision Liv had of holiday gatherings. Plus, was she required to provide all the food and drinks for the entire crew? Her sister and brothers weren't noted for their generosity and the ones who were, had married cheapskates.

Liv got dressed and walked down to the breakfast buffet. No one else was there and the room was cold. A bleary-eyed Lilly appeared to fetch coffee and make eggs for her. It showed seven o'clock am and none of the tours had reset yet so everyone must be catching a few extra winks. Liv had stuff to do though.

She pulled out her phone and started a list. She needed to find out how close to the plasma she needed to be to use it. Why did it make her so tired and could she fix that?

"Can I rent a vehicle for the day?"

Lilly dug into her apron and handed Liv the keys to the truck.

"Could I get a lunch and a thermos of coffee? Thanks."

Lilly disappeared into the kitchen area, returning faster than Liv could believe, with a bulging cloth sack and a battered thermos. "Just Cheese, sausage and bread."

"Perfect. I'm going back to where we were. To practice."

Lilly cast her eyes down and nodded. Liv could see in the reflection of the glass that Lilly crossed herself when she turned.

The drive was short and the twilight pressed down upon her. Bits of fine ash rained straight down but not in a torrent, more like soft gentle rain. The sky glowed red as the atmosphere reflected the color of the many open vents. The air smelled less burnt and Liv didn't have to cover her face this time.

She pulled into the shoulder area and cut the engine. The volcanic activity was supposed to be low tonight, according to the website she'd consulted. Liv wondered if there would be enough plasma available for her to practice.

She got out, pulling her hood up to keep the ash out of her hair, and took a couple of deep breaths. She knelt and put one hand on her chest and the other onto the hardscrabble of the lava and tried to summon the plasma to her.

Liv felt a trickle of apprehension when just a flutter of plasma touched her fingers. She directed it at the same pole she had before. A quarter-sized red spot appeared in the middle of the pole. It just glowed, nothing more. Some weapon.

So if an eruption wasn't active, she was helpless? That can't be right. What was the list of the other plasmas? Liv remembered fire, neon, lightning, and stars were all considered plasmas. The only thing available to her now was starlight. It was worth a try and nothing else came to mind.

Liv put one hand on her heart and the other reached to the sky. Was there a slight pull or did she imagine it? She directed the energy towards the pole but nothing happened.

So, when the big bad came she was basically defenseless? She pulled out the book and flipped the delicate pages open. Each time she opened the book, it was different. She sat in the truck with the light on and puzzled out the page that was presented. It showed one of the monks with both hands raised to the heavens. The next picture showed one hand up and one hand out at a target. Lightning flowed from the sky through the monk and then out the outstretched hand.

Could it be that her hand position was just off? Liv got out and felt the little specs of ash come down on her, soft like kisses. She glanced around to make sure there wasn't anyone watching her and moved her feet in the accumulated ash to ground herself. Liv stretched one hand up to the stars and the other at the pole.

Again, she felt energy in her fingers and she concentrated on fueling that energy. There was no accompanying pain in her chest. Liv went back and sat in the car. She opened the book again and chewed on some of the hard bread Lilly supplied her with. The pole began to smoke. Liv stopped chewing and held her breath. Maybe the battle, when it came, would be in slow motion. The book remained on the same illustration.

Was it an order thing? Liv got out again and positioned herself. She pointed at the smoking pole and then reached up to the stars. Fingers tingle, check. Smoke stopped coming out of the pole.

She took a moment to enjoy the scenery. The gray sky had lightened and Liv guessed this was one of the four hours of daylight they were allotted today. The valley spread out dark before her like a velvet cloak. A point of light that might have been a farmhouse hung against the horizon. The red glow of vents pulsed across the landscape.

Liv put both hands on her heart and reached out to the light at the horizon, not expecting anything. Flames erupted across the horizon. The farmhouse, framed by the light, exploded in a silent flash. Liv gasped and moved her hands away from her chest. The fire spread quickly, crawling like an ant and Liv struggled with how to stop it. Liv prayed no people were hurt because of her foolishness. She made fists out of her hands and turned away from the destruction. She shoved out her hands at the stupid pole. If it had only burst into bits like it should have, Liv would have been spared the destruction of the farmhouse. The pole shot up like a candle flame and fell in a heap of dark ash.

Liv looked at the flame in the distance and reached out her hands, visualizing pulling the flame back from where it came and dispersing it. She breathed a huge sigh of relief when the flames stopped their destruction. Had she caused the fire? Liv thought so but her denial of magic made her unsure. She hadn't believed in magic since she was little.

One early morning when she was young, around six, she thought she saw a fairy in the garden. It was a tiny, ephemeral thing with slender wings. She could still see it in her mind. She told her sister, who laughed at her and her brothers who had mocked her relentlessly. Finally consulting her father who had told her there was no such thing as either fairies or magic. Liv went to the window and tried to find the fairy again, but it was nowhere to be seen. Liv convinced herself that she'd imagined it but her family teased her about it for years. It was the first time Liv recalled thinking she was separate from the rest of her family, somehow not belonging.

Now she was in a country where everyone seemed to believe that magical beings were alive and they were not to be offended. If nothing else, at least the superstitious innkeeper provided her with good coffee regularly. Did she believe in magic or was this all coincidence in a country with erupting vents of lava?

Liv drove back to the inn and saw the ladies of the Esbat were eating lunch in the common room. They looked up when Liv came in. The innkeeper was beaming.

"The tour will start again today, assuming no more volcanic eruptions occur," the Innkeeper was clearly thrilled his charges were leaving.

"Do I need to settle up with you for the extra stay?" Asked Liv.

"No, it's all part of the tour, no matter where you stay. Enjoy lunch and then pack up. The van should be here at two. He rubbed his hands together and then looked frightened for a moment before smiling at her. "It's all good, right?"

"You've done a great job under trying circumstances," said Liv.

"Yes, yes. Enjoy lunch." He gestured at the lunch table and left for the kitchen.

Liv got her food and sat at a small square table in a corner. She located the original itinerary in an inner pocket of her jacket. They had missed two days and she wondered where they would pick it up.

Mr. and Mrs. Volks came down and looked rested and refreshed. They nodded hello to Liv.

When the van driver had them all packed in, he told them they would drive a portion of the Ring Road with only one stop for a rest break. The Volks seemed eager to get on with the tour.

The van driver, Galen, stood up before them at the front of the bus.

"There are only a couple of major roads in Iceland. The Ring Road circles around the country. We'll be back on track and the next stop is Thingvellir, where the continents meet." Galen started the van. "Let us hope nothing bad happens there!"

Liv sat across from the Volks and they exchanged worried glances.

Two hours later, they pulled into a paved entrance and stopped in a parking lot. The building was just visible in the haze. There were only a few other cars in the parking lot that Liv could see.

The sign said Thingvellir and had an arrow pointing towards the trailhead and another towards the visitor center. Everyone in their group went into the visitor building, but Liv held back in the parking lot.

If she had to fight right now, what would she use as plasma? Fire, lightning, starlight, could she force an eruption and use that?

Nothing seemed available in the gloomy landscape. A neon sign glared in the murky light. Liv glanced around. No one in sight. Liv reached out a slim hand to the light and one to a wooden rail alongside the entry. She concentrated on the part of her chest that held the amulet and gritted her teeth. She expelled breath from her abdomen and then blew out more until she was an empty vessel. Then, Liv filled herself with power until she couldn't hold anymore.

She turned her gaze to the wooden rail and took everything that was inside her and shoved it at the rail. It blew apart in a shower of fiery splinters. That was more like it, Liv thought and hurried back inside the center, hoping no one had seen her.

She examined the rightness of what she felt during this last use of the power. A smile came across her face. It felt great. It hadn't made her tired or weak. Just the opposite. Liv tried to remember that feeling, engrave it in her muscle memory. She wondered exactly what was going on from the little physics she remembered. Nothing came to mind to explain what she had done.

When the group left the small tourist center and moved towards the trailhead, light was beginning to show in the sky. Liv's glance shot to the wooden rail. It was in several pieces, some laying in the parking lot. She hid a smile at the results of her work. She still couldn't call it magic. Magic was a ridiculous concept, except that it was so accepted here.

Liv and the Volks walked down the path where the two continental plates meet. There was a light covering of moss on the rocks that had been there longest but most of the crust was brand new and fairly shook with plasma. Liv felt better than she had the whole trip. She vibrated with energy like everything around her.

Liv saw her first raven. Amazed at how huge it was. She'd seen plenty of crows in her life but this thing was like the size of an eagle. It crouched twenty feet above the black rocks that formed each side of the passage.

Weren't ravens a sign of good luck? No, wait. Death and rebirth, Liv corrected herself. She was due some rebirth and renewal. And the post had burned at her command. Jin and Jane turned off onto a part of the trail where the Raven sat.

"Not bad," she said to herself as the others followed the paved trailhead ahead of her to see Thingvellir.

"Not good, either," someone said.

Chapter Ten

"Sorry, I didn't hear you come up," Liv knew she was babbling but couldn't help it. She couldn't see who had spoken. Only that it was a man in darkness. His face was obscured, backlit by the slight morning light.

"You really need help. Didn't you read the book?" He was tall and very thin and she could see his inky black hair absorbing what little light there was. It was tousled loosley down to his shoulders. Girls would kill for that hair. His face seemed very white, almost transparent. Was he an Elf? Didn't they all have white hair like her? Maybe it was a misconception, like the one that all Icelanders were blond. It probably started out that way but now, they had the regular variety of hair colors, from what she had seen.

"What book?"

"Could you possibly be any stupider?" His disgust was evident. "Hard to believe they've chosen an idiot as the Elf Warrior. The book in your pocket."

"It's in Icelandic."

"Try Elvish. You can translate it, if you will it."

"Elvish?" Liv hadn't thought of that. She knew the words were too short to be Icelandic. Elvish hadn't occurred to her. "So, I just will it?"

"Yes," the man strolled next to her down into the Thingvellir rift. It started out as a gentle trail, with vertical ridges that rose up on either side of it. A fine mist hung over the trail where the snow met the warming air. This was where two plates, the Eurasian and the North American tectonic plates meet. Liv had read about it.

"This area is where the Althing, an open-air assembly where people could drown women and hang men who transgressed. Lovely place, no?" He gestured with one slim hand into the fog. A slight valley appeared before her through the dampness in the air.

Liv pulled out the bound book and let the book fall open where it wanted. Some words appeared in English but some were still in Icelandic. The drawing was of an assembly of stick figures. More detail came in as she focused, women underwater and men swinging from scaffolds. Liv slammed the book closed.

"Thanks for the tip about the book. I will have to work on it but it's nice to have a confirmed direction to go. You're the first one who has had any constructive advice."

"Look at what a little helper I am." He spread his hands wide as if she should walk into them for a hug.

"What's your name?" Liv took a step back.

"Nigbor, at your service," he scraped a mock bow. He was slim with an athletic build, big shoulders tapering to small hips. He wore black pants, black T-shirt and a casual black jacket.

"Just Nigbor? No last name?" Liv put up her hood to keep the moisture from sliding down her neck.

"No," he looked confused. "Do I need another name?'"

"People in my world have two names. There are so many of them, there are doubles and even triples of names. So we need the second name to narrow it down."

"There are not as many of us. We go with the one name. Each is unique."

"And who is 'we'? The Elves all were blond and pale."

"Not all Elves are blond although they do tend to be on the paler side when you see them. Part of it is because you aren't in their world. You're only seeing a portion of them," Nigbor told her. "Like me. You're only seeing a slight portion because I haven't really come into your realm all the way. I'm just kind of projecting a faint image."

"I see but why are you coming into our realm at all?"

"To see you, of course. You looked like you could use some help. You asked and here I am! I can't stay long though. I have to get back. Things to do. Other realms to visit."

"Other realms? How many are there? And do you know what happened to the Esbat witches? What burned them?"

"Those stupid women summoned forces they didn't understand and got burned. Haha, get it? Burned."

Liv frowned. What a jerk. No one deserved to be mistreated like those women. Liv remembered the dark bruising and claw marks on their clothes. A small shudder shook her whole body. His thin beautiful face began to look like a skull as the fog thickened. His fingers, just for an instant, appeared to be talons with long, sharp nails.

Liv grimaced and took a step backwards. Her throat constricted so that she could barely breathe. Menace radiated from him and his smile, which she previously judged gorgeous, was terrifying.

"I'll be going then. People to torment. Women to abuse." Nigbor faded gradually into the mist until she couldn't discern him any more.

Liv clutched the book to her chest and noticed the amulet in her chest was burning. She walked quickly back to the trailhead and stayed in the small souvenir shop until the rest of her tour returned.

Chapter Eleven

That night, Liv woke to darkness but she knew she wasn't alone. She couldn't remember where she was. First, she sorted out whether she was in a single room or a double. She was sure this was the cream building so she was in a single room, no bathroom. Someone occupied the comfy chair. Anger made her bite her cheek but when it passed, she sat up and sighed. Her night vision picked out the wild hair before she saw anything else. Minerva!

"Minerva! What are you doing here? Can I revoke your permission to enter or anything? Is there a removal spell that I could pay the Esbats to do to get you out of my room?"

"I've come to do you a favor, girl. You're no match for what's coming. I've seen it and I wanted to warn you. Get out before you get hurt. There's no shame."

"And you're doing me this big favor why?" Liv touched the book in its hidden pocket.

"Hey! I like you. We were fellow travelers before I found my vocation. I've got a dog in this fight, as they say. You're just a tourist."

"So what do you want from me? What do I do to renounce this gift?" It would be good to know if she got in too deep.

"Give me the book and you just have to leave the country."

"My trip isn't over yet. I paid a lot of money for this."

"The price could be your life," said Minerva. Her eyes glowed slightly in the darkness.

"Now you're just being ridiculous. Maybe that's true and maybe it's not but you aren't all that intimidating with your glowing eyes and your dark robes."

"You have a large family, if I remember. Maybe their safety could motivate you?"

Liv laughed. "My sisters-in-law would tear you apart with cuticle scissors all the while critiquing your lack of style and advising you on which spinning classes to take and who could help you tame those awful eyebrows of yours." Liv made her decision at that moment. She was going to take on this harridan and destroy her forever and her boss, if there was one.

Minerva stood and smoke rose from her clothes. Her body vibrated with rage and Liv smothered a giggle.

"You're doomed. I tried to help you but you're on your own now," spat Minerva.

"I've wrestled grants that are tougher than you. I can sit in an office with only paper for entertainment for months on end without human contact. I have relatives who are vicious and can cut with words and looks that could wither you in your tracks from your poorly cut hair to your unfashionable shoes. Begone demon." Liv waved her hand and the air shimmered and glowed. Her chest squeezed tight and Minerva dissolved in a flash of embers. The look of surprise on Minerva's face matched the one on Liv's face. She most likely wasn't gone for good but it was a pleasant respite.

"I did that!" Liv pumped her fist once.

"By accident," said a deep male voice.

"Why is my room Grand Central Station tonight?"

"You're the most interesting thing on this continent right now," Nigbor laughed. His dark hair was shiny against his pale skin. His eyes were sparkling and an odd mix of green and brown.

"How do I get into another realm and why would Minerva suggest I should?"

"You can enter through what we call a Shimmer, but why enter one? They're boring and stuffy, but if you went with me, I could help you sort out your power."

"Can I get out once I get in? Is it like a door?"

"No, not like that. You have to make a decision to go in. You might not be able to come out."

"But you do!" Liv said.

"I'm Nigbor," he said as if that would explain everything. "Nigbor can go in and out and travel through worlds. I own the knowledge."

"Knowledge is what I need most."

"Let me help you. You'll find out how to use your power much easier in the portal. Come with me."

"But you aren't sure I can get back. I might lose my life, my family, everything that's important to me in this world."

"Yeah, not saying it's an easy decision. You don't have to make it right now. There's still time. I can show you some things but, like the book, it won't work as well as if you went through the Shimmer, into my realm."

"How long before I have to decide?"

"What is time?" Nigbor replied. "Your people have portioned out the hours, minutes and seconds until they barely have meaning anymore."

"What can you teach me on this side?" Liv countered.

"Tour leaving in twenty minutes," the van driver called from the hallway, knocking on doors as he went.

"You're going to miss your tour," Nigbor said with a lopsided grin.

Liv paced across the room but when she turned, Nigbor had gone. Evidently, there wasn't much he could teach her on this side. If she went to the other side, she lost everything. Maybe.

Liv touched the book in her pocket and got her things ready. The breakfast bar was slim pickings and she got a couple of crunchy protein waffles and an apple to stuff in her side pocket.

When was she supposed to do battle to save the Elves? Was it on Nigbor Time or Earth time? It would help to know how much time she had to learn to use this power.

It was a white-out day and Liv was surprised they didn't cancel the tour. Snow covered everything and the van was only identifiable because of the larger lump it made in front of the building.

She got in the van and closed her eyes when the driver started. How could he see in this whiteout condition? This was suicide driving in weather like this. A headache crept up her neck and made her temples throb. Liv focused on the inner problem of how to get the power without losing her world. If she went into Nigbor's world, what would she do after the battle assuming she triumphed? What would she lose if she failed?

Until Nigbor returned, she didn't have any answers, only stupid questions. The book wouldn't fully translate and she risked misinterpreting the partial translation.

"Amazing that you're so terrified of the snow when eternal damnation is just a walk through a portal." Minerva sat next to her and Liv stole a quick look to see if anyone else could see her. By the way the Esbats stumbled to the back of the bus, she believed they could. The Volks kept their eyes on the road ahead.

"I'm not afraid of you," said Liv

"Bull crap."

"I'm more afraid of dying on the road from this maniac's driving," Liv told her.

The van slid off the road and jumped on the roadside rubble as the driver fought to pull the vehicle back under control. At no time did he decrease his speed.

"OK, I'll give you that one," said Minerva as she held onto the seat headrest in front of her.

"The eyebrows look better," said Liv.

"I waxed them. Hurt like hell, but it does look better."

"You know how it goes: first eyebrows then Brazilian bikini wax."

"No, never. Come through the portal with me. You'll never have to worry about that stuff again."

"So how come you can move back and forth through the portal and Nigbor can but I've got a one way ticket?"

"It doesn't have to be one way. But, I think once you step through you won't ever want to go back. You know how we trashed our resources on earth? Polluted all the water and the ground and the air? The other realm isn't like that. It's pristine, like our earth should have been."

"So why are you all singed and beat up? And why isn't Nigbor singed?"

"Nigbor? He's not the type you should be paying attention to," Minerva said.

"But what is he? He's not an Elf, at least he doesn't look like the ones I've seen."

"You've only seen the highborn council and you haven't seen them in their realm at all. I wouldn't worry about it, but Nigbor isn't your best resource."

"So far, he's been my only resource," Liv said.

"You have the book!" Minerva said.

Liv kept her mouth shut. She didn't want Minerva to know the book wasn't translating completely for her.

"It just helps to have someone to discuss it with. The images in the book are so foreign," Liv finally came up with when Minerva kept looking at her.

"Then use me. I can sort out anything you need," Minerva smiled at her.

"I'll keep it in mind," Liv pulled a breakfast waffle out of her pocket and opened it.

Minerva sighed. "I'll touch base with you later. Don't listen to Nigbor. He modifies the truth extensively. Take your time to make this decision and make the right choice. Go through the portal with me, not Nigbor." Minerva dissolved and Liv was alone in the second row of the van. She closed her eyes and prayed, while the storm tossed the van across the road.

Liv could tell when either the wind changed direction or the van did. The driver pulled to a stop. Liv's stomach began to unclench.

"I know you had specifically asked for the tour to include the witchcraft and sorcery museum, but the building is out on the fjord where the wind and snow will be more. I can do it if you really need to see this museum but I prefer not to in this storm," he said.

"We'll skip it," called Bea from the back with her clutch of frightened women around her. Were they afraid of Liv, Minera or the man's driving? Hard to say.

"Good," the driver slammed down the gas pedal and sped off turning left which alleviated some of the wind on the van. He picked up his radio and spoke rapidly, receiving an answer despite the weather. Liv drew in a breath as he raced even faster with the storm pushing him.

What if she entered the portal and never saw her family again? Would they miss her? She knew they would trash talk her because they did that when she was present. Would anyone miss her? At work, they'd hire a new grant writer for half the price. They'd be thrilled. It would take the new person five years to get three weeks of vacation. What about her dream of getting everyone together at the Lake House for holidays? That was a joke. No one wanted to go. The house held tons of memories but bad ones as well as good. The Lake House definitely wasn't her style. It was best described as comfy clutter meets rustic cabin.

She had a couple of girlfriends she would miss but that was the total sum of her social life. No man dangled in the distance. It was hard to meet anyone when you worked in a renovated closet.

The snow stopped like a switch had been thrown, when the van turned into the house where they would be staying. They would go to Vik tomorrow. Liv thought she may as well finish the tour before passing into the Shimmer portal. She really wanted to see the Blue

Lagoon and a black sand beach. Those were her top choices on the tour of what might be her farewell tour.

Liv wanted to write to James too. At least he wouldn't worry so much about her fate if she couldn't come back.

They stumbled into dinner, exhausted from the van ride, Minerva's visit, the weather stress or a combination of all three. They moved to their rooms without much conversation. It was dark, of course. They were well past their four hours of allotted sunlight today.

Liv got into bed and found sleep almost instantly. No dreams marred her rest.

A knock on her door shocked her awake, clutching her chest and shaking. "Auroras are out," someone was yelling up and down the hall. At first, she was annoyed that someone interrupted her sleep but she hadn't seemed to need as much sleep during this trip.

Liv stumbled out of bed and into her outer clothes. They definitely needed a wash. Sour sweat rose from them from all the stress she'd had on this trip. Another chore to do before entering the portal or would the smell just vanish?

She followed the Esbats and other guests out into the freezing chill, but it was worth it. The splendor of the dancing green and purple lights elicited a gasp from everyone. It was like there was a beautiful beast in the sky. Liv was so glad someone had woken them. She took a picture with her camera, but it would never do the scene justice.

She moved to the back of the group and concentrated on the glowing sky and moving waves of light. With one hand on her chest where the brand was, Liv felt energy rushing into her. She visualized translating the book. She slipped one hand inside the secret pocket and found the book to be warm, almost hot.

Liv tore herself reluctantly away from the dancing aurora and hurried to her room, locking the door and drawing the shades. She took out the book. It was still warm and she opened it to a random page.

There were words in English! She snapped a photo of each new page with her camera before taking the time to read through them. The story it told her was ominous. The portal was one way to show her commitment to the upcoming battle with the Evil One. It was felt that if things got tough, the Elf Warrior might just jump ship back to some place and not fulfill their quest.

The text kept referring to the cost of doing magic. What was the cost? When she'd seen the fairy in her garden, which she totally believed now, her family had taunted her and shamed her relentlessly and for years. But, in her heart, she knew she'd witnessed a privileged thing.

And damn her family for not believing her. How would her life be different if she hadn't been labelled as crazy, time and time again? Maybe she wouldn't be the introvert she was, hiding in a closet for work, if someone had given her the benefit of the doubt.

Chapter Twelve

The usual light breakfast and coffee fortified Liv for the short trip to Vik. Black sand beaches, bring them on. As soon as she stepped off the van, she felt the strong connection to the land and sea. The sea was rough and dangerous here. Just black sand forever and crashing waves. A cute little town skirted the sea and the earthquakes and auroras seemed far away from this quiet place.

A shimmering door opened to her right and Liv debated going through it. She couldn't see anything past the shimmer. Was this an opportunity to go home? What did she really want? Did she want to go back to her family and the Lake House? The house had become a burden of projects falling in line: roof, windows, walkways, dock. The list was never ending. None of which her relatives would help pay for or appreciate. On the flip side, she would never see her nieces and nephews grow up. What to do?

"So, what are you waiting for, stupid girl?" Liv looked up and saw the crow was above her.

"For advice from a wise raven?" She was being sarcastic but buttering the bread never hurt either.

"About time. Up to now, your advice givers have been ill-advised." The raven cocked his head to one side to look at her, then the other. Liv looked down the path to see if the other travelers were seeing the talking Raven.

"Really? What advice would you give me?"

The Raven squawked and flew off.

"Nice," Liv said.

The Volks came down the trail and Liv smiled at them. They had the same rambling gait of people with upcoming hip replacements. They looked adorable and Liv waved as they came up to her.

"Were you just conversing with that Raven?" Asked the woman. Her hair was tightly curled and close to her head. She and her husband sported matching coats but different colors. Her husband's hair was short and white also. She judged them to be in their eighties but they might be older. They had hit the stage where they fell into the category of "Old" in Liv's mind and age was non-specific.

"I was speaking to the raven," Liv admitted. "He wasn't very helpful, either."

"What did you need help with? I've heard ravens can be as intelligent as a three-year-old," said the woman.

Jane led the way to a large rock that looked far from comfortable. She and Jin sat side by side, prepared to hear and help.

May as well have strangers' opinions. She would never see these people again, she thought. "I've been offered a chance to travel but I can never go back to my family or my job, ever, if I take it. I guess that's the cost of going off and being a hero. I can't decide if it's worth it."

"Why can't you go back home eventually?" Asked Jin.

"It's a one way portal. If I don't agree to never go back, I can't go at all," Liv said.

"Like a magic portal? I say no," said Jin. "Magic always has a price tag attached."

"It depends where the portal goes, I would think," said Jane.

"See, I don't really believe in magic. I used to, I think, but it was beaten out of me," said Liv.

"Common Magic is all around you," said Jin.

"I was just speaking to a raven," Liv countered. "That's kind of like magic, don't you think?"

"Either that or you've gone loopy, " Jane said.

"You may regret what you gave up later in life," Jin said.

"Well, that's a stupid thing to say. Are you regretting choosing me over your family?" Jane snapped.

"Why are you bringing this up again? Is this whole trip to be marred with your insecurities?" Jin struggled up and walked down the path away from them.

"Maybe I wouldn't be so insecure if you ever listened to me!" She yelled at him as he progressed away at an even faster rate. Jane pushed up and followed him. Calling, "Have a lovely day," as she left.

Liv watched them for a moment. Jin upped his pace and may have been running or as close to running as an eighty-year-old could get. Jane was chugging right behind him like the little engine that could.

"OK I'll go." Liv stood up but whether she was going through the portal or leaving the trail was unclear. Liv turned to where the portal had been but it was gone. Nothing but clean, clear air in the space the Shimmer had been. Missed opportunity. Maybe for the best. Liv walked back to the visitors' center. She knew there were spectacular things to see but she had no appetite to follow the trail of arguments of the older couple. Liv hoped to see the raven again but it had flown off.

Liv climbed down to the beach and sat watching the waves. Various signs had warned her of a vicious cross current. She was hidden under an overhang of rock. She dug deep and pulled the plasma from the ground. Her other hand rose to the aurora. It was there, she could feel it through the cold layers of atmosphere. She pulled on its power and dragged it into her amulet. Liv felt the ignition of the two different plasma as they joined in her chest, sparks flying and she tore open a portal right in front of her. Liv smiled wickedly and stepped through. Here's to you Jane and Jin and unknown adventures!

"Stop, what are you doing?" She heard the croak of the raven but the portal sucked her through strongly once her fingers touched the surface of the Shimmer. As she passed through, she realized this Shimmer was red gold, not icy blue. What the heck had she done?

Chapter Thirteen

Liv choked on the smoke and she couldn't see two feet ahead of her. She reached back blindly and struggled to find the portal behind her. It wasn't there. She'd just passed through it! Where was it?

She could hear the squawking of the raven, but it got farther and farther from Liv until she couldn't hear anything but the roar of the hot gasses as they swirled around her. Her vision began to adjust to the smoky red light and she saw lava dripping from the mountains in sizzling fountains in the distance. The smoke left sooty smudges wherever it touched her and tasted like oil.

Liv walked forward, feeling her way with her feet when a searing pain cut across her back. The cut burned like salt was in it and she turned in time to see the whip coming at her again. It glowed like it was on fire. Liv screamed in anger and fell forward to lessen the force of the blow. It still hurt like the devil on her forearm.

"Oh look. It learns! How delightful." The creature was humanoid looking but without clothes. It wore thick boots on its legs, but that was its only concession to modesty. It wound up the cord of sparkling fire to lash Liv again. It had enormous bug-like eyes and a tiny mouth. The nose had two thin slits. Its skin had a dark gray green cast to it.

"Why are you attacking me?" Liv asked.

"And talks too. What a joy you'll be," it cracked the whip in her direction and Liv dove at the creature, hitting it in its mid-section, just like her brothers had taught her to fight. Liv had a moment of nostalgia which passed as she battered the creature under her strong thighs. She didn't want to kill it, just subdue it and that was probably where she erred. The thing was sinewy and strong and able to get out of her grasp. It lost its whip in the fight and the two combatants scrambled up and stood facing each other.

"Who are you?" The greenish skin looked like it was fading to lighter splotches. She hoped that meant it was in shock or injured.

"I entered the wrong portal. How do I get back out?"

"Portal? How would I know? The creatures are sent. We round them up and mark them

and harvest them as needed."

"But most of them don't talk."

"Very few. We cherish these. Sometimes they are allowed to graze for a time before we use them." The thing walked over to retrieve his whip.

"If you try to hit me with that again, I'll kill you," she told him.

"But this is what I do! You are the cared for and I am the caretaker."

"How about you leave here and forget you ever saw me. I don't intend to be here very long anyway and probably none of your brethren would believe you."

"I don't wish to be removed from this place," he said. "I have been very diligent to get this place over the muck hole I was tied to before." The thing puzzled over the entirety of what Liv said and turned away, tapping his fiery whip on his free hand.

"What if you just came with me?" He paused and asked. "We could ask the others what is right."

"Nope. The portal was here before. I have a better chance of finding it here again. Get on with you."

He walked down a red trail of dust that rose and moved with each motion. Liv could see a flock of small creatures that reminded her vaguely of sheep, farther down the valley. Liv climbed the ridge behind her and found a place to hide. Not a cave exactly but not exposed to a casual observer with a fire whip. The wound on her back almost caused her to cry out as she moved during the short climb. A tear fell off her cheek and sizzled in the hot sand.

"How do I get out of here?" Liv said it almost as if it were a prayer and pulled out the book. A rock fell somewhere above her and she caught a glimpse of the creature with a fiery net in his hand. He was hunting for her. As badly as the burn on her back hurt, how much more would a net of fire hurt on her already damaged back? The only weapons available were rocks and Liv found a baseball sized rock that fit well in her hand.

Liv had spent years as the pitcher for her brothers when they were in baseball. She could have joined the girls' team but declined. Her pitching speed was in the mid seventies to low eighties according to the pitching cages. Sure that was fifteen years ago but did you ever really lose the good stuff?

She warmed up her shoulder, making a wide arc in the air and causing pain to scream down her back. She wound up and fired the missile. It made a satisfying screaming sound as it traveled through the thick air and hit the creature square on the back of the head as it turned away to scan behind it. Liv scrambled up the hill, hoping to finish the job but it looked like her first pitch had done it. Green fluid leaked out of the back of his head, smoking as it hit the hot sand.

Just in case he miraculously resurrected, Liv wound the flaming net around his slight body. It sizzled where it crossed his flesh.

"Why are you here? No, let me guess, you tried to open the portal and went through the wrong one." Nigbor sat on a rock watching Liv wrap the creature. The net burned her hands and relief at Nigbor's appearance flushed through her. She smiled at him and hoped he had the answer to her predicament. He looked almost solid in this realm.

"I didn't know there was more than one portal," she said, surveying her handiwork.

"How are you going to get out of here?" Nigbor asked.

"By asking you nicely for a ride?"

He laughed. "I can't take passengers. What else have you got that you could use?"

"I was just going to ask the book."

"Simpler than that. What do you work with? Your so-called power is driven by what?"

"Plasma." Liv waited but Nigbor just smiled at her. The dusty red smoke didn't seem to bother him in the least. She noted none of the greasy residue clung to him. He looked good with those warm hazel eyes, pale skin and dark hair. She smiled back at him. It hit her: lava. There were waterfalls of it in the mountains across from her. She could use the lava to take her back.

Liv felt a little like Dorothy in the Wizard of Oz. "Take me back," she chanted, digging her consciousness into the lava and reaching up for any ionization in the atmosphere. Lightning danced across the red sky and Liv grabbed for it. The pots of lava began to bubble and geysirs of molten rock shot into the air. Liv strained to gather it all. Her body stretched and her back arched as she felt tendrils of need grab the Light.

The inferno raced through her like a drain unclogging and she felt empty.

The air was clean and clear again and Liv sucked in a huge, filling breath. Nigbor sat on a rock near her smiling at her. There was smoke clinging to her clothes and her white hair showered soot when she shook it. Exhaustion ran through her bones and she began to sit and rest for just a minute but Nigbor pulled her up to her feet.

"Time to go back to the van, my sweet."

"I am so tired," said Liv

"And stupid, don't forget stupid," croaked the Raven.

"You were zero help. Thanks for nothing," Liv yelled at the bird and picked up a handful of stones to throw at it. Nigbor took her hand and opened it up. The stones fell to the trail. She glared where the bird had been but it had flown off.

Nigbor pointed her at the van but wouldn't step on the asphalt. Liv trudged to the vehicle.

Liv struggled to get up the three stairs of the van, collapsing into the first seat. Neither the Raven nor Nigbor had followed her after the parking lot.

"Hey, Liv! We were worried when you didn't follow us. Where did you end up going?" Asked Jane.

"Nowhere pleasant," Liv replied. "I have some more work to do."

Jane and Jin were sitting together, arm in arm. Jane nodded. Jin nodded off and Liv examined what she'd learned. There was more than one portal but how many? Was there a way she could get a preview before she committed to going through. Nigbor was watching her. Was that comforting or alarming? Hard to say.

The driver put the van in gear and the little shuttle lurched off. Liv dozed off several times, only waking when her head fell. She finally slumped to the side, waking with a cramp in her neck when the van driver squealed to a stop in front of the inn.

Chapter Fourteen

Liv ate dinner and went up to her room. Some of the inn's guests were starting a card game but she needed a shower and bed. In the shower, black soot ran off Liv's body and hair. After changing into her sweats and t-shirt, which doubled as her bed clothes, she paid for a wash and a dry at the machines down the hall. Liv could barely stay awake as she waited for her clothes to be done. She should send a quick email to James.

Dear James

Have had some adventures here in Iceland. Frolicked under the northern lights with a group of witches on the tour. Stood between two continents and imagined them ripping apart. Watched an eruption blanket the island with soot and new rock. We're trying to get out but so is everyone else. Gigantic winter storms stop everything except the maniac tour van drivers. If I don't get back, I'll be recycled as volcanic ash! I found out when tourists get lost, no one really looks for them. These Icelandic folk expect you to know to stand back from lava and not breathe the fumes. You're kind of on your own to watch out for the dangers. I'm being careful! Take care, Liv

Liv felt better for having hinted to James that things might go awry. She laid her head down and smiled.

"Sleeping? Do you really have time? When are you going to realize you aren't just a tourist anymore?" Nigbor sat on the edge of the bed, finally resorting to shaking her to wake her.

"I need to be rested. I barely got the soot stink off my body and ate after taking the tour of one of the levels of hell. I need to sleep."

"Tomorrow, we will do some exercises. It's not like you have all the time in the world, you know." Nigbor disappeared. His voice came from the ether, "I want you at your best for the finale."

"Did he say something about not having all the time in the world?" Liv laid her head down.

The next morning, the storm was gone and Liv got dressed in her bathing suit and then put her clothes over it. The itinerary was going to the Blue Lagoon, about a two hour trip.

She packed the rest of her clean clothes in her backpack to change into after her swim. Despite what Nigbor said, she was determined to do touristy things and get some enviable photos for those back home.

The van ride was filled with happy voices. The Blue Lagoon heated waters were one of the highlights Liv had been looking forward to seeing.

The smell of sulfur reached her nose as soon as they stopped and began to unload the van. She changed.

The waters were a bright cerulean blue under the light blue sky. The smoke from yesterday had cleared this area. The black volcanic sand everywhere else made the spot seem otherworldly.

Liv touched the warmth and felt herself slide into the mineral water. There was a bar available in the water as they had been told and she floated over and bought a drink. This must be what it is like to be rich.

"Enjoying the lagoon?" Asked Jane, Jin in tow. "Hard to believe there are vents erupting all across the continent."

"Well, we can't go home so we may as well enjoy it," said Jin. They bought drinks too and settled in next to Liv. She hoped they weren't in the bickering mood today. Liv just wanted to relax for one more day before she took on the warrior challenge. She remembered that Nigbor had stopped by to get her to go out and practice last night, but she had been too exhausted.

"I wonder where this beautiful water comes from," said Jane.

"It's waste water from the geothermal plant, dear," Jin said.

"You're kidding me," said Liv, instinctively rising up.

"It's not polluted. It had too many minerals to run through the municipal water. I read it in the travel book." Jin said. Jane, with a frown, gulped down her drink and set the container on a counter in the water.

"It kind of takes the shine off, you know?" She said.

Liv smiled and moved away with her drink. The Esbat witches or pagans, whatever they were, were around the next rock outcrop sipping their wine. It was good to see them enjoying themselves, even if she hadn't gotten to know most of them. Bea waved to her and Liv waved back, although a little shocked at the gesture. Maybe the Esbats didn't know it was waste water yet.

"So, make any decisions yet?" Minerva glided up next to her.

"About what, Minerva?"

"Whether you're in or out of our own little game of thrones, sister."

"Do I get to fight you?" Asked Liv.

"No, but I would practice with you, if you want," Minerva said.

"Why would you do that?" Liv finished her drink and set it on the counter.

Minerva shrugged. "To know your weaknesses. And maybe some of your glamor would rub off on me. I'm small potatoes where I'm at but elevated just because I even know you. If some message has to be delivered, it comes through me because I've already used the pathways to get here. After yesterday, you know how easy it is to miss the right portal. So it's in my best interest to stay in contact with you."

Maybe the idea that they were ripping off tourists for almost $60 a piece for bathing in wastewater had reached the boiling point.

"I'm going."

"Want company?" Asked Minerva.

"Sure, I'm going to walk through the gift shop and then go through the town. Not very exciting but you're welcome." Two could play the intelligence game, thought Liv. Minerva just might let something vital slip that Liv could use.

The gift shop overflowed with mud and other facial items made with the healing waters. Liv could appreciate the hype but soap and water worked just fine for her delicate skin. Minerva browsed but didn't buy either. Was she really there in the same plane as Liv? Hard to say. No one had interacted with her but Liv kept an eye out.

They walked into town discussing Game of Thrones and the different characters. Minerva was a good companion despite being a mortal enemy.

"A witches' shop! Let's go in." Minerva steered them across the empty street into the quaint shop that looked right out of Diagon Alley in Harry Potter. Minerva exclaimed over charms and spell books.

Liv kept one hand on her own magic book inside her coat. No telling if this was just some crazy plot to get her to bring it out so Minerva could wrestle it away from her.

"Are you a witch?" Asked Minerva. The shopkeeper, a short pale woman of ample girth, started to explain the difference between Wiccan and Pagan and Witches with Minerva sharing her enthusiasm. Liv continued to wander the shop, finally stopping in a dark corner where a young woman was weaving a bracelet out of wool.

She slid a couple of charms onto it that looked like bleached bones with holes drilled in them. The girl turned to Liv and Liv realized she was a grown woman, not an adolescent. The woman tied off the bracelet and reached out for Liv's hand. When Liv hesitated, an ancient crone had replaced the woman. She took hold of Liv's hand and slid the bracelet on Liv's wrists. "This can only help you and will do no harm." The crone's hand felt like sandpaper. The old woman sat back down in the shadowy corner, stringing more wool on the small loom. Liv looked at the bracelet. It was simple and beautiful. She looked up to thank her and now the young woman sat at the small loom. She muttered some words and Liv felt a bolt of energy race through her.

"Remember this as a help when you need it," the young woman told her and when Liv looked down to examine the bracelet, and then back up, there was no one in the corner. The bracelet began to glow and then the pain raced up her arm to her amulet. Her whole right side throbbed with energy. Liv cried out and cradled her arm to her chest.

"What's wrong?" Asked Minerva.

"Nothing," Liv said. "I stumbled over something; I think my own feet." The bracelet
melted into her wrist, leaving a faint line of raised skin.

"Did you see anything you like?" Asked the shopkeeper.

"Very nice stuff but I'm not buying gifts this trip. It's too expensive to get them home and my family doesn't need more stuff in their lives. They're all in a rage of decluttering these days."

"You should probably get back to the van," said Minerva.

"Are you going back through your portal to report?"

"That's what I do, my new bestie. Are you going to be practicing later today?"

"Yes, I will and you're invited. Do I just summon you?"

"That would be dandy," said Minerva. "Every time you call me, it makes our bond stronger and I become more useful to the powers that be." Minerva smiled.

Well, that could come back to haunt her, Liv thought. I won't be calling her any time soon, she promised as she got on the van. Liv was sure that Minerva's strengthening bond would be used against her when it really mattered. The young girl/woman/crone from the witch's shop bothered her. How had she known that Liv would come to that shop? Whatever it was, Liv would take all the help offered. She fervently hoped it was help the Three offered her.

The van drove with the same reckless abandon as before but it didn't bother Liv the way it had. She rested her eyes until some violent random moves shook the van.

"Everyone out!" The van driver yelled. "Earthquake." Liv was in her usual spot up front and was second out of the van. She held onto the stair railing with one hand and helped the others out. The ground trembled under her feet and the vibrations knocked her to her knees. Her chest felt like an elephant sat on her and she rolled onto her back, writhing in pain. A roar rose up and Live grabbed her ears in agony. The sound went through her.

Liv saw people running past her but no one stopped to see if she needed help. Liv squeezed her eyes tight against the agony that snaked through her. The ground movement stopped and Liv was able to take a breath as the pain subsided.

Jin and Jane knelt by her. She saw their lips moving but couldn't hear the words. Each one took one of her hands. Peaceful feelings soothed up her arms.

The van driver was crouched on the ground a few feet away. "Are you ok, miss?"

"I think so. It was probably just a panic attack," she rolled over and dusted off her pants.

"Don't get up yet," Jin warned Liv. "It may not be over."

Liv crouched down. Something inside her told her it was just beginning. She felt an upwelling in her stomach and a fiery glow inside her chest. Somewhere there was a huge amount of plasma moving.

A crack split the ground and Liv screamed again, covering her ears. Every nerve-ending in her body seemed on fire. Smoke billowed out from the horizon. Missiles of lava shot up and looked like rockets against the darkening sky.

Liv got herself under control. She trembled as she fought to stand upright. There was too much plasma in the atmosphere. Jin and Jane helped her up.

"Get back in the van. Everyone OK?" The van driver hustled them back aboard and any serenity they'd gotten from the blue lagoon vanished. Jane helped Liv up the steps and Jin took the other side, escorting her back to her seat.

The driver sped towards their hostel and Liv's apprehension increased. "We shouldn't go this way," Liv told the driver. Just as they turned into the city, the lights of a police barricade lit up the inside of the van. The van pulled to a stop and waited in line with other vehicles.

The police holding the barrier conversed with the driver in what might have been Icelandic or Elvish as far as Liv was concerned.

"OK, we're evacuating to the school in the next town over," the van driver told them.

Various complaints rumbled through the van, until finally the van driver said, "Enough. There is an active eruption. It may be something and it may be nothing. We're getting you one step closer to the airport in case there's trouble. I've been here during eruptions and it can be pretty scary." He turned away from them and stomped on the accelerator.

They drove around the city and on to the next little town. The van driver pulled into a school with all the lights on. "Here we are." Liv could see the lights of Grindvik below them and hoped the higher altitude might keep them safer.

It was full dark now and Liv wondered if the other passengers could see the smoke curling up in the atmosphere like she could. The Esbats were complaining amongst themselves about the inconvenience, blissfully unaware of their danger. Jin and Jane smiled at each other and held hands, apparently unbothered by the eruption.

Liv could feel the magma forcing itself up through the brittle rock and exploding as it touched the cold air. Huge pieces of rock were flung into the air and battered Grindvik below them. Liv hoped the residents of the town below them were safe.

The people who had been evacuated stayed in a gymnasium. Wrestling mats were beds and the people in town had contributed blankets and what food they could but it was slim pickings.

"There isn't enough food," said Bea.
"You foreigners are too fat anyway," laughed the van driver.

Liv thought a fist fight might ensue. If the Esbats could really cast spells, the van driver would have been in real trouble. As it was, they muttered angrily for a few minutes and then the Esbat group got up and moved their mats into a hallway for more privacy. Liv lost interest in watching the group as they wandered off. Liv finished her protein bar and stepped outside into the smoke.

The plasma energy was overwhelming and shook every part of her body.

"Fun, isn't it?" Nigbor walked out of the smoke towards Liv, with a jaunty step, breathing evidently not a problem for whatever species he was.

"It's overwhelming. I can feel it vibrating through my body." Liv put a portion of her scarf around her mouth and nose. "Now, if I could only breathe."

"You can. You just don't realize you can. The more you manifest or accept the plasma, the more you step into our realm. Try it."

Liv stood a moment, trying to reason it out. Then, she shrugged and took off the scarf, breathing in deeply on faith. Her lungs expanded and the gritty air moved in and out just fine. A little heavy on the sulfur but Liv could breathe it easily. She almost smiled at her newfound gift.

"Mind over matter," said Nigbor, tapping his head.
"What else do you know that I don't?"

"Soooo much," Nigbor smiled. He was cute but not in a conventional way. In a Nigbor way, all angles and high cheekbones.

"Let me rephrase that. What else can you tell me that I need to know to survive?"

"I wish I had the time. I'm not even really supposed to be showing you anything but I know you have the translation problem with the book."

"Three questions. Give me three before you fade off into wherever you fade off into."

Nigbor pointed his finger at her. "You're a sneaky one. I should leave now."

"Big bad Nigbor afraid he'll get in trouble?" Liv had learned the power of mocking from the moment her two younger brothers could respond to taunting. She was at an expert level at poking at the soft core of male ego.

"How do I win the coming battle?" She asked.
"Good question."
"I'm a researcher," Liv smiled. "I get paid to write good questions."
"I can't see in the future, but I think your best chance is your spirit."

Liv pursed her lips, disappointed. "Too general to help. Tell me something helpful about how to use this power."

"Much better, more specific question. You need to bring the power to your body before attempting to use it. Once your body accepts the power, only then can you direct it. It's up to you to gauge how much power you're capable of handling."

"Last question: After this battle is all over, can I go back home?"
"If that is what you want, of course."
"Well, that's a relief. Wait, why wouldn't I want to go home?"

"That's four questions. Time for me to fly now." He wiggled his fingers and faded into the smoke.

"What possible reason could there be for me to not want to return home?" Liv couldn't think of a reason. The normalness of the Lake House and her job started to look more appealing.

On the plus side, she could consider a career as a smokejumper, since she was impervious to smoke inhalation. Would sitting in a cubicle putting together reams of paper reports satisfy her after this?

May as well try out what Nigbor suggested. Liv relaxed, closed her eyes and tried to open herself to the plasma force she could feel all around her. She drew it in and held it. She swelled as the power rushed into her. She was overfull but still she took it in. Rational thought fled and she only knew the plasma.

It was alive but not in a way that Liv understood. Each piece of it knew all the other pieces, and they communicated. She was part of the whole and it accepted her.

"Getting your practice in without me? Naughty girl," said Minerva, walking out of the darkness.

The fullness, the belonging was shattered. Something ripped itself from her. Liv fell to her knees and gasped.

"Sorry about that, dear heart. Did I ruin your little moment?" Minerva leaned down close to Liv's ear. "Don't forget to summon me next time you have a little training session. I can help you manage it so it doesn't kill you." Minerva hovered a foot off the ground and then faded.

A fine layer of ash covered Liv and she struggled to find the strength to get up. Liv stumbled back to the gymnasium.

"Lights out in ten minutes," one of the organizers called. Liv glanced to where the Esbats' mats were grouped, but none of them were there. Probably chanting their chants and lighting their black candles. Liv cleaned up as best she could in the locker room and dragged herself to her mat.

She had never been so grateful to lay her head down. Ever. Was that the effect of the plasma overload or the breaking of her contact? Minerva had indicated Liv was in danger but it felt like Minerva had put her there, not the plasma. Liv remembered that Minerva needed Liv to forge a link that would get her brownie points with her boss, whoever he was.

And that was the real question she should have asked Nigbor. Who was her ultimate adversary? And when did the whole contest start so she could go home? The questions never ended and she fell asleep tossing and turning on the wrestling mat.

When she woke the next morning, it was dark out. The volunteers were setting out breakfast and Liv tried to sit up. Her body seemed to be one massive muscle spasm. She breathed through it until she could move again and eventually was able to get up on her feet. The Esbats were either gone or had never slept. Their day backpacks were still in the same positions as yesterday, so she guessed they hadn't slept. Where were the little witches? More breakfast for her.

Everyone seemed subdued, whether from the darkness or the disruption of their trip. The van driver found her while she slowly chewed her energy bar.

"Where are the others?"

"Not sure. I'm not really with them," Liv said for the umpteenth time. Did no one listen?

"Well, if you see them, we're leaving in ten minutes. We're taking everyone to the airport for evacuation."

Liv was ready at the door of the van with her few things. Eating had helped her regain her equilibrium. She wasn't anxious to try touching the plasma again. It was like she'd been sunburned all over but on the inside as well.

She relaxed slowly into the seat of the van and closed her eyes. She could hear the van driver yelling at the other vans if they had the missing women. One of the coordinators checked the open corridors, but they weren't located.

The van driver finally climbed into the seat and turned to Liv. "And you have no idea where those idiot women went?"

"No, I'm not really with them." But Liv wondered if Minerva had something to do with their disappearance. Had Minerva known they would be evacuated today and had taken them somewhere? Liv rescued them once, should she try using the power to rescue them again? The first time it had just been 'wishing' but this time, she had more power at her disposal. Maybe they went willingly or were happy with their whereabouts. Liv dreaded reaching out to the plasma again.

"I contacted the authorities. The plane is full and the next two planes are also full. Maybe your friends will find their way there. You have a better chance of getting on a plane with the whole tour group. Otherwise it's too hard for the officials to keep track." He gave Liv a bottle of water and a protein bar.

Chapter Fifteen

Liv sat in the crowded airport and frowned at the granola bar. Was it better to eat it or save it? She knew she'd be tempted to give it away if she kept it so she opened it and chewed it slowly feeling the crumbly oats and dark chocolate.

Did Liv really want to leave Iceland at this point? She didn't see how it would solve any of her problems. She had to learn to work the plasma and this was the place for it especially with an eruption.

About an hour later, the van driver found her.

"Any sign of your friends?" He was sweating and scanned the growing crowd constantly.

"No, I haven't seen anyone I know."

He nodded and walked through the crowd to the other side of the airport. It wasn't very large for all that it was an international airport. He came back in a few minutes. "They aren't here. I'm going to have to go back to the school and look for them. Do you want to come with me?"

Liv hesitated. They weren't her friends and she didn't really care what happened to them. They hadn't been nice to her; just the opposite. Still, it would be more exciting than sitting here while the tourists piled up.

As she got into the van, she wondered if Minerva had taken them. Why would she? The only thought that came to mind was as a trap for Liv. Did she assume since Liv had looked for them before, she would again? The farther they got from the airport, the more Liv felt Minerva had been the author of their disappearance.

They stopped at a police checkpoint and the driver got out to talk to the police. They let the van through. Liv sat watching the interaction from the front shotgun seat. The plasma was very active, almost jumpy. Liv's fingers tingled and the last bit of pain floated away.

"Now, I'm going to check inside the school. Stay here so you don't get lost too," Galen said.

"Let's split up so we can finish faster," Liv suggested. The plasma was different than she'd seen before and she didn't want to miss a chance to gently see if she could work it without getting fried. The driver went off with a small bow and Liv went the opposite way to a warren of hallways.

Liv drew a modest amount of the sparkling plasma into her and held it. Her throat was scratchy and the noise of energy crackling filled her ears.

"Came back for your little friends, didn't you?" Minerva manifested in a dark corner.

She was darker, maybe from the smoke but almost like she'd been burned around the edges. Her clothing was frayed through in places, showing her pale, stretched skin and her eyes were glowing red all the time now.

"No, I just got tired of waiting in that crowded airport. Minerva, you're looking a bit ragged. What's going on?" Liv reinforced a line of energy in front of her, between Minerva and herself.

"I'm perfect thank you! And I suppose you don't care if the rest of the tour group is suffering unspeakable torment?" It was meant as a taunt, but trailed off into a question. Minerva was losing it.

Liv looked inside herself, at the plasma that was everywhere, communicating and making new pathways within her body. "Sadly no. I know in some way, I should be desperate to help my fellow humans but I'm just not feeling it today. You were the only one of that group who was ever nice to me, Minerva."

Minerva made a noise that sounded like the squawk of a goose and blinked out of the hallway. In the space of a heartbeat, the

Esbats appeared where Minerva had stood. They were naked and soot covered and looked confused.

Galen rounded the corner. "I heard a noise. You found them!" The van driver stared at the group of women who stood huddled together like sheep. "I'll get some clothes from the locker rooms. You stay here."

Liv still felt the strong pull of the plasma running through her and began to let it slide away. The van driver brought back a cardboard box full of unclaimed clothes from the locker room and encouraged the women to find something that would fit. Liv walked into the adjacent cafeteria and found bottles of water. She also nabbed two boxes of granola bars and brought it all back to the newly clothed Esbats.

The group looked uncomfortable in the tight clothing of Icelandic teenagers but there were enough sweatpants and hoodies to cover all the important bits. They murmured amongst themselves but didn't make eye contact with Liv.

"You saved us," Bea came up to her with downcast eyes.

"I told Minerva I didn't care what happened to you and she lost interest, I guess."

Bea's red rimmed eyes met Liv's. "You look a little detached," Bea said.

"Detached? How?"

"I'm not sure," Bea said. Gale approached from the group.

"You almost glow in all this darkness," Gale said.

Bea nodded. "You're luminous."

Liv raised a hand but it looked normal to her. "Hey, am I glowing?" Liv asked the van driver.

"You're not even clean, much less glowing. Maybe they think you're glowing because you are so pale. Everyone, let's get on the van now, and I'll take you back to the airport."

"I don't want to go back there. There's no food and nowhere to sleep. No planes are leaving just yet. You can take these ladies but I'll stay here," Liv told him. There was a mounting excitement, no not excitement, more like anticipation. Like she was at the top of a slide and ready to go down into what? Darkness, thought Liv. Whatever was going to happen was happening sooner rather than later. Better she be here, near the eruption, than the airport where so many innocents could suffer.

"I'm not going either," said Bea. "There's food, at least these granola bars, water and even showers. We can sleep on the mats and all our stuff is here. No one is going anywhere until the eruption is over anyway."

"I'll go back and tell the police so we don't lose track of you," the van driver said.

"Remember to come back and get us at some point," said Gale.

He left and Bea started organizing her people to lay the mats down. Liv noticed one mat a ways from the cluster and knew that was hers. All Liv wanted to do was work on her plasma and she didn't feel like she could do it with the women watching her.

"I'm going outside." The women exchanged looks with Bea but no one challenged her. It wasn't like Bea was their leader, but she was definitely in charge. The group ate their bars in a circle and then laid down. Liv couldn't blame them; they looked beat. Like someone had beaten them with a stick all over their bodies, they had cuts and bruises everywhere.

Liv breathed a lot easier, despite the heavy smoke, when she got outside. Funny how she actually had to think about it if she wanted to breathe. She brought some plasma in and felt instantly more relaxed. Nigbor was sitting on a large decorative block of lava.

"Getting right to it, I see. You really gave Minerva a turn. She's not nearly as clever as she thinks she is. She dropped whatever spell she crafted when you didn't respond to her taking the women. Nice play."

"I'm not worried about Minerva or even those poor souls in the gym. I'm worried about being ready for whatever is coming. What is coming?" Liv asked.

"Have you looked in the book lately?"

"Can't you just tell me? I'm so sick of you telling me to look at the book, then I look at the book and it doesn't make any sense."

"You're so much stronger now, though."

"I haven't had a moment to myself to look through it," Liv said. She pulled the book out of her pocket.

"Make it into something no one would look twice at," Nigbor said.

Liv frowned at the book and it shimmered and turned into a People magazine. She leafed through the pages, delighted they were in English. When she looked up to thank Nigbor, he was gone. She sat next to the building with the solid bricks at her back and began to read.

Chapter Sixteen

The first chapter told a story about how the Elves came to the world and lived side by side with men. Not usually mating because the humans were stupid and repulsive and the Elves were so far above them as beings. Liv stopped and smiled. This history was obviously written by the Elves! Or maybe they were around prehistoric man, in which case Liv forgave them their snobbery.

The Elves preferred the colder, more remote regions, and the humans stayed in the more habitable spots. A lot of flowery words, but the basic text said Elves improved the world, but men befouled it. There were some wars which, of course, the Elves won and a lot about several great heroes. She wondered if the book really had any knowledge for her to gain to help her in the future conflict.

Why would the Elves choose a human for the Elf Warrior?

If they were as superior as they said in the guidebook, they should pick a glorious Elf from their ranks to represent them. Not some grant writer whose family treated her like an unwelcome alien.

The next section of the book dealt with technique. That was more to the point. The first skill was bringing the plasma into your body. Nigbor had helped her figure that one out. She concentrated and was able to fill herself half way.

Liv held it there, marveling at the way the plasma felt coursing through her body. None of the burning or stinging bothered her like it had before.

"That's because you're getting used to it." A flat voice rang in her head.

Chapter Seventeen

Liv turned to see what she assumed was an Elf. It wasn't what she expected. She could see crystals in the planes of its body. The smooth, glassy contours of its face and sinewy muscles in its bare arms and legs looked masculine.

"And who are you?"

"Anthor. Your guide on this journey." It wore what might have been dark leather skirt and a breastplate of silver. Its skin was crystalline like new fallen snow. Anthor wore knee-high boots that tied instead of buckled.

"My guide? Where have you been? I've been struggling here, really struggling."

"Apologies. I was not sure you were worthy."

"What about Nigbor and Minerva? They thought I was worth it. They've been subbing in for you. I couldn't translate the book at first." Anger rose in her and she could feel the plasma becoming excited in her body.

"Not surprising. I'm here to help now."

"Liv!" Gale called from the door. "There are more eruptions coming."

"Thanks, I'll be in soon." Liv called. Evidently, Anthor wasn't visible to regular humans.

"Your deadline is approaching," Anthor told her.

"What deadline?"

"The battle for the Elves," he explained. "You read the history. The great battle is ahead. Not too far ahead either. We have much work to do to get you ready."

Although that was exactly what Liv had hoped for, she was still hesitant to trust the white warrior. "When?"

"Time moves differently in your realm, but it is soon enough that we need to gird ourselves and prepare."

"I'm ready to gird," Liv affirmed. Since she was stuck here, she may as well use the time to prepare.

"This is not a lightly made decision," Anthor told her. "I was once like you and then I chose to take up the mantle of a warrior. I have known chaos and decided to set things right. Just as your current work might set things right for an age."

Liv said. "How can you be like me? I'm human," she said.

"Part human," Anthor told her.

"Part? Which part? Was my mother an Elf or my father?" Liv pictured her short, dark haired parents who were built stocky like all of her kin. Liv stood out as a pale slim weed.

"Neither your mother nor father had any idea. It has become difficult for Elves to reproduce. Each generation becomes weaker. So the decision was made to cross pollinate, as it were. You were placed in your mother."

"That's why I couldn't translate the book. I didn't have the full Elf set of chromosomes. I never felt a part of my family. Not really." Scenes from her past washed through her mind: simple things like looking at the moon and going on field trips with other kids. They knew Liv didn't fit in. But did she believe this apparition? He had appeared out of the ether. Did she trust him?

"As much as your tour mates wished to see magic, they did not understand how to gather it to themselves. They afforded evil a pathway, but had no say over it once they were ensnared. Even now, they hold the seeds of betrayal and destruction for you."

"It's not like they're friends. They're more like pesky sisters you can't shake."

"Just beware. If you try to count them as allies, they will fail you. If you don't account for them, they will attack your blind side."

"Untrustworthy, check. I can totally see that."

"Form a knife with plasma," Anthor said.

Liv concentrated. A nub of something white and shimmering formed. Liv struggled to get it to shape properly. She knew the moment Anthor took control of her mind and guided the formation of the blade. It was a foot and a half long, sharp and wicked, curved like a scimitar.

"Try again." The blade dissolved.

"Does the thing I'm fighting have any sweet spots?"

"Vulnerabilities? No, although the light blades will cause it discomfort."

"How do I kill it?"

"It cannot be killed. True evil can only be repulsed until it is driven back from the gateway."

"So I have to defend a gateway?"

"It's a passage to the Elf realm but to you it may appear as a gateway or a bridge." Anthor smiled. "For me, it was a log over a fast flowing river, but that was when the Elves wandered the earth freely."

"When I've finished the challenge, assuming I drive this thing back, can I go back home?" Liv fashioned an almost perfect knife, following the inner pathways that Anthor had shown her.

"Home? Once you've accepted the mantel, it will be difficult. If you felt like you were different before, you won't fit in at all in your new representation." He made a beautiful curved sword that glittered in the smoke.

Liv started with the knife and tried to lengthen it. Once again, Anthor took control and carved a pathway in her mind and body so she could replicate the weapon.

Anthor dissolved the sword and created a small moving target 25 yards away after clearing the smoke away with the wave of an arm.

"Throw the light to destroy the target as it moves."

Liv struggled but she couldn't force the ball of light from her fingertips. Anthor showed her how and she was able to throw the light inexpertly. She only hit the target one out of four times.

"I'll leave you to work on these basic skills. My energy is low. I'll come back when I am able. We need to spend as much time together as possible to prepare you." He dissolved into thin, white smoke.

Liv practiced the knife, the sword and the targets for what seemed like hours. The impression she got from being immersed in Anthor's brain patterns was that she was fairly hopeless. When she felt her own energy ebb, she went inside to find what they had to eat.

They had some pre-packaged snacks and Liv tore into them without regard for taste. She just needed fuel. She stopped eating when she realized she wasn't hungry. Did she live off the Light now?

Gale stood in the kitchen doorway watching her. Liv sensed her without looking. Liv reached out and tried to locate the other Esbats. She had a vague idea where they were but couldn't pinpoint them. She would practice that skill too.

"Liv, have you got a minute?" Gale asked.

"Sure," Liv continued eating her granola bar as she turned. Gale looked haggard. Her purple bruises were turning yellow, and she had dozens of sharp cuts on her limbs, too many to bind.

"If Minerva comes for us again, will you protect us?"

Liv considered and made a harsh decision. "No, I can't."

"Why not? You're the only one she's scared of!"

"No, there's someone behind her. I'm training to fight that thing, whatever it is. You chose to side with Minerva."

"But we could help you," pleaded Gale.

"You will ultimately choose to save yourself. I can't blame you for that. I have other priorities." It sounded callus to her ears. Almost inhuman.

"Save us! We were playing at being witches. Haven't you ever made a wrong decision? I admit, we erred, but we still deserve to be saved."

Liv thought about when she tried to force the green jello on her family to build closeness and laughed.

"It's not funny. I want a life. Was it so awful to want an exciting vacation? I don't deserve torture and despair," said Gale.

"I wasn't laughing about that. It was about a memory." Liv smiled. She knew she would cherish the jello moment forever, part Elf or not.

"You have a duty to save us. I know you can," said Gale.

"You guys have some magic, I can sense it. Why not try to save yourself?" Liv asked.

Gale glared at her. "Thanks for nothing! Just abandon us like we're vermin. Are you even human or are you filthy scum, like Minerva says?" Gale paused a second and then stomped off.

"Filthy scum? I can live with that. What does that make you and Minerva? Celestial beings? You look like you've been put through the ringer."

Gale turned and gave her the finger. "We need your help!"

Liv smiled and fashioned a solid glass-like knife. "Not bad for a filthy scum." She brushed some of the soot off her hand. Her hand looked paler than usual.

Maybe she didn't want to go home. She really wouldn't fit in after she got done with all this training, would she? What if her sister-in-law said something snarky? Would Liv cut her with the plasma knife? Would it even hurt her? Something to ask Anthor in their next round.

Liv washed with soap and water, scrubbing the soot off. Her hands were a shade lighter than her arms. She pressed on her fingers. They seemed more solid than usual. Was she turning into the cold, white plasma-thing like Anthor? Liv's gut rolled and she got an unsettled feeling.

At what point had she agreed to this? Could she back out now and did she really want to? Could she really go back to the former closet that barely held a desk, chair and a filing cabinet? She would miss her family though. She'd grown up with them and had tons of memories both good and bad. It would be tough to just disappear and never contact them again.

Liv couldn't answer these questions so she worked on creating the knife and the sword, improving her time. Eventually, Liv was able to create different shaped swords and she finally fashioned a crude mallet, of which she was outrageously proud. She put a slice of apple on the stainless steel counter and smacked it with the mallet. It exploded into a million pieces. The counter remained unharmed.

Liv spent twenty minutes cleaning up her applesauce mistake, all the while wondering why the counter was unmarked. Maybe it didn't hurt the counter because she was concentrating on the apple. It was her working theory at this point and she was reluctant to try again unless she was outside. Plus, someone else might want an apple. See, she told herself, she was considerate even if she was filthy scum.

Chapter Eighteen

Anthor was waiting for her outside. Liv could feel it and sighed. She was tired and thought the mallet should be enough of a triumph to get her a break. Evidently not. Liv considered ignoring what could only be called a summons. She was sure that wouldn't fly.

Liv pushed open the door to the outside and a flurry of ash flooded in. She had to clear the bottom before the door would close. The air was full of ash and smoke and a red tint colored everything.

Anthor was just out of her limit of sight. Liv closed her eyes and used her plasma to clear the smoke.

"Are you ready for some simulated battle practice? You can create a knife and a sword, as I recall. The next is to see if you have the will to use them. I'll set a perimeter. None can observe or tamper with your practice. I noticed that the shade, Minerva, has been hampering you. She is just a distraction." Anthor drew an arc in the sky and Liv watched a shimmering shield form a dome shape around them.

"Before we start, I have a question: When did I agree to do this or is it still OK to back out and go home?"

"What? When you received the book, you agreed to be the representative!"

"How did I know that?"

Anthor formed a curved sword and cut through the air. He came at her, and she faltered for a second before creating a mallet. He was on her with freakish speed, slashing and hacking at her. Liv recovered and found some deep-seated anger to fuel her attack. She stopped retreating and pressed forward with the heavy mallet, countering the blade that Anthor wielded.

He grunted with each swing of his sword and Liv found she was exhaling in rhythm. Once she realized it, she changed her rhythm to a half count. When he swung on a beat, she came in half way through, like dividing a whole music note into two half counts.

Her mallet got inside his guard and struck him a solid blow to his side. Anthor bent double, breathing through his mouth. He held up a hand. "I'm not as nimble as I used to be. You've done well. I wasn't prepared for you to show so much fight. It will hold you in good stead. I'll have you fight the warrior." A man-like shadow appeared across from Liv.

He attacked her, using two knives that he fashioned from thin air. Liv responded as if her brother was attacking her with paint brushes. She sacrificed one of her arms in a defensive ploy so that she could move in close to him and drove her mallet under the warrior's chin. He staggered back under the blow but recovered.

He charged at Liv. Liv, veteran of years of having two younger brothers, turned her body sideways at the last possible moment and hit him a stunning blow on the back of the head with the mallet. The smoke warrior dissolved.

"I see why you were chosen," Anthor said. "Although it defies reason that a woman should be so adept."

"That's pretty insulting. Why shouldn't women fight as well as men?"

"You are weaker," Anthor said.

"Women are stronger. Maybe not arm strength, but we can handle more pain. What's next?"

Anthor crouched and touched the ground. A white cloud gathered around him and spread out towards Liv. Pale lightning arced in the cloud and it rushed at her. Liz tried blocking the lightning, but it got through all her defenses. The white cloud reached her and blanketed her so she couldn't see or breathe, and a spark of panic grew in her chest. Liv fought through the solidifying mass, but it tightened around her. Liv flailed, but her arms became imprisoned tight against her body.

Liv couldn't clear her head to focus. The white stuff suffocated her and infiltrated into her body. She didn't give up but her struggles became weaker and weaker as her terror grew.

Chapter Nineteen

Liv awoke, laying on the frigid ground, in the dome.

Anthor plunged a pole into the ground across the dome. "Try encasing the pole with Light, like I did to you," he said. "When you succeed, the dome will vanish, and you'll be done with today's lesson." Anthor walked out of the dome into the suffocating red smoke.

Liv lay where she was, gathering her energy and sat up. Her throat and nose were raw where the white crap had invaded her. Liv wished she had some water with her. She'd gotten cocky. Anthor has been hitting it hard for a long time if his singlet and armor were any indication, even his weapons were old. That didn't mean hers had to be though. She had to practice with the deadly cotton candy first to get out of here.

Liv pulled plasma into herself and felt better, cleaned out somehow. Did it heal her? Could it? Her body seemed stronger with the plasma filling her, although she was careful not to take too much in. Liv formed a small cloud within her hands. She'd taken a Reiki class once and the man had them form energy balls in their hands. Liv always felt the energy but now she could see the little mass of clouds.

Liv gave it a push towards the pole. It moved four feet. How did he get it to explode and cover her like expanding foam?

She pulled it back and reformed it into something like a tank shell, or what she imagined a tank shell would be. Liv concentrated on hardening the casing until it looked like white metal. How to propel it? Liv created a missile launcher, over the shoulder tube. She firmed it up and put the shell into it. Liv concentrated her whole being on applying force to the shell.

It exploded out of her launcher and wrapped around the pole. "Nailed it!" She yelled. The dome dissolved and Liv waited for Anthor to congratulate her. After a few minutes, she gave up and went inside to find water. He really wasn't the cheerleader type of mentor. Not that Liv needed constant reassurance, but a "You go, girl!" would do wonders for her confidence.

The Esbats sat in a tight triangle, joined by heavy chains on their hands. Was this one of Minerva's tricks to wear her down? It didn't look like they could see her and Liv was almost too beat to care. She couldn't sleep in the same gymnasium, knowing they were sitting somewhere suffering so she found an empty hallway to sleep in. It was a cheap trick and she hated Minerva all the more for her pettiness.

Liv stopped off in the kitchen and rummaged through the boxes of supplies: water and a couple of granola bars it would have to be. Eating was a habit she wasn't ready to give up yet. Ditto, coffee. She burned, thinking of the innocents that Minerva was dangling in front of her. Liv stalked to the gymnasium where the Esbats were suffering, Liv could tell by the expressions on their faces. Liv thought why not combine practice with ruining Minerva's little pain game.

She gathered her plasma. The mallet? The sword? The tank missile? Liv formed a curved sword half the length of her body. She smiled and put some oomph behind her swing. The chains shattered and the women cowered on their mats.

"Everyone OK?" Liv asked.

"Thank you for saving us. I knew you wouldn't let us die in there," said Gale. She held Banya's hand.

"I saved you so I could get some sleep," Liv told her. "I've been practicing, and I think this was just one of Minerva's little soulless tricks to see what I've been working on." The use of the plasma, just the act of cutting the chains, made her feel better, reinvigorated her.

Liv felt energy coursing through her body but something was off. It felt like little strings of goo were tying her to the Esbat women. She forged a jagged knife from plasma. Liv concentrated on making it as sharp as possible.

She turned and sliced the air between Gale and herself. The connection didn't sever. Then, she tried cutting the bond between Bea. Nothing happened.

"And thank you, Liv, for falling into my little trap," said Minerva. "Welcome to your new assistants, or baggage, as I like to call them." Minerva threw something in the air and Liv could see the lines connecting her with the Esbat women. Not only was she physically connected, their thoughts entered into her consciousness. She knew Gale was afraid of her and Bea just wanted to get home and see her grandkids, Banya was literally blank, in shock. Liv tried to clear her head and concentrate but too many random thoughts and emotions crowded in.

Liv stumbled around the room, holding her head, trying to physically force the images out of her mind. She screamed in frustration but the images just kept bombarding her. The internal voices rose in volume: grandchildren laughing in the sunlight, someone crying for her mother and Minerva's cackling over it all. The noise in her head was deafening.

Her hands were wet and Liv pulled them away from her ears and found them clammy with blood. She had to do something to save herself. The noise was damaging her. What would Anthor do? Liv choked back a sob. This kind of shit wouldn't happen to Anthor.

First, Liv stopped stumbling around without being able to see or hear. She stilled herself and then sucked plasma in, blanketing herself with it, including her mind.

Liv willed the plasma to expand like the foam that Anthor used on her. Everything slowed down, and she found she could function without physically being able to see. She reached out with her inner eye. The horrible noise found a chink in Liv's defenses and rushed in to overwhelm her. The force of the noise beat her to her knees and Liv calmed herself and forced her body upright again.

Liv immersed herself in a sauna of whiteness, sinking deeply until the crap that was in her head, was forced out through sheer volume displacement. The sharp knife was still in her hand and she wondered if she should kill the Esbats to combat this from happening again. Surely, Minerva would come up with something new for her next volley.

Instead, Liv cut the ties that linked the women with her and scraped the residue from her mind and body. It worked this time. She felt like she needed another bath. There was something cloying and oily about the magic that Minerva did. The white plasma felt clean, and she wondered if it repulsed Minerva. She hoped so. She meant to sicken Minerva with the suffocation Anthor inflicted on her.

Liv walked back to where the Esbats sat or laid on their mats.

"You need to leave when the next opportunity comes. When the van driver checks on us. I can't have you in the way when the battle starts."

"I don't think we can, Liv. Minerva said we're linked to you like belling the cat," said Bea.

"I unlinked us. You'll need to get out of here, first chance so she can't do it again."

"Is that why I feel so blah like I can't concentrate?" Bea asked.

"Yes, I think that would be it," Liv said. "When you were in my head, I couldn't concentrate. Are you guys with Minerva or against her? Just curious."

"Against, except when she's there, it's like well, I can't speak for the others, but I can't do anything but what she tells us to do. Like I'm powerless."

Chapter Twenty

Liv expected Minerva to make her next move right away, but it must have tired her, all the tethering in the spell. It was good to know her adversary. Liv was confident she could best Minerva again with a little luck.

Liv wondered where Anthor was. She was eager to show off her expertise and be secretly pleased with his praise. She tried calling him with the plasma, but wasn't sure how to do it. Still, she tried. What good was a mentor if he didn't mentor?

Liv went inside to the gym again and tried to nap but was too excited about her victory over Minerva. Liv really only had four weapons: mallet, knife, sword and suffocating cloud that worked occasionally, and an unreliable lightning ball. She wished Anthor would show so she could ask for more weapons. Oh and the bazooka. That was cool and she'd done that on her own. What other weapon did she need?

In the movie 300, the guys had a spear, sword and shield but they had their brothers to help. In Gladiator, he allied with the other fighters. What about Alien or Predator? Neither of them worked out for the protagonist very well. Maybe a net? She could make a net and try to have it constrict tighter and tighter. Or a rope like Wonder Woman.

Liv decided meditation would do her the most good. Her mind was whirling and she still felt the tendrils of the Esbat women in her brain murmuring. In her meditation, she saw a vision of Anthor, naked and chained to a wall. He had holes in his body where the red of the wall showed through. One arm was mangled and he mumbled in a coma-like state. Liv tried to wake him in her meditation, but couldn't.

What was strong enough to beat Anthor, Warrior of the Ages and what could Liv do about it? She'd mounted a rescue of the

Esbats, couldn't she do the same for Anthor? Or was that exactly what Minerva expected? What would Anthor want her to do? As a teacher, he left much to be desired. How would she approach it from a grant standpoint?

OK, big bad grant that she wanted for some school X. How would she go about it? Research everything about school X and the grant givers. Liv pulled out the book and got a bottle of water.

Liv paged through the history, looking for any clues about techniques Anthor used in his time. He fought with honor and bravery, yada, yada, yada. She saw something and flipped back a page. Anthor had been tricked and was losing but he had laid a couple of snares and the Big Bad fell into one and was trapped.

Liv sat back. So, Anthor never defeated the Bad, he just trapped it. Liv concentrated more deeply. How had he trapped it? Some kind of closed portal. It could go in but it couldn't get out. She'd practice making a portal and sealing it. Maybe use that net she imagined creating.

A shiver ran through her body. Portals were dangerous. She could get stuck as easily as Minerva. Did Minerva really have that much power, or was she the frontman for the main act?

She paged through the book, concentrating on portals: opening and closing. There was some scrawled writing going vertically up the binding, in very small script. Concentrate and open the portal like a soft flower opening, close it like your fist. And squeeze.

How to choose the portal though when she didn't know what was out there? It seemed like some realms were already there but some were just created. Liv imagined the ideal realm: no plasma. It would be tricky to open because she could very well get caught in it with no plasma to get her out. Last time, Liv created the portal where she stood. The next time, she would attempt to open it as far away as she could get it without losing control. She could even fashion a pole to keep her from sliding into it, to anchor herself.

Was plasma what made Minerva tick? Good question. What provided her life force? It was red, she believed. Lava? Fire? What was the opposite of plasma? Something negative. Ions? Liv concentrated and went back through the book. The book called the plasma: Light and the other force Dark. Black Hole? Made sense for as much as she knew about Black Holes, basically nothing or whatever Star Trek told her.

What overcame darkness? More light. What could protect her from the overload she experienced before? Liv fashioned the anchor pole and a vest to hold the extra Light with vents in the back in case it got too much to handle. Liv was only now appreciating how much imagination and belief mattered in this game.

"Ready to play?" Minerva walked out of a wall and Liv gasped. She looked awful, ragged, with holes in her person where the light showed through. Her hair was dried out and stick-like. Smoke fell off her clothing. Her eyes were totally dilated and rimmed in red.

"What's happened to you? Minerva, have you seen yourself lately?"

Minerva stopped, mid-rant, and saw a mirror on the wall over a sink and stared into it. Smoke rose from her clothing, what was left of it. Minerva frowned and smoothed her hair back. Several chunks broke off and fell to the floor. Minerva whipped back around to face Liv.

"I'm manifesting my internal power, skank. Deal with this." Minerva threw her hands, almost like jazz hands. The hot squiggles that flew at Liv were absorbed into her chest pad that still had some Light stored in it.

Liv concentrated and opened a portal just behind Minerva. Minerva reacted instantly, flinging herself at Liv and wrapping her arms around Liv. They tilted and Liv screamed as they tumbled through the portal that glistened like a seeping wound. The world was water, only water, at least it looked like water. The smell burned in her nostrils, like ammonia or something else caustic. The smell reached into her sinuses, and Liv covered herself in plasma, her shining suit gliding over her head and the rest of her body. She could only hope it protected her. It had some buoyancy in whatever the liquid of this world was and she scanned the area for Minerva.

Between waves, she caught a glimpse of the ragged red hair. Minerva was making her way through the waves to her, looking like a ghoul. Liv examined the amount of Light left in her chest pack. She reached out, closed her eyes and imagined drawing herself to the pole she attached near the school. Liv slowly pulled herself out of the liquid of the sea. It took all her energy and concentration. It was happening as she'd imagined it and her speed rose toward the portal that slitted open in the sky above.

Then she stopped rising and looked down, Minerva had both skeletal arms dug into her leg. Liv sighed. If she saved herself, Minerva was going to be saved too.

Liv dissolved the Light coating her legs and Minerva floundered for a moment but Liv saw she had dug into the skin, not the suit. They popped through the portal but the energy tried to pull them back and both Minerva and Liv clawed for purchase in the hard lava soil.

They were gasping, their breathing ragged and harsh. Liv took in Light and her breathing regulated. Minerva staggered towards her with bare bones where her fingers had been flesh before the caustic sea.

Did Minerva mean to strangle her? Liv created a sword and hardened it just before Minerva rushed her. Liv cut her straight across the waist. Minerva stopped a second, confused by the cut, but renewed her attack without any consequences. Had the sea dip helped her? Liv could see where the sword cut through her stomach. It was a grim and ugly gash through the pale flesh and whatever remained of her clothing.

As Minerva closed the distance, Liv tried to push her with the Light. Minerva stumbled back but kept coming like a zombie. If she'd had time, Liv would have consulted the book and gotten some answer as to why Minerva seemed unkillable. Maybe it was a spell she'd done. If it was, Minerva had to offer something for it, especially if it was powerful. Had she sacrificed the Esbats? Gale had mentioned she couldn't refuse Minerva.

She had read a little about those instances. The book specified they couldn't be sustained indefinitely. Liv was exhausted from physically beating off Minerva's attacks.

Liv wrapped Minerva in a cloud of suffocating white Light. The shrieks sent chills down Liv's spine and she could feel the control breaking away from her hold on Minerva. Minerva popped and was gone. Must be nice to be able to scoot when you're losing, Liv thought.

To be sure, Liv needed the chance to rest. Dealing with zombie Minerva engaged her physically and mentally. It was an effective strategy, Liv admitted. Minerva might be softening her up for the next act. Maybe Liv could learn something from the tactic. Liv found the physical fitness locker on the far side of the gym. She kicked in the double door, at the lock where it was weakest. With the usual assortment of balls, hockey sticks, hula-hoops and scooters, she found what she was looking for: clear poles used for fitness routines. Rounded poles five and a half feet long. Perfect. She paired it with a slim sharp knife from the kitchen, taping and tieing the knife in place at the end of the shaft. The tape was some kind of wunder tape that would keep roofing intact and holes in glass from spreading. She just needed one solid jab. Maybe a real spear would work where her one fashioned of Light hadn't.

Chapter Twenty One

Liv went outside into the smoke. The eruption was proceeding, she could feel the lava oozing over the lip of the rift. She pulled the Light into her and regained some of her energy. Her fingers looked like stalactites of white crystal. Her arms seemed very white. Was she turning into the Light? Was that how Anthor was? Would she revert to normal once this task was done or stay as an alabaster statue? She wanted it over now so she could get back to her life.

"Been going through a rough patch?" Nigbor asked. He lounged against the wall of the school.

"Are you aware of what's been going on?" Liv asked him.

"Vaguely. I keep my finger on the pulse. That Minerva, wow, tough ah, whatever she is." He shook his head and whistled. His hazel eyes sparkled at her and he'd grown a scruffy shadowy beard.

"Beard looks good on you," Liv said.

"I am glad you like it. How can I help you?"

"Tell me how to end Minerva. I think once we get past her, I can go home."

"Still on the 'going home' business. A sad refrain."

"Are you saying I can't go home?" Liv felt grit in her eyes and she brushed a tear away.

"Why so upset? Was home that great?"

Liv sat down on a rock. "I think it's all the changing rules. I mean, I cut her in half, you'd think that would have killed her. Instead, she just welds herself together and keeps coming."

Nigbor came over and sat next to her. "Don't forget, she's a thing of magic more than flesh now."

"Did you see her? She's like a zombie. Skin and flesh hanging off her bones. How do I kill something like that?" Liv shook her head.

"She's a tough little fighter, that one."

"Not helpful. If you can't help, begone. I'm going to study the book some more," Liv waved her hand and Nigbor popped out of existence. He had a look of anger on his face in the last unguarded moment before he popped away. Liv wondered again what kind of thing Nigbor was. He had the rosy glow that everything did right now. He looked human. Cute to boot but he definitely wasn't a human. The Esbats were either naive or working actively against her. No one wore their true face.

Liv heard a sizzling noise that brought her back to the present. It was like the sky ripped apart. Huge balls of fire shot into the air, for hundreds of feet. Although Liv could feel the huge influx of plasma, this time she could also see the fireballs rising up against the horizon. It occurred to LIv that the van driver had taken her the perfect distance so that she wasn't overwhelmed with the amount of plasma but was close enough to learn to use it. Another ally and she could scarcely ignore any advantage. He hadn't come back for the witches, either. Perhaps he knew they were tethered to this battle for the Elves.

"Do you care about them?" Gale stood next to her. Liv jumped.

"Sorry, I didn't hear you come out."

"I heard you talking to yourself. Did you fight with Minerva?"

Liv nodded, not about to tell this emissary of evil anything. "It's nice that you came out to talk to me."

"I think we might be safe now. Minerva didn't even try to use us. If I hadn't heard you talking, I wouldn't have known there was a fight."

"Don't discount Minerva, remember she was human, and she seems impossible to kill."

"That's not good."

"Excuse me, but I have some research to do." Liv stood up and Gale reluctantly went back inside. She needed Anthor before whatever was coming got to her. She could feel it moving closer to the surface, like the magma. She was overconfident dealing with Minerva, but what if whatever was coming was much worse?

Liv turned another page of the book and saw a list of things with plasma. They included: lightning, aurora, comet tail, solar wind, earth's ionosphere and magnetosphere, neon, static electricity and welding arc. There were a few others Liv wasn't familiar with that didn't strike her as useful.

Lightning would be awesome but she'd have to time it right to use a bolt of lightning. Something to keep in mind though. Aurora, she knew and had used. Comet tail, how exactly was that useful? Solar wind, ionosphere and magnetosphere. Wow those were reaching back to middle school for what they were. Neon, not useful, ditto welding arc. Static, now that was a powerful force that could be generated anywhere. Come on, science, help me out here!

As she pondered how to use these sources of power, the image of Anthor came to her. He was bound and suffering. He looked up at her and he knew she was watching. He mouthed "No," and shook his head.

Gale had asked if she really cared about the Elves. She cared about Anthor, even though he hadn't given her much reason to care about him. He was noble somehow and expected the same of her. Liv wanted the opportunity to learn about the people who hid her among a short, dark haired family of humans. Which actually turned out not to be such a dumb idea, after all.

Liv already knew trying to rescue Anthor at this point, wasn't an option. It would deplete her energy and Anthor didn't look like he had much energy to add to the mix. No, it was all on her this time. The Warrior Elf Hero didn't matter. Neither did rescuing the Esbat witches. All that mattered was defeating Minerva and whatever forces helped her.

The next page turned in her hands. The book had gone back to pictograms and Liv saw a sequence of pictures that showed a monk traveling to the rift towards Grindavik. Once there, the monk raised his hands in some ceremony that, of course, wasn't described. Power flowed into the monk and he redirected it into a black cloud on the edge of the page.

Liv went in and stuffed her backpack with bars and water and picked up her spear. Had a thought and then cut one of the soccer nets so she had a net with her. Just in case zombie Minerva came at her. Gale called out to her, but Liv waved and left. She didn't need any of the Esbats communicating her plan to Minerva.

Chapter Twenty Two

Liv enjoyed the simple pleasure of walking. The smoke got thicker as she went toward the eruption. She figured she was within ten miles and her long legs ate up the miles. Using her Light vision to enhance the way allowed her to cross several cracks in pavement and in the lava field. The more she relied on the Light, the sharper her vision became.

Liv swigged some water and looked down at the slight valley before her. The undulating lava showed cracks twenty feet across, maybe more. Smoke rose from several places along the rift and Liv felt the magma rise and fall like it had a heartbeat.

She set down her backpack and looked at the book one more time. The pictures were detailed more clearly. A heart was evident on the monk and the black cloud was almost entirely driven off the page.

Liv connected with the magma and raised her hands to the heavens. She visualized forcing the black cloud away. The rift shook and opened up, shooting balls of red lava into the air. She stepped back. She didn't want to cause more eruptions. She wanted to wield more power to defend what? Herself? The Elves she'd only met once and briefly at that? Her will failed but the eruption exploded.

Rocks rained from the sky and Liv ran for cover. Everyone had evacuated and she huddled under the solid concrete portal of a building. The ground shook and crumbs of concrete rained down upon her. Steam screamed out of the vents in the ground. Liv collapsed and covered her ears. She tried to pull up some Light to help protect her but she couldn't even find the plasma within her. Liv moved farther away as the concrete began to rain more heavily. She worried she had exhausted her luck and she ran.

The Sight left her and she had to work with human vision. The thick smoke choked her and her eyes watered and tears ran down her face. She took a tumble over something but rolled with it and came up running. Blind panic rose in her and she flew like a startled deer. Agony slammed into her shoulder and she found her arm was on fire from a glowing ash on her sleeve. She patted it out and checked for other cinders.

Liv swung around a building and found an open door. She collapsed inside and sucked in the relatively clean air. The smoke hadn't bothered her before but now she choked.

What the heck was she going to do? Had she lost the gift of the plasma or just the nerve? She took out a water and drank deeply, watching the heavy smoke roll past. Bombs of molten rock crashed into nearby buildings and Liv shook at how brazen she'd become and the hubris of thinking she could harness a volcano to her will.

There wasn't any magic. Nothing but dumb luck up to now. Had her mind constructed all of this? Was she going insane? It could be possible her family was right to question her sanity. The ground vibrated and the windows of the building rattled. Liv went back further into the place and found a coffee machine. Such a small thing, but Liv wept at the chance to make a pot of coffee in the office and said a prayer as she took the first sip.

Maybe this would all be over soon and she could go back to the Lake House and leave this cursed country. Elves? Who was she kidding and who would believe her that she'd rescued a Little Person who gave her a magic amulet? The tears ran freely now and Liv sobbed. Eventually, despite the shaking and screaming from the vents, or perhaps because of it, Liv crawled under the sturdiest desk she could find and curled into the smallest ball possible. She slept.

When she woke, she wasn't rested but instead weary. Should Liv pull some plasma into her? No, that stuff was ridiculous. She argued with herself back and forth. It did make her feel physically better. Maybe it was like yoga or something. Liv argued herself into it without a lot of trouble.

She stood and pulled in the Light or plasma, whatever it was, and felt herself reviving with better energy. Definitely like yoga, although she had never personally done yoga. So, what Liv imagined yoga would feel like. What was the difference between yoga and the Light? The analytical part of her brain stretched and Liv felt more like herself than she had since coming to Iceland.

You couldn't feel yoga or see it, much like the Light. Both made you feel better, so why didn't she believe in the Light? She believed yoga existed. Did her cast of odd characters exist only in her mind?

Minerva, Anthor and the Esbat sisters? Liv ran her hand without thought, over the raised skin of her chest. That was real for sure. Liv wished James were here so she could talk to him. She got out her phone and penned a short email.

Dear James,

Things are weird here. Went to see the eruption and realized this is definitely NOT a tourist stop. I'm currently hiding in an office with a coffee machine so I'm safe, but it's been so long since I had brewed coffee, I may just stay here for a while. Everyone in Grindvik is evacuated or hiding, so it feels spooky and empty.

What do you think about yoga? Is it real?

Your sister, Liv

He had written back after her first email: a newsy holiday centric post with hidden meaning layered behind it that only Liv would understand. The family was angry about her trip. "Oh she can go to Iceland but not Acapulco!" Liv could actually hear it in her head. "Did she even ask if the baby is alright? There could have been an injury that showed up later and she doesn't even ask about it."

Liv didn't need her family to be present; they had permanent residence in her head. Nice that she hadn't thought about them for almost a week. It had been a true vacation for a few days anyway. She thought about the Lake House but it felt more like an anchor than somewhere she wanted to live out her life. All her futures had centered around a living, supportive family meeting at the Lake House. Lights burning warmly through the windows (which need replacing). In her vision, smoke rose from one of the three fireplaces, unlike from the ground. The fireplaces needed to be inspected for soot buildup. The list was endless and disheartening.

There was a lull in the eruptions, should she head towards Reykjavik and a flight out? It would be nice to know what she wanted to do with her life before she got back.

Liv filled her empty water bottle and left the office building. The ground still vibrated with small quakes and she used the former spear to help steady herself as she walked.

Minerva manifested at the edge of the road. Liv gasped. "You aren't real! Get out of my mind. What happened to you?" Minerva looked down at the arms bones stretched thinly with skin. A patch of hair dropped off her scalp and fell on her shoulder. Minerva brushed the hair off her shoulder as if it were lint.

"Not a good look," Liv shook her head. No way could she have made up the specter of Minerva: the patchy missing hair, rags for clothes and gray hollowed out face. Liv remembered the sweet Minerva who had first spoken to her, all excited.

Minerva glanced at her reflection in the windows of the building and shrieked. Then, she preened and ran her hands down her arms and thighs. It was vaguely sexual.

"Ewww," said Liv. The moment gave her time to gather as much Light as she could into herself. She didn't try to gauge the amount she took it, just opened herself to the Light and let it fill her as it would. Liv didn't rationalize it or try to break it down into ionic particles that behaved along the lines of science.

It thrummed through her, in tune to the waves of earthquakes that swarmed through the earth. Liv created a net from the Light. It shimmered like a lacework of diamonds in the red light of the rift. She thrust her pole into the ground and it vibrated under her hand.

Minerva ran at her, her hands like claws and her now sharp teeth bared in a grimace of hatred. Liv's net of glimmer repulsed her, leaving Liv untouched. She felt great and powerful, as if she could fill the world and push the clouds of ash away.

Her mind moved slowly to Anthor. She reached out through the portal and dissolved his chains, guiding him through the path to her. He was broken and she laid him on the warm ground and flowed healing over him.

Minerva shrieked and came back at her. Liv wheeled her arms and a great white wind arose. Minerva flew out into the smoke, spinning through the air. She scuttled back on all fours like something out of a bad horror movie. Liz cast the net at her, catching her neatly. It wrapped around her just as Liv had imagined it would. The thing that had been Minerva, hissed and spat at Liv.

Liv moved a portion of the smoke, grabbed onto her stake and opened a portal to hold Minerva forever. Liv must have been thinking about the caustic lake because that was the world that opened. Deceptively blue and beautiful, Liv shoved Minerva into the opening and watched her sink beneath the waves. Minerva's bony face was contorted in rage but no sound came out. Her open mouth filled with the blue chemical. Liv closed the portal and then collapsed next to Anthor.

"You did well," Anthor whispered.

"Are you going to be alright?" Liv asked, kneeling down next to him. A voluminous robe appeared on his body.

"I'm not sure. I have never felt this way before. I could not escape the place I was trapped in. It was a strange feeling." He labored to sit up.

"Well, we've got time now, with Minerva gone."

"Someone controlled Minerva. She existed to drain you of power, to show your weaknesses to the true evil that is coming."

"What changed your mind about me? Why did you show up so late? We could have been training all this time," Liv said.

"I feel remorse about that. I was sworn to do my duty to mentor you and I failed."

"And what changed your mind?"

Anthor sighed, waiting a beat. "I wasn't sure you were worthy until I saw you fighting. I apologize for my tardiness. I was wrong. It was wrong of me, not worthy of a warrior."

Liv gritted her teeth. She'd expended her energy to save someone who tried to sabotage her. She should have left him to rot. That was basically what he'd done to her. Liv pulled out the book and sat on the warm lichen.

"Let me repay your generosity." Anthor struggled to his feet and raised his hands to the heavens. His body lengthened and he pulled a bolt of sizzling lightning out of the dense black clouds. Anthor bent his body into an arc and threw the lightning. When it struck the ground, thunder crashed and Liv could see a large burn crater.

"I'm not at full strength, but you get the idea." Anthor sank back and propped himself against the bench by the tee area. His breathing was uneven and he closed his eyes. His being stilled and he seemed like a statue with his pale smooth limbs and white coloring.

Liv was tired but she had a shot of energy from dispatching Minerva. It hadn't been easy but she concentrated on pulling the lightning out of the dark cloud. It didn't work for her. Liv could feel the sparks in the cloud but couldn't get it to form. How could near-dead Anthor do it and she couldn't?

Liv blew out a breath and then filled herself with Light. It sputtered and refused to cooperate. What was going on? Liv stamped around, trying various techniques she could do in the past, but without the filling Light, they didn't produce the desired results.

Anthor had faded out, possibly he went back to the Elf realm to recharge.

Nigbor stepped out of the smoke and smiled at Liv. "How's it going?"

"I think Minerva is gone but somehow it doesn't feel satisfying."

"You should be out dancing! That's quite an accomplishment. Minerva was no push over." Nigbor sat on the bench where Anthor had been.

"Yes, it was tough."

"Are you sure she can't escape wherever you put her?"

Liv looked around as if Minerva might suddenly appear. "I am pretty sure she can't leave where I put her."

"I could go take a peek at her, just to make sure, if you want," he smiled at Liv. "You'd have to describe the realm to me though so I could find it. Or I could pluck the image right out of your mind, with your permission."

Liv considered his offer. She pulled enough Light into herself and then used that Light to really look at Nigbor. He liked to watch her flounder. He'd never helped her, had he? He looked a bit aged about the edges, almost like he'd been burnt and refinished many times. Why did she need him to look at MInerva? If she wanted, she could do it herself. Liv was pretty sure this was a scam to get her to show him where Minerva was hidden. With any luck, the ocean had dissolved her by now.

"No, I think I'm good, but thanks, Nigbor." Liv concentrated on healing and kept an eye on the Elf or whatever he was. As she watched him, his cute smile slid off center and she saw teeth. Liv frowned and lowered her eyes from his face to his hands. The well shaped strong hands had claws for nails. Liv had meant to ask him why her power was pulsing or unavailable, but a lump formed in her throat. She turned away but kept him in her mind's eye. Liv saw him lick his thin lips with a red reptilian tongue. He snapped out of her existence without a goodbye. She heard a snarl as he left, and smiled.

He'd told her some valuable information. First, he didn't know what portal she had opened. Second, he was a liar. Liv couldn't believe she thought the guy was cute. He certainly hadn't helped Minerva, who was on his team. Why would he help the other side? He wouldn't. Dumb question.

Liv examined the few contacts she had with Nigbor. He wasn't evil, more like ambiguous, digging for information. Liv didn't know much, but she was getting more wily by the minute. Liv concentrated on Anthor again, hoping he wasn't imprisoned. She wasn't sure she'd have the energy to deal with a trap.

Anthor appeared but Liv noticed he was almost transparent. He sighed with exhaustion, and Liv felt a pang of regret over their miscommunication. Only a small pang as it was his fault, not hers.

"Sorry, I winked out for a moment," Anthor said.

"When you 'winked' out, Nigbor winked in," Liv told him.

"Nigbor? I am not familiar with him," Anthor shook his head.

"Great looking guy, hazel eyes to die for, dark hair, wearing that attractive glamor over something ugly with claws and really sharp teeth. He's been visiting me since the beginning. Always supportive, offering help if I would just let him in my mind and heart. As I get stronger, I'm starting to see the chinks in his disguise. And why is my power blocked right now?"

"Blocked? Explain what you mean."

"I can fill partially up with Light but then I can't use it. It sputters."

"You have to sever each time you use it afterward or you end up with too many ties. Just think of each instance and then cut that tie. I think that must be the problem." Anthor stood up with difficulty and leaned against the bench near the road, for support.

"That would have been nice to know a little earlier when I was fighting for my life," said Liv.

A fluorescent green vine snaked out of the smoke. When it first touched her, Liv shrugged it off. Anger bubbled through her. Not only had Anthor screwed her over by not teaching her to work the Light but he never told her to cut the ties that drained her power. She paced up and down until something held her foot immobile.

Liv frowned and saw the green vine moving quickly up her leg to her torso. It burned where it touched her pants, to find the white flesh beneath. The vine or whatever was rapidly slithering its way up her chest and pinning her arms. The green vine was transparent and she could see things inside of it as it swarmed over her.

"Keep your arms free, you must!" Anthor tried to help her by grabbing one of the vines but it divided into two vines. Liv grabbed his hand, but the plasma force barely made her arm glow.

"Help me!" Liv cried. The vines wrapped and re-wrapped until Liv could barely stand and every inch was covered except her neck and head. She fought the vines off each time one tried to grab at her cheeks.

"Sever the ties. You must, to get your power back," Anthor's hand was torn from hers. The burning consumed her and her flesh sizzled where the vines touched her. They burrowed a half inch into her flesh; enough to incapacitate her with pain.

Liv fell to the grass, unable to break her fall. Her hands were free but only from the elbows down. She fell facing away from Anthor but heard him fighting something, someone. The sizzle of a portal opened and despite the searing pain it caused her, Liv rolled over. Anthor was struggling with a shadow. He manifested a massive sword but the black shadow was nimble and seemed to be toying with Anthor.

Liv could see Anthor was losing ground. It was difficult to concentrate when such a struggle was being fought next to her. She thought of the last time she'd used the power with Minerva. She imagined the ties and broke them one by one. The power trickled through her limbs with a tingling pinpricks sensation. It hurt but she embraced the pain and felt the vines loosen.

Liv imagined the previous time she opened the portal and then cut the links that bound her to it. She was aware of Anthor's struggles and of his sacrifice so she could regain her power. Liv used every moment to clear the ties that lessened her power. The vines fell away and she saw Anthor cast into a portal. He clawed at the edge, trying to stay in their world but the shadow grew denser and stronger and forced Anthor back into the portal. Just before he disappeared, he threw something to Liv.

"No!" She yelled as the amulet he'd tossed her, buried in her hand. It burned its way in and Liv screamed in pain, her breath difficult to pull in and her chest exploding with the power Anthor entrusted her with. She could see images, feel the waves of his energy as he gifted his power to her. She knelt, unable to rise against the tides of power that crackled through her.

Doors opened that she hadn't known were there, then they flooded with Light. Something ran through her veins, like plasma with the activated ions pulsing and racing through her. Her vision turned white and she felt rather than heard the portal close with Anthor lost to her.

White plasma poured out of her and the shadow thing retreated, stunned. The shadow dissipated into smoke and disappeared.

Liv bent over and tried to balance the power that moved through her. She concentrated to get control. The Light had stopped streaming out of her, but she was over capacity and had that feeling again like she would be torn apart. Liv started breathing in and out deep breaths. In through the mouth and out through the nose.

The brand on her palm glowed red and Liv relaxed as much as possible and invited the talisman into her for safekeeping. She hoped she could return it to Anthor someday.

The vent was erupting again and Liv blocked out the plasma that filled the air. She saw lumps of ash rain down but they didn't touch her, sliding off like she had an invisible barrier. She cut the ties of her recent struggle.

Liv concentrated on what she'd seen of the portal Anthor was shoved into. Maybe she could find him. All she saw was green, bright green behind him as he fell. Her body shook with the stress of accepting all the plasma and she brushed her hair back. Her arm was white with crystalline structures within it. She was becoming like Anthor, some white crystal structure, like some frickin piece of rock. She tried to cry but nothing came out of her eyes.

Liv sat on the bench and drank the last of her store. She had no allies and one nasty demon thing after her. She had no idea how to harness the vast amounts of power she had without killing herself but maybe that was the point. She could destroy the demon as well as herself. End of a sad fairy tale. And weren't they all sad anyway?

So that was her great, strategic plan for victory? Blow them both up? Liv went back to the office building and made more coffee. She sat down to read the book, not at all surprised to find it in English, the pictograms replaced by detailed drawings.

She flipped through pages until she found pages she hadn't seen before. Evidently, she could kill this 'Ellt,' as they named it in the book. Even its name meant 'evil' in Icelandic. It was ageless and timeless and it rose up once every millennium to see if it could take over the world. It either got beaten back by the Elf Warrior or destroyed the Warrior and it wrecked havoc on the magic system. It ruined magic. No one ever felt that special glow when they saw a sunset. The delight of living was taken out and the Elves would disappear, just fade out and the humans would cease to find delight in anything. The warm glow of a fire. A family laughing together. Everything would be washed in a curtain of gray despair. There was more at stake than just the destruction of the Elves.

Liv thought of James and the special thing he and his children had. That connection that made every day worth living. Liv read on. The next page talked about the importance of talismans. Each warrior had their own special sigil. Liv looked at her palm. Anthor's was Power. Hers was Adept.

But now she had two. The book said nothing about having two sigils. It said that each Warrior was given one. Then there was the bracelet the Norn women had given her in the magic shop. Liv had three markings. No wonder she was a mess.

She rationalized that she was only holding Anthor's until she could find a way to bring him back. The bracelet the Fates gave her was personal, not Elvish, she reasoned. So she was left with Adept. Liv held the book and wondered how to access her "Adeptness."

The book hadn't lied to her yet so she tried on the concept of accepting that she, Liv Hermes, was an Adept magic user and by the way, an Elf to boot.

The only way she could continue was if she thought Anthor was still alive and eligible for rescue. Even if it was someday and not soon, she needed that. His welfare had become entwined with her future life. And she didn't want that end to be trapped, helpless in a portal not of her choosing by something like Nigbor.

Chapter Twenty Three

Liv reached out to Anthor. His essence was faint but she could find him out in the universe so that was encouraging. Liv explored down the thread that located him and began to strengthen the tie between them. He was too depleted to help but he still had a spark flickering so he was alive.

Encouraged, Liv poured herself into the bond. She tried to lift him and pull him towards her world but he was tethered to where he was. Liv pulled harder and strengthened the bridge between them but Anthor wouldn't budge.

Liv tried to jerk him to her, but saw that his white crystalline body tore, with half of it staying locked to the world and a fissure opening from his shoulder down to where his stomach might be. She stopped abruptly and released her hold on him, watching while his body mended itself. The tie still connected them.

"Hey, Liv, how is it going?" Nigbor smiled at her. He had shored up his image, but Liv could see the edge of his sharp teeth. His fingers blurred when she looked at them between slim hands and claws.

He squatted on a chunk of lava, jumping up and down slightly, like some kind of monkey. Liv tried to sever her connection with Anthor, confident she could find him again, but she was stuck. The bond that held them wouldn't cleave. It drew more power from her and thickened the bond.

"Gotcha!" Nigbor chanted, delighted with his work. "The bond will get stronger and stronger until you and your mentor, who left you out to dry, are bonded forever and always."

"I stopped Minerva. I'll stop you," Liv struggled but what he said was true, the bond was thickening and worse, pulling her into wherever Anthor was.

"Minerva was human trash as they all are. After I secure you, I'm heading to your Lake House to kill your family."

"They aren't there, loser, only the realtor." Liv tried putting all her Light into pulling Anthor to her but he was like a part of the planet. Liv lost a precious inch as she was dragged towards the portal. Her breathing was shallow and she could see her destination. It was a world of bright, transparent green. It looked like, no, it couldn't be. Whatever it was that Nigbor had concocted, it absorbed energy like thick cotton.

"What is a realtor? No matter, I'll kill them too. Then, your family. Eventually, they'll come to your precious Lake House to look for you. It will be so sweet. I might let you watch, if I can remember."

"I'm not sure you could handle a realtor. Some of them seem like the undead but are endlessly cheerful and energetic. What's your goal, Nigbor?" Liv relaxed for a moment and focused on the demon or whatever he was.

He stopped gloating and looked at Liv. "What do you mean, goal?"

"What are you trying to get done here by beating Anthor and me? I mean, I tried to ask the book but it doesn't work that well for me."

He snarled at her. "That's because your mentor failed you. That gave me the opening I needed. The Elves will be gone. They'll fade out. I'd enjoy destroying them but they'll leave before I am ready for them. Magic will leave your world. Wars will begin. People you love will despair and die. I'll kill everyone you ever knew. I'll make sure you have a great view of everything."

"So you're the main event, not Minerva? I really thought Minerva had that leadership stamp about her." Liv stuffed as much Light as she could sneak into her chest pack to use later. While Nigbor droned on, she crafted a small knife she hid in her coat and filled it with Light, too. Getting the bad guy to describe his evil plan is always good. Villains love to gloat.

The bond between Anthor and herself strengthened until it looked like they were joined Anthor's front to Liv's back by a thick green stem. Nigbor took some of the sticky green goo and wrapped it around her waist and hands to secure her.

"Yuck, this stuff is gross. What is it?" Nigbor tried to get it off his hands but it clung to him.

"You made it. You tell me," Liv said.

"I took it out of *your* memories of horrible things," Nigbor complained.

"I think it's lime jello," Liv said. "It's something you eat."

Nigbor frowned and stuck one slim claw into his mouth.

"Gak! Poison." Nigbor spat and coughed.

"It's an old family recipe! My mother made it every year," Liv complained.

"Bah," Nigbor scoffed. "Liar."

"Baby Jane liked it," Liv yelled at him.

"Then this Baby Jane is a liar too! Minerva was a tool meant to drain you of power and show your skills. Every warrior has different gifts. I always like a preview." He struggled to get the rest of the jello off his claws. "Time to go now, I've enjoyed meeting you. Gotta go prepare to kill a bunch of people you love and this realtor. Oh, enjoy your Baby Jane Jello." Nigbor grinned and let the portal close.

She couldn't see Anthor or much of anything although he was directly attached to her back. It was all green, endless jiggling green. Occasionally there was a chunk of something in the mess. The bond was thick around her waist, like unending wads of hard foam.

Everything was the same noxious green color. She became disoriented. She couldn't see the portal opening anymore, just vast expanses of vibrating stuff. There was no sign of life from Anthor.

Liv oriented herself to up and down. Everything was soft and yielding to her touch at first, then it would harden. First, she rested. She felt stuck, well and good. Liv tested the goo around her waist and arms. It was solid and getting more so as she contemplated it.

Liv thought of Anthor. What would he say? Refer to the book. Only she couldn't reach the book, not with her hands bound from her shoulders to her elbows, anyway. Concentrate! She could visualize the book in her mind: its ancient cover, the thick pages that more often than not, appeared blank. Liv closed her eyes and opened the book. The pages fairly leapt at her. She relaxed and let the information seep into her.

She read the words, but they didn't make any sense, at first, just gibberish. Then, Liv heard a melody in her head, or more like, through her body. She hummed along, like she had known the tune since birth.

The green goo around her torso loosened enough she could get her hands out. Liv sang louder until a patty of the goo slapped across her mouth. As she suspected, it was lime jello. Low blow, Nigbor. She continued to hum as loud as she could. The green stuff shrank slightly. It fell off her mouth and she sang the ancient foreign words. At first her voice fell onto the jiggling world without incident, then, the jello-like substance began to recede. Anthor had disappeared.

Before too long, she had a space around her and the stuff touching her body turned into powder and crumbled away. Liv found she could push on the clear, green material while singing and mold it to her wishes. She made a bench that she could sit on. She might as well be comfortable while she puzzled her way out of this realm.

She had a flash of what Nigbor might do to the people she loved. Would he hesitate to kill children? She didn't think so. What a miserable world it would be without hope; with only war surrounding every corner of her beautiful earth.

Liv reached out to Anthor but there was no response. Liv sang the song and forged forward with a path, thinking of Anthor. Liv held her hands out and closed her eyes. She tripped over something. A pair of pale legs were wrapped in hardened jello lay at her feet.

She sang and put her hands on his bound legs. It was Anthor. He seemed very thin and shrunken. The bindings turned to dust. Liv called his name. His body was pale, almost colorless. She worked her concentration up his body until he was free.

Anthor's eyes fluttered open, and he appeared to nod. "Glad you are still among the living," Liv said.

He coughed, dryly. "I haven't been among the living for a very, very long time, child." He raised a hand and patted her arm. She waited until he sat up. She created a second bench and helped him onto it.

"Thank you," he whispered. "This is truly the worst of all the realms I've been in. The way the material moves and clings," he shuddered. "And the taste! By all that's holy, some got in my mouth. I thought I was dying."

"OK, that's enough about the green goo. Do you want your amulet back now?"

He shook his head. "You, it's for you. You need it to vanquish the one you call Nigbor."

"I thought I was done once Minerva was captured. Now, I have to defeat Nigbor too."

"But first, we have to get out of here," Anthor looked around at the jello. Liv could see bits of horseradish and pineapple.

"Any thoughts on that problem?" Liv sat next to him. "I asked the book and it showed me the song, which led me to you. It can push back the gross stuff."

"What did Nigbor say to you?"

"He's going to make the Elves fade away and cause Earth to lose all its magic and become embroiled in war. Nice, huh. And kill everyone I love."

"It's unusual that the Evil One would make it personal," said Anthor.

"Lucky me," Liv said. "Any thoughts on getting out of here?"

Anthor shook his head. "I have never been here."

"I apologize. He took this place from my memories. How would you begin to get out?" Liv asked.

"I would concentrate on the problem. Here, I'll show you. As I'm doing it, I imagine the portal ripping open and me stepping back into the realm I want." Anthor moved his hands, like a swimmer doing the breaststroke. He sank back onto the bench. The effort exhausted him.

Liv rolled her shoulders and concentrated on creating a portal. Nothing happened. Liv suspected that this realm had very little plasma. She would have to use what she had stored inside her.

Liv blanked everything else out of her mind but the portal creation. There was no family waiting for her, no Esbats, no Anthor. Nothing but Liv's will.

She opened her arms like Anthor showed her and gathered every swatch of Light she could. She found spots inside her that she'd flooded previously. Liv added them to the whole of plasma she gathered in her center. When she judged she had all that she would get, she focused the energy on opening a portal back to her realm. Liv pushed her hands forward like Anthor demonstrated and then swept them back like a breast stroker. She felt the space move and a small portal opened. She tried to look through but couldn't see anything. Anthor motioned her forward.

"I'm not important now. Get your mission done. You can find me later."

Liv narrowed her entire being on getting back to Earth and stepped through the portal. The small slit barely accommodated her but Liv was grateful. Light filled her as she opened herself to the force and replenished herself, healing the burns that the vines had caused and fixing any damage and fatigue from the green goo squeezing her.

Whole again, Liv sent out her senses, searching for traces of Nigbor. It felt like he was everywhere. She adjusted her sight to visualize the most recent trail. Well, that narrowed it down to four paths that looked equally recent. Liv stopped. Did she really want to be chasing someone, or would she rather be proactive? When she did grants, and found a mistake after it was submitted, she preemptively sent a letter with a corrected page. Hopefully before the granters found it and canned the whole grant request.

How could she be proactive here? Nigbor had the advantage if she was chasing him. What could she do that would draw him to her? Give him more targets? Liv found a van with the keys in it. Icelanders were such trusting people. Of course, where could you go on an island? She went back to the office and grabbed the coffee maker off the counter and several cups and coffee packets. She could run on coffee for a long time.

She drove to the gymnasium where she'd left the Esbats. The dark smoke parted for her, allowing her to see the road. Liv opened the door and saw them freeze, like deer in headlights.

"How would you like to learn some real magic?" The Esbats looked at each other. Liv felt they were leary but there was a spark of interest and she tried to fan that spark. "I'm going to get Minerva back and see if I can help her."

Liv could see the fleeting thoughts of the Minerva they knew: bright, bubbly and naive. Who wouldn't want to help her?

Gale and Bea stepped forward and then the rest followed. "We will help," said Gale.

Would it be better to go to the other building or stay here? "Is that a coffee maker?"

Gale took it from her and set up a pot. "I've missed coffee so much."

"Let's talk strategy while the magic beans brew. I can bring Minerva out but I need you guys to work with her and pull the real Minerva out of whatever it is that she morphed into."

"How will we do that?" Asked Bea.

"First, coffee," said Gale. "It's all I can think about right now." While it brewed, they kept silent. Liv watched them inhale the coffee fumes and then sip their treasure. She knew how they felt. Gale made another pot.

"I'm more of a tea drinker, but I confess, this tastes marvelous. Like home," said Bea.

Liv drank some of the second pot and sighed. It was good. She thought about the Light. She thought it was generated by the lava and eruption, but it wasn't on the list of plasma generators. So, it must be the aurora and lightning, whether they could see them or not.

"When you're ready, form a circle" Liv said.

"You aren't part of the circle?" Asked Gale.

Liv considered. "No, I was never really part of your circle. It will be stronger with just Esbats."

"Are we going to die?" Bea's voice shook.

"I hope not. I think this is the first step to protecting our world and everyone in it we love. Otherwise, we're just trapped here while things get worse and worse. At least this way, we're trying to do something good." Liv was using them for bait, but she didn't want them having that fear as the basis for their circle. The three of them sat.

"He might come for her if I grab her," Liv said, "She was one of the things he bragged about. If he does, ignore him and concentrate on making Minerva back to the way she was: a delightful girl who liked everyone. Her survival depends on all of us. We can't break concentration. Know that you are going to see awful things. Smile and keep the Light moving."

"Tell us about this Light," said Gale.

"I'm going to start it and send it to you. You guys keep it moving around the circle with your positive thoughts. Then, I'm going to drop Minerva in the center. She's going to look like a zombie or worse but I think we can heal her and bring her back to us as the Minerva we know. Got it?"

Nervous nods. The ladies sat in a circle and Liv could see them compose themselves. She was pleased that they were able to gather their focus. Maybe they were used to doing it from trying spells. For whatever allowed them to put aside their personalities, Liv was grateful. She could feel the solidness of it.

Liv put her hands up and sang. She wasn't sure about the song she was singing. The words didn't make any sense but the melody sang in her body and gathered the Light. Liv imagined her sharing the Light with the Esbats, bathing them in it and then allowing them to take a miniscule portion of the Light inside of them.

"Concentrate on the wonderful Minerva you knew," Liv whispered. As the three women focused on the lovely moments of Minerva's life, more white plasma flowed into them and Liv started it in motion around the circle so the memories of one became the memories of all.

Liv gathered a separate piece of hard plasma, reshaping it into a pole with a chain. She drove it into the ground inside the Esbat circle. Then, she sent a single thought to find the portal that held Minerva and had held her for a time. It was a deceptively beautiful world with a clear blue ocean of who knew what vicious chemical. No land that Liv had seen. And she couldn't find Minerva. Had she dissolved? Nigbor had said she had a really strong will. Minerva was integral to

Liv's plan. She didn't know the path yet but she knew Minerva had a part to play if she was to succeed.

Liv found a single human thread in the depths of the killing sea. Minerva? The thread was too weak to respond but who else could it be? Liv banished the errant thought and concentrated on Minerva, only Minerva. A pile of viscera joined the thread. Liv hoped it could still support life.

Liv sent Light through the portal to help the thing that had been Minerva. The women of the circle screamed as a pile of wet guts landed in the middle of the circle. Liv's white circle was the only thing that kept them together. Sweat gathered on her face but the connection held.

A leg bone appeared into the circle and some rags of flesh clung to it. Liv could feel the collective group swallow and renew good thoughts of Minerva. More bones appeared and Liv saw most of the circle close their eyes. She could feel their thoughts of how sweet and nice Minerva had been.

Sinews and connective tissue realigned and loose skin flapped around like wrapping paper. It was gruesome but can't look away stuff. Liv was certain this scene would replay in her subconscious forever. Slowly, Minerva was rebuilt. She ended up more of a lump with an angry seamed face. She was on all fours. She hissed at them and crawled about the circle, looking for a way out.

She stopped in front of Liv, who continued the low singing for a moment. "Minerva," Liv said quietly, "Come be with your friends. Look away from evil and put it from yourself."

The thing in the circle screamed and clawed out for Liv. It couldn't get through the hard, crystalline white of the circle.

"Minerva, you're in there, I know it. You can fight this evil. What has it ever done for you? Let it fall away like snow off a roof. You aren't this thing. You are a good person." Liv channeled some of the whirling memories of the Esbats into the thing. The thing screamed but the exposed arm became flesh instead of smudged darkness. The Esbats were tiring. The memories came fewer but were more impactful. Only the best of the Minerva they knew, remained in their hearts. Liv funneled them into her. At this rate, it would take hours to get a fully functional Minerva back, if they could at all. Liv sighed. What else could she try?

Black specks of lava battered her like a tornado, and Liv covered her eyes to protect them. There was a roar and Liv's Esbat circle scattered. When the smoke cleared, it was Liv with a mangled Minerva on the floor behind her in the red smoky realm Nigbor seemed to like the best. Minerva was still in Liv's white circle.

"Look what you've done to my magnificent Minerva," Nigbor walked up to the thing in Liv's circle. He was wearing what Liv thought of as 'The Smooth Guy' facade. His thick dark hair was perfectly styled and his hazel eyes were warm and compelling. He was dressed in a tan Cashmere sweater and charcoal gray pants. He looked great.

"You could change places with her," Nigbor offered. "If you're so concerned about little Minerva." He rested his slim hands on his thighs as he squatted and looked at Minerva. "That would be the Christian thing to do." He waved a hand and they were back in the gym. One of the Esbats screamed but Liv didn't know which one it was. She kept her focus on Nigbor.

"And how would you even know that?" Croaked Liv. Her voice was dry and broken. If she could still cry, she would have. Another thing she had lost in this battle.

Nigbor shrugged as if he didn't care but Liv could see his eyes glowing red if she looked past the warm hazel. The thought that he was annoyed, pleased her and gave her hope. Nigbor turned and grabbed her arm. Nothing happened for a moment and they both looked at her white, solid arm and his hands that brimmed with red.

The pain began slowly but was more intense than Liv had felt before. She screamed and fought to break the grip Nigbor had on her arm. "Poor Liv. You never were strong enough. or loved enough or desired enough. Your family didn't want you and neither did anyone else." Nigbor's smile was showing his sharp teeth. Liv was surprised the pain was on the inside, not in her arm but in her heart. Was she really worthless? She half believed it or he could never have gotten to her.

The Esbats ducked under Nigbor's outstretched arm and recreated the circle around Liv. They closed their eyes and sang the song Liv taught them. They pummeled her with good thoughts and visions of her kindness. Things Liv didn't even remember. She forgot about Nigbor and happiness welled up within her. The Light and music became one thing and she felt joy.

Nigbor screamed at them and picked up Minerva and threw her at the white circle. The circle closed over her and accepted her as part of their group even though she had strayed under Nigbor's influence. The white circle exploded.

Liv opened her eyes and saw an ugly red scar on her arm. She looked around. No Nigbor. The other ladies were strewn about in a circle. Minerva was among them. She was horribly thin and her skin showed gray and dusky where the limbs were exposed. Smoke rose from her clothes but when she opened her eyes, it was Minerva who looked out, not the thing.

"Well, thanks for the rescue," she said.

"No problem," said Liv.

"It sure looks like it was a problem," Minerva said looking at the unconscious bodies littering the floor of the gym.

"They are all alive," said Liv.

"Hey, thanks and all but don't trust me. There's still a part of me that the evil one controls. I can feel it. He broke the big bond, but there seem like a million tentacles in my body, all bad."

Liv smiled and got up. She held Minerva's arms and ran as much Light through as she thought the woman could absorb. Minerva fell into her arms, unconscious. Ok, a little too much, perhaps.

"So, she's mostly ours but we still can't turn our back on her," said Gale, sitting up and watching.

"Yes. We need to surround her with as much Light as possible. It will also strengthen your bond with each other," Liv said.

"Wouldn't it just be better to, you know," Bea sliced a finger across her throat.

"She could still play a part in this drama. Nigbor needs to have his failure of Minerva, thrown in his face as much as possible. I think his huge ego is his soft spot. Let's think how we can play on that."

The other ladies regained consciousness and they regrouped in the kitchen with coffee and granola bars. Liv felt confident she could find and bring Anthor to them but was now the right time to give up the second amulet?

Liv went to a corner with a chair and pulled out the book. Minerva looked in her direction and Liv decided to go outside, instead. A moment later, the metal doors let her know Minerva had followed her.

"You have to fight the tendency towards evil, Minerva. You know it's still there and active. You should focus on the Light."

"Was that in your book?"

"I've been making some notes for when this is all gone."

"Let me see it," Minerva's eyes grew wide and glittered in the twilight.

"Go back inside, Minerva," Liv said. She gathered some Light and bathed Minerva in it. Minerva choked and brushed the white residue off of her skin like it burned.

"Thank you," she murmured as she went back into the gym. Liv wondered whether she was sincere or whether Liv had just given her some sort of weapon.

Liv hid in the shadow of the building and opened the book. What should her next step against Nigbor be? The book showed her legends and some text about building and sanitation, as far as she could tell. Liv leafed ahead a few pages and let the book fall open where it would. Just blank pages. Great.

The gym door opened and Bea came out. She looked for Liv but she didn't have the Elf vision that Liv did. Liv didn't want to have to deal with her right now. While they had helped when Nigbor was here, they still were swirling with doubts and questions that Liv didn't have answers for. She needed to concentrate on getting her own focus straight.

"Bea, I'm over here," Liv slid the book into her inside pocket.

"Well, I hesitate to bring this up, but Minerva said you have a magic book that is helping you know what to do. I think it would be beneficial if we all had access to that book." She wrung her hands in front of her, betraying her nervousness.

"It is in Icelandic that I can translate sometimes. I think it is a gift from the Elves. You wouldn't be able to read it."

"But you could read it to us. We've already proved we can help, we have some power. What happens if you fall in battle? We'll have to carry on, right?"

Liv hesitated to tell them that most of their power came from her boost of the Light. Already Minerva was driving a stake between them.

Liv drew it out and flipped open a page. She brought it to Bea so she could see the image the book displayed. It was an embellished triangle. The Light was on one side and the Darkness was on the other side of the triangle. They both peered closely at the third point of the triangle. It resembled the Yin and Yang symbol but was more elaborate and obviously Elvish. "The Elf Warrior," Liv told her.

"What do the words say?" Asked Bea.

"The key to existence or something similar, may be balance, I'm not sure."

"Listen, I'd like to keep this information, whatever it means, from Minerva. I'm afraid she might be an information conduit for Nigbor."

"Like a spy?"

"But she may not know it. She definitely has some pockets that reek of him. Her eyes were glowing when she demanded the book. So then she planted the seed with you and you found a reason to see the book. I just want to be careful. The book may be the only advantage we have."

"Who exactly is this Nigbor? Where does he come from?" Asked Bea.

"I thought he was a bad Elf or something else at first because he came to see me when my mentor didn't come. I thought he might be a good guy. Now I think he's the main event. He's been brewing evil and war and hate forever. I don't know if we can defeat him entirely. The previous Elf Warrior only fought him to a draw."

"And you're the Elf Warrior this time?"

"I am. I didn't know until this all started."

"And what will happen when it ends?" Bea asked.

"I hope that Minerva is restored, you guys can go home and maybe I can too."

"Your skin has changed. Look how pale you are and there are crystals in your arm like you're becoming a rock or something," Bea said.

Liv looked down at her arm and saw the sparkle. What was she becoming?

"I don't know what's with that, Bea. I just know that he's going to destroy our world and the Elves if we don't stop him."

"I didn't even believe in Elves before I got here and I don't much care about them now."

"The same for me until I found out I was one," said Liv. "I'm the only one who can use the book. Sorry."

Minerva slid out of the gym while they were talking. Liv put the book back in the inner pocket, away from Minerva's red stare.

"You think you're so special, but you aren't. You never were. I've seen your life, he showed it to me. You're so ordinary, it's sickening."

"And you were pretending you were a witch. How ordinary is that?" Liv shot back and admonished herself. Don't engage. You aren't a teenager on the street yelling from your car.

"You are such a prima donna," called Minerva.

Liv smiled at her and pulled some Light together. She blanketed Minerva in it. Minerva's tirade shorted out and she shook her head and walked back inside.

"I see your point. I don't need to see the book."

Gale came out. "What did you wammy Minerva with? She looks all blank."

"She was channeling her inner demon again. I hit her with a blanket of Light. You guys should team up and practice that. I'm sure you can manage it," Liv said.

"I was just thinking about this Nigbor guy. He hits, makes a mess, and then takes off," said Gale. "If you could trap him here, it might drain him."

"Good thought," said Liv. "I think he's too powerful for me."

"How about 'us'? You aren't alone. I feel like our circle solidified or maybe even magnified your attack."

"Let me think about that. I'm not sure what I felt during his visit. It's hard to keep to my game plan when he's all sparky and smoky," Liv said.

"Maybe together is the key," said Bea. "We Esbats do have some power, you know."

"Do you think you can take him? Maybe you should lead the attack the next time he comes around," said Liv. A weight lifted off of Liv. Had she been going about this all wrong? Anthor hadn't said anything but he hadn't been the most reliable teammate. Were the Esbats provided to help her and she'd been assuming she was the lead when they were supposed to be in charge?

Not only did Liv feel relieved to step back from command, a weight of dread also sank in her gut. Was she relinquishing the position because she was scared or because she really thought the Esbats would do a better job?

"Let's get organized, ladies! I suggest the Dance of Denature," said Bea.

"Do you want me to do anything?" Asked Liv.

"No, just stay out of the way. Minerva, we'll need your positive energy, join the circle."

The Esbats formed a small circle and walked around it at a stately walk, chanting a low mantra that Liv couldn't hear. Minerva walked right with them and kept her red eyes downcast. Bea looked at Liv and nodded at Minerva as if to say, "See, we control her."

It was impressive but Liv questioned whether they really had a hold on Minerva or was she playing o'possum? Liv shrugged. Liv had given over control to Bea and had to live with it now. Liv really wasn't the leader type anyway. She preferred to be on her own and responsible only for herself. Liv sat back on the floor of the gym to watch. What were they doing anyway? Some kind of protection spell? Liv hoped they included her in the weave.

She pulled out the book, filled herself with Light and let the book fall open to share its wisdom. Minerva's head slid to Liv. Liv could feel her eyes on the book. Her instinct was to go to a deserted hallway, away from prying eyes, but she needed to keep an eye on Minerva for possible mischief. She glanced at the page and got the impression of chaos. Had she made an irrecoverable error? Bea and the ladies sure seemed to be thinking they were on the right track. Liv slid the book back into its inside pocket and sealed it with Light, just in case. When she looked up, Minerva's red eyes were on her, burning with interest.

Bea stopped the circle and raised her hands to the heavens. She said something and then the women started around the circle again. Nigbor appeared around the circle. He wove in and out of the circling women. Liv tried to shout out a warning but couldn't make a sound. The women kept circling, apparently not seeing him.

He had some moves, Liv almost smiled. He was shaking it and gyrating. Minerva shifted her eyes from Liv to the center of the circle almost as if she could feel something but not see it.

It was a show meant only for Liv. He did a little Charleston and a couple of pirouettes.

When Liv didn't react sufficiently, he appeared and the women screamed and scattered in the gym. Bea frowned but was rooted to the spot. Nigbor grabbed her arm and swung her around, launching her like the end of a whip. He went back to dancing, shaking and gyrating his hips to music only he could hear.

"What? All of a sudden you guys are all wall flowers? Liv, I was looking forward to partnering with you in particular." Nigbor made one more circle and put his hands on his thighs as if exhausted. Liv rolled her eyes at him, mocking his pretense to be human. How many beings had he watched to get the details right?

"We're having some fun now," Nigbor continued. "You know, I'm really not your enemy." He pulled forward a folding chair and draped his long, lanky body across it. "Let's talk about what you really want? I can make it happen, like that." He snapped his fingers.

The Esbats moved back towards him. Liv could definitely see the allure. His charm or whatever he was blanketing them with, seemed to be swaying the women who had been chanting against him, just a moment before. Liv could see the tendrils of smoke circling them.

What really decided Liv and snapped her out of his funk was when she saw Minerva smiling, like a cat.

"Enough!" Liv stood up and walked to the circle. The pole and chain she created earlier were still available to her and she pulled the pole and chain to her. Liv meant to chain Minerva later when they all slept. Now she slammed the pole full of Light on the ground, generating shock waves of Light that traveled through the gym. Bea, Gale and the others shook the cloud of smoke from their heads. Minerva hissed as the smoke evaporated.

Minerva launched at her, but Liv was used to evading her younger brothers in football when she was younger. A claw scraped her leg and it sounded like fingernails on a chalkboard. Was her leg crystalline too? Liv thought she'd have to do an inventory when she had a moment to take an assessment.

Liv smiled grimly. Minerva couldn't be anything more than a nuisance.

"How exactly are you not an enemy, Nigbor? You threaten my family, my world. What's in it for you?"

"What's in it? I get a kick out of you," he sang. "But, really, if you want to get philosophical, I provide the expression of free will."

Liv wrapped the chain that she'd created for Minerva, around Nigbor's wrist. He screamed at her and struggled. He shook his hand and yanked on the chain on his wrist. He sat on the ground and pushed against the restraint with both feet and his one free arm. Liv was excited to see that she'd created such a strong bond.

When it shattered, Liv saw Nigbor rub his wrist before he disappeared. Minerva dove into the portal after him.

"We just weren't ready for him to manifest in our midst," Bea said.

"I'm hoping I hurt his wrist. He was rubbing it before he popped," Liv ignored Bea's excuse. It was clear to Liv that the power was in her hands. Maybe the Esbats had some magic of their own, but it couldn't force Nigbor back. Not like Liv's magic could.

"Too bad Minerva got away," said Gale. "I really thought we had her convinced to jump to our side."

Liv thought there was zero chance that Minerva would side with them. "I'm going to take a shower." She picked up her back pack and went to the locker room. Liv hadn't forgotten her skin and its progression into crystal. She pulled the drape closed and took off her clothes. Liv wrapped a scratchy towel about her and shoved her clothes into the washer.

"I really don't like the witches. Can we get rid of them?" Nigbor was sitting on the washer.

"Then I will keep them just because they annoy you," said Liv.

"Your skin is really pretty, all shimmery and white."

"I'm a little concerned it's going to stay this way," Liv said.

"Yeah, you should go home with the witchy women. The eruptions are over for now and flights will resume tomorrow."

"And you know this how?"

"I listened to the weather earlier," said Nigbor.

"You're a good dancer," said Liv. It couldn't hurt to stroke his huge ego a little.

"Oh, it's nothing," but he smiled.

Liv glanced at his wrist and saw a pale ring around the one she had encircled. It pleased her to have hurt him.

"I can have the van driver pick you guys up in ten minutes," he offered.

"You can take the witches, but I'm staying to see how this turns out. I can't really go back home looking like this." Liv showed him her arms and saw the lower part of her legs had crystallized already.

"You can go anywhere. Find a realm that's sea water and sand. Or go to somewhere on your world. You don't have to go back to your old boring job."

"It's not just the job but my family too. I'll miss them."

"They treat you like crap! I can pull a dozen memories where if you analyze them, they are lousy to you."

Liv had to admit it was true. Her family had never treated her like one of them and the sisters-in-law just made things worse. She felt they might have stuck her with the Lake House so they could have more money, sooner. Of course no one realized the extent of repairs the old house would need. Even James had been shocked when Liv started getting estimates for the roof, the driveway, painting and woodworking report, not to mention the dock had to be pulled up and stored for winter. Or maybe her sister-in-laws weren't shocked.

"Stay out of my head! I'll deal with my own life, thank you." Liv fashioned a NFL style helmet out of Light.

"The Elves are pretty much dead. You and I could take over their realm. It's really nice, very forestry and water filled."

"Did you forget? I am an Elf. I am an Elf Warrior, to be specific."

"You aren't all Elf. Have the Elves ever done anything to make your life easier? Even now, they stay in the shadows, ready to jump whichever way I let them. You deserve better than that."

"Waaa! Poor me. I'm tougher than that. So what if the family rations their love and attention? So what if the Elves left me on the doorstep to die or thrive."

"And what about that jerk Anthor? He withheld vital information from you that could've helped you deal with all this crap better. I even felt bad for you when no one came to help you."

"All of it is true. All of it is sad. But it's in the past."

"Come spend some time with me," Nigbor said as if it just occurred to him that this was a good idea. Liv was sure he'd been planning this. If he hadn't suggested it, she might have to get a view into his world and his weaknesses.

"Is this a trick? I wouldn't be trapped in your realm, would I?" Liv added a note of longing into her voice, as if this might solve all her problems.

"I swear, you would not be trapped or restrained in a visit to my realm," Nigbor held up one hand that turned into a greenish claw while she watched.

"Let me think about it," said Liv.

"You LOVE to make life changing snap decisions! They make you feel empowered. Like coming to Iceland, throwing the jello, taking the Lake House as your share of your parents' legacy. You knew all these decisions were lousy."

"And this one is different how?"

"You're with me! I control everything in my own realm. I'd be delighted to show you around. I've been working on it for millennia. Maybe just for this moment. It's fate, kismet, destiny, whatever."

Liv could tell the moment his argument started to make sense to her. It was like a noose tightening around her neck. Was it his eagerness or his 'Gosh this would be so neat' earnestness. Whatever the perfect combination was, he'd located it and pressed Liv's 'sucker' button. She turned away before he could see her smile.

"Maybe later," Liv dismissed him with a wave. She felt the book in her pocket. If he controlled everything in his realm, would he control her book if it was in his realm? Tough one to answer. "I know Minerva didn't have an easy time there." Liv used some Light to bring up an image of Minerva. She looked ragged and tired. Greasy smoke swirled around her and her eyes glowed full red. She didn't look happy.

"Minerva doesn't look like she's having a great time in wonderland," Liv showed him the image.

"She's a piece of work, I can tell you that. Totally pledged herself to the realm and then decided it wasn't for her. Reneged on the whole deal."

"So it's all on Minerva now? All her fault?"

"Well, no, when you put it that way. I'll take responsibility for my part. I'm just saying, if Minerva is unhappy, she's responsible for her own choices. Isn't everyone? Aren't you?"

That stopped Liv. "You're confusing platitudes. I don't have any reason to go to your red realm. I don't want to end up all greasy and missing parts like Minerva. No thanks."

"You're stronger than she is. It won't happen to you," Nigbor scoffed, wiping away Minerva's image.

"Face it, Nigbor. There's no reason for me to spend any time in your realm. It doesn't do anything but make me weaker." Liv turned away, breaking away from the haze Nigbor had about him all the time.

"If you could understand why I do what I do," Nigbor pleaded. "Maybe we could avoid this senseless war."

"If you don't want war, just stop," Liv said.

"It doesn't work like that," Nigbor said. "War is coming and I don't think even the two of us can stop it. If I don't attack, the Elves will or maybe humans will kill themselves off. I can't see the future." He shook his head and the dark brown curls fell around his face.

"The Elves definitely don't want a war," Liv said. "That's just stupid. They hid me among the humans so you wouldn't find me."

"Or so one of them couldn't find you and kill you," he said.

"So now you're my savior?" Liv laughed. "Nigbor, you are entertaining, I'll give you that."

"I can prove to you that the Elves are the villains, in this case. Just come with me."

"How can you prove the Elves are the bad ones?" Asked Liv.

"Everyone is bad, not just the Elves."

Chapter Twenty Four

She was going and it was stupid. She couldn't say why she was going, only that something was prompting her to find out everything she could about her situation. Maybe it was the researcher within her, but she needed to know everything to make an informed decision.

Nigbor was fairly dancing with glee. He turned to Liv as if he would say something, shrugged and put a hand on each of her shoulders. His face changed and the demon showed through. Pointed teeth protruded from his mouth and his eyes were slitted like a goat's. He shoved her. She fell into a red portal, through smoke and ash. As she fell, she envied how easily Nigbor had opened the portal. It was always so difficult for Liv. Then, in the space of a moment, she smashed into the ground, feeling her shoulder go numb as it compressed. She lost consciousness as the pain washed over her. When she opened her eyes, Nigbor stood over her and the portal was closed.

Liv struggled up and dusted the red particles off her. She cleared her vision with the Light and looked around the Realm. It looked like Iceland, except everything had a reddish tinge. Liv had filled her chest pack and sword with as much Light as it would hold in case Nigbor double-crossed her. Or more accurately, when he double crossed her.

"See not so bad," said Nigbor.

"If it's not so bad, why did you have to push me in?"

"I get impatient," he explained, kicking a stone with his boot. A flaming waterfall of lava sparked in the background. With her Light-improved vision, Liv thought it beautiful.

"Rude. You know, if it weren't so smoky and dark, I could live here. Maybe I'll take over, what do you think?" Liv was joking but she saw a glimmer of something behind the demon's yellow eyes.

The trap was coming and it was all Liv could do not to call Nigbor on it. Once she defeated him, would it all be over? According to the book, he couldn't be defeated, only detained for a time and drained of power. Why did she even think this was a good, fact-finding mission? Maybe she just wanted the whole thing over.

So when the trap was sprung, she barely flinched. Nigbor threw a smoldering net over her and shoved her into a portal that appeared in the wall. The net didn't burn her but she shrugged it off anyway.

"What's with all the shoving?" Liv yelled. "Really, is that the best you can come up with?"

The space closed in on her and she expanded her Light to keep all the area she could around her body. At least Liv didn't have to wonder when the other shoe was going to drop. Liv took a moment. It wasn't exactly the same as the white room puzzle, but Liv thought it showed a marked lack of ingenuity. Instead of white stuff, the room was red and smokey. Was he just tiring her out again?

After she got out of here, she had to find a way to trap him that lasted for as long as possible. She had no idea how to do it. Well, job one is getting out of here. She wondered for a moment, just a stray thought.

"Minerva? Are you here somewhere?" Liv whispered but let the words reverberate through the smoky chamber and imagined it going through the walls and finding Minerva. Liv sensed Minerva was startled at the contact. Liv explored the bond and strengthened it. Minerva didn't reject it but instead, held it and examined it to see if it was solid.

"Listen, I'm trapped in a cell by our mutual friend. How are you doing?" Liv made it conversational and focused on Minerva, the way she thought Minerva would receive it best.

"I came here. I thought it would be so much better than those draggy old ladies, but it's boring. At least there I was the bad girl.

Here, I'm mediocre girl. I'm not powerful enough to cause any real trouble and I'm just kind of ignored here."

"I hear you. I think I know a way you can move up to bad girl, but never mind, I don't want to trouble you."

Liv felt the uptick of interest. She just had to wait her out.

"What did you have in mind?" Minerva thought.

"I think you should break me out. I think that would really aggravate Nigor."

Minerva considered. "Yeah, that would certainly piss him off."

"What's the problem?"

"Maybe that would make him too angry."

"What's he likely to do if he gets too angry?" Liv could feel the apprehension building in Minerva, tinged with fear. Liv tried to scrape images of fear off Minerva's mind. Was she underestimating Nigbor? The room seemed to solidify around her.

"I don't want you to be afraid anymore, Minerva. You are meant to be a happy, joyous young woman finding her way through love and stuff."

"I don't have anything to fight him with. It's not like I have the white stuff like you do."

"You probably do have it, it's just buried deep."

"Not anymore, if I ever had it." Liv felt Minerva's despair. "What good is it anyway?"

"You can make a weapon, for one thing. Something to defend yourself against Nigbor."

"No, I don't think that is something I can do." Minerva's consciousness was withdrawing.

No help from that quarter, Liv sighed. She picked up the net in her hands and felt the energy Nigbor expended to create it. She reached out and grabbed some of her prison. If she concentrated, she could feel how Nigbor created the folds of the walls and did the magic to make it collapse closer to her body. Liv smiled. He had done it hastily and left holes in the fabric of his magic. She enlarged an existing hole and forced a small amount of light through to widen it.

She carved out more room for herself. It didn't change her situation, but it did change her perception and gave her a feeling of more control. How much Light did she have stored? Enough to get out?

Chapter Twenty Five

Liv reached out to Anthor but couldn't get through the interference. Should she work on getting out or opening a portal? Liv felt she had tons of Light left so she took a chance and forced her way out of the clingy cage Nigbor had put her in. Liv visualized tearing open a small hole in the wall and was surprised how easily she was able to get out. Was she that much stronger, or had Nigbor not spent a lot of time crafting her jail cell? She suspected a little of both.

Once out, she reached out to Minerva again but that connection was dead. She just couldn't reach her. Minerva was a part of the solution. Liv was sure of it even if she didn't know how she fit in. Liv opened her Light enhanced vision and the ever present smoke dissolved. The bare red corridor had lava-carved walls. Liv saw them branch out ahead of her and used a tiny bit of Light to see if there were any corridors more promising than others. She followed the flow of her Magic and found a throne room of sorts. All it really had was a raised chair, more of a lounger and some chains attached to the floor (ick).

Liv sensed Nigbor wasn't here in the realm. Was he wreaking havoc on Earth or somewhere else? What was the point of this stupid play by Nigbor? He had half convinced her that his cause was just and the Elves were in the wrong. Now, he'd blown it with a clumsy trap. Liv started opening a portal back to Iceland when she saw a shadow move against the wall.

"Minerva, do you want to go back to Iceland?"

Minerva scuttled forward. At least she wasn't on all fours and could walk upright. Liv drew a circle in the air and called upon the Light she had stored. The portal opened and she took Minerva with her through to the bright sunny clean air of Iceland.

Delicate tendrils of smoke rose from random spots in the lava. No trees were visible, just lichen and snow and lava. Mountains christened with white caps of snow sparkled in the distance. Although it was stark and forbidding, it felt welcoming and clean to Liv. Minerva shrank from the cold air and coughed as the smoke came up out of her lungs.

"Do you want to be saved, Minerva?" Liv breathed deeply and found residue of the greasy smoke residing there. She did a deep cleansing breath and coughed up something nasty. Great. Not going there again. And the worst thing was she hadn't found anything of significance. "Maybe I should have rephrased that. Would you rather stay in that realm or here? Or we could try somewhere random, kind of like spin the wheel? I haven't found many good realms but I'm sure it could happen."

"Like that acid water world? No thanks. At least this place doesn't hurt my skin."

"Can you try to draw Light into yourself?"

Minerva screwed up her face with effort. Liv lost patience and boosted her with a gentle bump of Light. It was plentiful here, unlike in the red realm, and Liv accessed it easily. Liv used her Sight to look at Minerva's body. She found stunted pathways throughout the woman's physical being. Liv helped her as much as possible, but much of the work had to be completed by Minerva and Liv told her so. Her skin looked better. The scabs began falling off, and the new skin underneath was pink. Her hair, which was patchy, made her look ninety years old but her eyes had lost a lot of the red-rimmed look. They just looked tired to Liv.

"I could say I want to be saved but if Nigbor appears, I know I'll come running. He has his hooks deep in me. You go on and save the world. I'll wait here," Minerva said.

"I wish I knew how to save the world. I feel like I'm dithering. If I was really the hero of all heros I would know how to save the world, right? I can't even find Nigbor." Liv reached out and scanned for Nigbor. He wasn't in Iceland, thank goodness. At least Liv could get some sleep, except for Minerva. There was no telling which side Minerva would work for.

Where would she be safest? "I'm going to go looking for Nigbor. You want to stay here?"

"No, that doesn't seem very smart. I'll go towards the airport. Maybe there's coffee there."

"Or you could try the gym. The rest of the Esbats are probably still there unless the van driver picked them up."

"Nah, I'm not the most popular person with them. I'm partially responsible for what happened to them," said Minerva.

"Are you going to revert to bad Minerva?"

"Not unless Nigbor comes to ask me to kill them all. Then, I'll be all in." Minerva shrugged.

"Yeah, OK then, try to resist that urge. I'm off." Liv said and gathered herself for opening a portal. Where would she be safest? It came to her in a moment and the portal slid open.

Chapter Twenty Six

Time to go visit her real home. One place she hadn't seen yet: the Elf Realm. She slid through the portal and stopped, stunned. It was brighter than she thought it would be, blinding in fact. And the very air made her feel, well grubby. The place was like earth but pristine. A clear brook bubbled past her and birds sang. It looked like a movie set. Liv crouched next to the water and washed her hands and face. Dark grease came off, leaving a film on the cold water.

Liv felt bad defiling the world. She didn't really fit here, did she? Every step of her heavy boot was an affront. Her skin seemed more human here, less crystalline, as if the human world in which she'd been raised had subtly altered her body chemistry.

Liv scanned to see if Nigbor was here. She couldn't imagine him in this world at all. If she felt unwelcome how much more would the land and air repulse him? Still, she meant to chase him down and get some answers for what he had done to her.

There were Elves here. Liv could feel them in the trees watching her. They didn't make contact or interact with her. Elf Warrior, welcome to sacrifice herself for them but not good enough to talk to.

"They are in awe of you, not afraid or unsociable," A tall thin Elf put his hand in the water and scooped out the mess she'd left in the water. "You are the first Elf Warrior of this age. They are curious but won't intrude on your moment." He made the film from the water disappear. His robes were light and floated over his body.

"I wanted to see this world I'm supposed to save. To see if it is worth giving up everything for, not that I've been given a choice."

He smiled but Liv didn't find it amusing. She found it disquieting that she didn't fit anywhere: not on earth and not here in the realm where she was created.

"Where do I fit in? It seems unfair that I have to do the heavy lifting and reap none of the rewards," Liv complained.

"It's a hero's destiny. You are special and a thousand thousand would trade places with you. You're chosen." He said as if it should be obvious to Liv that this was the best thing in the world.

"Any hints on how to take care of Nigbor?"

"Not a one. No one has ever had to deal with this except Anthor."

"I should see if I can spring him. I'm just really worried where Nigbor is and what he might have waiting me."

The Elf turned and disappeared into the forest without a word. How would she find Nigbor? And more, how was he hiding himself from her? Liv tried to imagine where to find him?

First things first, find Anthor. She focused on Anthor, but had trouble finding him as well. Had he given up or was her power weakening? She pulled more Light into her and focused. The portal opened a slit and saw Anthor slumped over, looking gray instead of white. Liv gasped and rushed to him. Anthor raised his head and said, "No." Just as the portal snapped closed on them.

"Well, that was a poor decision," Anthor said. "Now, we're both trapped."

Liv sighed. "Maybe. Maybe not. This Elf Warrior isn't ready to give up just yet." Liv tried to gather the Light but whatever the trap was made of resisted her efforts. Nigbor must have upped whatever it was that the trap was made of initially.

"So did he build it or reinforce it when you were inside or did it just happen and you didn't know it?"

"It must have happened when I was unconscious. I know at one point I was dead to the world. My captor did not appear, so I am not sure."

"Well, the material of this cell is different from what it was the first time I visited you. He must have felt it and realized that it wasn't strong enough to stop me."

"Can you get us out of here?" Anthor rose to his feet and gathered himself.

"Let me see." Liv tried to gather the Light but the material wouldn't let her. Her fingers tingled in a burning way, not a force gathering way.

"Try a sword," said Anthor.

"Good idea." Liv fashioned an ornate sword with a pommel handle. She admired it for a moment and appreciated how it felt in her hand. She picked a spot and swung it in a powerful arc at a protruding spot on the wall.

Liv's sword bit deeply into the wall of the room. Then, Liv dropped the sword and grabbed her hands, pulling them into her stomach. "Yeawww!" When Liv pulled her hands out and looked at them, there was pale pink blood everywhere: on her hands and on her shirt as well as dripping down from her shirt to her pants.

"OK that really hurts," said Liv. "It won't stop bleeding. I didn't even know I could bleed and why is it pink? I'm going to be this way forever, aren't I? Why won't it stop bleeding?"

Anthor went to Liv and grabbed her arms where the blood came out in twin long cuts running the length of her small white arms. Anthor was able to stop the flow of blood but it depleted the small amount of Light that he had left and he fell to his knees.

"What are we going to do?" Asked Liv. What was she going to do if her weapons backfired on her? Could she use her hands? Or would that backfire too?

Liv was shaky, her knees like jello. She walked forward and tentatively punched the wall.

Her body fell back as if she'd been hit. Liv gave a little gasp of pain and grabbed her shoulder. It looked out of joint. Liv had seen people pop it back in on TV but had no idea how to do it.

"Anthor, do you know how to put a shoulder back in a socket?" He grimaced and fought his way to her. He walked like the mummy or maybe Frankenstein, that stilted, foot dragging walk.

He touched her shoulder, just a touch and took her hand in his hand. When the whipping motion came and she knew it would, the crack made her jump. Anthor had her arm secured but the crack resonated throughout her body.

"Oh, that does feel better, thanks," said Liv. Liv pulled out the book but the pages remained blank. After what seemed like hours, she gave up and rested.

"We are well and truly trapped," Anthor said.

"Are you in pain?" Asked Liv.

"No, not really. I just can't find any energy to summon. This place seems to suck it from me."

"Then, we need a plan sooner rather than later." Liv wondered if she threw Anthor against the wall would it hurt him? Just to exhaust all options, Liv checked the book again but it was blank. This is where Nigbor spent all his time while he tricked me into that other cage. "If you formed yourself into a spear, do you think I could throw you against the wall to open a portal?"

"Good thought but I don't have the energy to form anything."

"I do though. Would you let me do it?"

Anthor considered and then shrugged. "At least we'll know if it fails, we have one more option crossed off of our possibilities for escaping."

"That's the attitude. Here comes the good stuff," she said. Liv gathered some Light from her chest pack and bathed him in it. Anthor took the Light and fashioned himself into a spear.

"Promise me something," he said.

"What?"

"Whatever happens, you'll try your hardest to get out of here. All our hopes rest with you. If it is my time to be destroyed, I've lived the lives of many men. Do not worry about my pain or well-being. Promise me. I think if you don't get out this time, you won't ever."

"I promise." Liv had already felt the Light draining off her in ripples. She prepared to open herself to collect Light but stopped. Maybe that was the error. This site might be rigged to take her Light. Liv slammed the pathway shut and looked within herself to generate the Light with everything that was within her.

It was the right decision. Liv felt the little threads of Nigbor's trap fall away from her in waves as she disconnected from the world she was in. Her emotions became distant and she took the weapon that Anthor had made of himself and hefted it. Heavy but not so much she couldn't throw it. Liv forced her own Light into the spear and visualized it breaking free of this greedy cage.

She threw it and followed it out as she formed herself to become the fuel behind the spear. Hardened as he was, Anthor pierced the wall and the two of them accelerated into a dark void of stars and nebula.

Liv lost concentration but Anthor held onto her.

"This is where we part, Elf Warrior."

"I don't know, we made a tough team, Anthor,"

"I can see Valhalla beyond that nebula. I am being called to my reward. You will do what needs to be done to save not only your world's moments of magic but also the Elf realm and others. Though you may never be part of any of them, you will live on to fight again."

"Goodbye and Godspeed, Anthor," Liv nodded.

Anthor turned his face from her and stood in space for a moment. Then, he smiled and moved towards the nebula to what only he could see. Liv said a prayer for him and one for her that she had as successful a life as he had. First, though, Nigbor.

Liv looked around and formulated her next move. She couldn't fly through space so she opened a portal. How easy was that? So much different than the struggle to get out of the cage. She drew on the Light from the nebula and the Light sang through her.

Liv went back to Iceland. It started there and she believed it would end there. She was stuck until she figured this particular puzzle out.

Liv reached out to locate Minerva. She was traveling towards the airport. No issue there. Now for the tough one: Nigbor. He was a resourceful bugger. Liv needed to consider setting a trap for him. She couldn't just react all the time.

What did Nigbor want? Besides attention. What did he need to survive? The dark energy that fed him came from where? Well, she supposed it was the flip side of the same energy she used. How could she turn the trap against him?

Would the same strategy he used on her, work on him? Suck the dark energy out of everything, like the Elf world. Could she plop Nigbor right into the Elf world? Would the elder Elf just scoop him up like the oily trash she had deposited in their water?

Liv took out the book and was relieved to see the pages fill in with writing and drawings. She'd lost Anthor but at least she had the book back. Now, for some coffee. The gym was within sight, so she walked over, hoping they had left the coffee maker. She smelled it when she opened the door. God bless Icelanders who left every door open in case someone needed shelter.

The Esbats were shocked to see her but came over eagerly to greet her. She was never sure which side they were on. Still, it warmed her to have smiling faces meet her when she felt so isolated. The coffee was great and she accepted a power bar even though she wasn't hungry. Did she even need food anymore? She had the Light and that seemed enough. She just wanted the warmth and taste of the coffee more than needed it.

"What's been going on?" Asked Gale.

"The usual. Trapped in a hell dimension. Fell into a trap from Nigbor. Fought my way out. Said goodbye to Anthor. The book came back to life."

"Sounds very exciting," said Bea.

"Maybe in the telling, but it was quite the struggle when it was happening. I need to create a trap for Nigbor. Any ideas?"

It was to their credit that they actually paused and considered it seriously.

"Can't you decapitate him?" Asked Bea.

"Probably, but I don't think it would kill him. He's not a vampire."

"Well, he kind of is," continued Gale. "He drains energy from people and I think he lives off of that. You go with him because he offers all this great stuff and he does deliver but once you get it, you find out it's not real. Like he would get you a great car and it would turn out to be a miniature of one or a cardboard cutout of the car. So technically, you'd get what he offered you but it wouldn't be satisfying."

"So you'll need some lovely chunk of energy with neediness attached to draw him in," said Bea.

"Kind of like Minerva was. She was very unsure and wanted to be part of the magic so much she was willing to make a deal. She got the magic but it wasn't good for her," said Gale.

"Nigbor really dropped her when she ran out of steam, you know," said Bea.

"I guess the rest of you didn't have anything you were desperate for," said Liv.

"Not like Minerva. Getting the Magic was consuming for Minerva," said Bea.

"He tried to make a deal with me," said Gale. "I have an autoimmune disease. I don't usually talk about it but I'm in pain a lot of the time. I asked him to cure it but leave me alive and well. He couldn't do it. He's not omnipotent."

"Wait, he tried to make a deal with you but couldn't manage it?" Liv asked. She got her second cup of coffee. This could be good information for her. At the very least, she could taunt him about it. She knew he hated failure and anything that distracted him was a positive for her.

"It's like I phrased it so he couldn't cheapen it and still fulfill my want. Not unless he cured me," said Gale.

"Well I have to say that I never noticed you struggling that much," said Liv.

"Be honest, you never noticed us much at all. You just got lumped in with us and thought we were all basically the same with the dark cloaks and sensible shoes, right?"

"Well, on the other hand, you guys weren't very friendly to me either. Minerva was the only one who would give me the time of day. I got the feeling it was because you guys ignored her too. She was just uber needy."

"Easy mark for someone like him," said Bea.

"So, he needs 'needy' people," said Gale.

"Who are prone to jumping without really thinking it through," said Liv.

"Where is Minerva by the way?" Asked Gale.

Liv reached out and found Minerva almost at the airport. Flights were supposed to resume today. Maybe she would get out. "She's at the airport."

"Go tell her you want her for an apprentice," said Gale.

"Not so much," said Liv, remembering the betrayals that Minerva had been a part of.

"No, but say you do," said Gale. "You might actually have to teach her something to make it real. What would Nigbor hate more than anything?"

"You converted his little pet to the side of Light," said Bea. "Is that fair to Minerva?"

"She's pretty much broken anyway, I think."

"Say we convince her, then what?"

"You spring your trap on him!"

"And there lies the problem. I don't have a trap."

"You could use one of your family as bait. Invite them over and hit Nigbor with a ball peen hammer of Light when he comes for them." said Gale.

"I've hit him with everything. He can't be destroyed, just like the Light can't be destroyed, only marginalized. I think from looking at the book that I have to trap him somewhere."

But how to do that was the big question. Liv couldn't see a net holding him for long or a hole. Another dimension would have to be it. Somewhere where Nigbor would be hard-pressed to find the negative energy he needed to fuel up and escape.

"Oooh, I just had a brainstorm. I went to the Elf Realm to see if he was there. They found me immediately and they weren't too excited that I was there, and I'm supposed to be the magical Elf Warrior. I wonder what they would do if he appeared in their midst and couldn't get out.

"Would they take care of him? Like kill him? That seems easiest," said Gale.

"I don't think they are equipped. They were aggravated that I washed my smokey hands in their stream."

"Too bad," said Gale.

"Yeah, I don't think that realm would supply any dark energy for Nigbor to get fuel."

"So, where else would keep him occupied for like 100 years?" Asked Bea.

"It has to have no dark energy. I just haven't been to enough places to know where that would be," Liv said. "I'll check the book again." Liv grabbed the last cup of coffee and put it in the microwave. She found a chair and opened the book but Gale and Bea followed her.

"What if Minerva gets away?"

"You mean, catches a flight and goes home?" Liv asked. "I'm not sure. I guess we come up with plan B."

"We could barely come up with plan A," said Gale.

"If I go convince Minerva now, we have to deal with her. Are you willing to be in charge of her, Gale?"

"Ugh. I see what you mean, but without her, the plan won't work," said Bea.

Liv considered their options. "I'm not really sure she can leave. I gave her some Light to make her whole, but she still has holes in her body that the smoke destroyed."

"You're the only one who can see them, though. She looks normal to us. Maybe a little run-down, but this has been a harrowing trip," said Gale.

"OK so say a couple of us go to the airport and look. I can't find her by myself. She is probably with a million other people, waiting to get a flight out," said Liv.

"I'll go with. I'll grab my stuff," said Gale.

"I'll stay here. I'm really beat. I think my traveling days are over. I just want to get home safely," said Bea.

"Unfortunately, I think we may all be connected until it is over," said Liv.

"If you get an opportunity to pick something else up, these granola bars are getting old and we're on the last box," said Bea.

Liv drove back to the airport. The roads were fairly clear, everyone had gone back home or to work except the tourists, who were worn out and just wanted to get on a flight. The airport was small for an international hub and they walked from one end to the other until they found Minerva, asleep on three chairs.

"Hey, girlfriend, rise and shine," Gale said. Minerva woke up groggy. There was no smile on her face for any of them.

"Every time I get standby or close to, something happens like an emergency or something and then I get bumped," Minerva said. She brushed her hair back and a wad of it came out in her hand.

"Yikes," said Gale.

"We don't think any of us can go home until this thing with Nigbor is settled," said Liv.

"Oh, that's so annoying. I just want to get home and forget all this," said Minerva.

"As do we all, but it isn't going to happen. We're on a mission here," said Liv.

"Mission from hell," said Minerva.

"Come back with us so we can finish this," said Gale. "We all want to go home."

"Do you have a plan?" Asked Minerva.

Liv and Gale looked at each other. "We have some ideas," said Liv. "Nothing definite and nothing we want to talk about in public. But we need your help. It's your chance to get back at someone who almost ruined your life and your trip of a lifetime. Help us, Minerva."

"They are giving out some food. Let's see if they have any left," Minerva led them across the concourse and they picked up a box of food for each one of the Esbats and Liv.

They boarded the van and drove to the gym in Grindvik. The others ate the food like it was manna from Heaven. Liv ate a little bit although she wasn't hungry. The bottle of water was welcome and she had more coffee when they arrived at the gym. The Esbat ladies were ravenous. They finished their food and Liv's. There was a community sigh of contentment with real food in their stomachs.

"Shall we sleep on it and figure something out tomorrow?" Asked Bea.

Liv looked at Bea and saw the dark circles under her eyes and the sag of her shoulders. She decided to read the book while they slept. Liv wondered if she would ever sleep again.

She read a lot of the history of the most recent conflict. Anthor had won, but the other Elves who existed had lost and lost badly. That explained why the present Elves she'd seen were weak and timid. It probably took them a long time to heal. Maybe they were used to losing. Liv was not used to losing. Her two brothers had instilled her with fierce competitiveness. How had Anthor won?

She opened the book, thinking of her question. She saw the book form a strong-looking man she assumed was Anthor. He formed lighting in his hands and then fashioned it into a sphere. He shoved the bad guy into the center of the brilliant lightning ball and then flung it into the cosmos. It worked. It had given the Elves as well as the humans several hundreds of years of peace. Liv needed to do at least that well.

So, lightning was a good option or anything with overwhelming energy. Liv thought back to the list of things that had light energy she could use: lightning, the sun, starlight, neon, aurora and static were the ones she remembered. And a comet's tail.

If Liv could tire him out and then open a portal to the sun.... It was as good a plan as any. Were there any comets moving by in the night sky? How far up in the atmosphere did lightning go? Time to regret not learning more in science. 'But when am I going to use this?' resonated in her memory.

The next morning, Liv started the coffee early. When everyone woke and had coffee, Liv started, "Any new thoughts on how to neutralize Nigbor?"

"He's like Dracula, right? Prince of Darkness. Can we chop him up and put him in different boxes?"

"Great idea. How would we cut him up though?" Asked Bea.

"Liv has a sword and knives," said Minerva.

"He's stronger than I am. Hundreds of years old and crafty," said Liv.

"Maybe if we did an Ides of March attack, it would get him. Surprise him," said Gale.

"Could you make us knives out of the Light? Would it work for us?" Asked Bea.

"Not sure. Let me try," said Liv. She concentrated on bringing Light to her and filling up her tank. It felt good and she sought to repair every corner that wasn't perfect. She had sustained a lot of damage in the different realms and fixed herself before she attempted the creation of weapons. Liv fairly thrummed with energy.

She created two simple knives and gave them to Bea and Gale, hoping they could maintain the weapons through their own power. At first, the knives remained solid and sharp. Then, moment by moment, the weapons faded into vapor.

"You have to pour your will into keeping the weapon intact," Liv told them. "Like you would sing to keep a spell turning, the same is true for the weapons. Let's try again." Liv reformed the knives and kept them tethered to her by a slender filament of Light. Bea and Gale were able to hold the knives for as long as Liv kept her connection.

"Better, but I was hoping you could draw upon the Light yourselves. This way, I have to be part of the engine. Maybe this is something we can try once we get him here."

"What if he doesn't come here?" Asked Gale

"He has to. We have unfinished business," said Liv. Was there any time limit? She'd ask the book later. "So if you suddenly find a white knife in your hands, stab him or cut him. Let's try it once." As they stepped up and Liv gathered herself, the door to the gymnasium crashed open.

Banya walked in with a smile on her face and a wave. She favored one leg over the other and had a light metal cane, but Liv thought she looked better, more whole than the other Esbats.

"Banya! How are you?" Bea asked.

"Been a long stay in a nice hospital. Since the planes weren't leaving, they lent me a bed. I had no idea where you guys were but the driver taking me to the airport said you were here and I decided to come say hi. You guys look a little worse for wear."

Liv said, "I'll make more coffee and let you ladies catch up."

"Look at you, all sparkly and white," said Banya looking at Liv's arms. "How?"

"Bea and Gale can explain."

Banya's bruises were turning a nice green and her arm was still in a sling, but her eyes were clear, lively and intelligent. Maybe this is what the group needed to solidify them as a team. "Minerva, let's see if I can get you a knife." Liv moved aside with Minerva and worked on putting a knife in her hand. Every time, it fizzled out a moment after it appeared in Minerva's hands.

"Yipe! That time, it hurt," said Minerva.

"OK, we're done for now," said Liv. She walked back to the group. "Is there any magic you guys can pull together to make a stronger connection between you?"

"Well, we have that one circle," said Gale. They formed the circle, almost touching shoulders, and Liv ducked in so she could be in the center. Liv pulled the Light, filled her tank and then tried to form simple knives in each of their hands. Minerva's sizzled and dissolved but everyone else had a knife for a couple of moments.

"Let's try it with you guys farther apart," Liv said. They moved farther apart, eight or ten feet diameter and sang their bond while Liv conjured knives for them. The knives faded in and out of solidity but Liv thought in a pinch, she'd be able to get it done. She would call it the Dracula Defense.

"What happens after we cut him?" Asked Gale.

"The goal is to cut a piece off, like an arm or the head. Think Dracula. Remember, he's not human and he's hurt all of you. I'll open different portals and see if I have the juice to shove the pieces into the portals. Hopefully if his hand is in one portal, and the rest of him is in twelve different places, he won't be able to manifest for a long time."

"So that one is our Dracula Defense. Any other ideas? Minerva, you must have learned something in all your time with him," said Gale.

"I didn't spend a lot of time with him. Just in different cages he made for me," Minerva said.

"Any other thoughts? No? I guess we'll go with the Dracula Defense unless someone thinks of something else." Liv walked away and went back to the book. She needed some kick butt ideas or allies with power to stop Nigbor. She felt him waiting out there, could almost smell him. The book didn't offer any additional wisdom.

Liv checked her phone and saw a message from James.

Dear sis, Worried about you. You sound a little crazy. Made the mistake of telling the sisters in law. They are taking this whole issue to the next level and may make a grab for the Lake House. Come home please. I don't think they have the stones to confront you directly, but they have contacted a lawyer for the possibility of declaring you unfit or something. I've erased your emails and replaced my hard drive and you may want to leave your phone in Iceland.

Love James.

Great, that was all she needed to add to the stress. How could they take her house? She guessed if she heard that her brother was fighting Elves, she might have a moment for pause.

Dear James,

I'm having a great time. My vacation isn't over for another three days and flights have just started getting out of here. Believe me, with the eruptions, they are backed up with everyone leaving so I may extend my visit until I can get a flight out. Take care, Liv.

See? The email did not comment on Elves, no dark Matter or evil one. No Minerva or Esbat witches. Nothing to see here but an ordinary vacation. Tears blurred her vision and Liv's chest heaved with sobs.

Something touched her on the back of her neck. Liv tried to shove it away like it was an insect but the soft thing clung to her, keeping her hand pinned to her neck. The strips of darkness flew around her like dark flannel bats. The next one covered her mouth as she thought to scream for help. Her legs were bound, as well as her arms.

Nigbor had taken advantage of her distraction. It had to be Nigbor. The material threatened to invade her eyes, ears and mouth. A part of her, the part that was a small, terrified child, curled up against the assault. Liv's mind blanked and she lost the will to do anything and closed her eyes against the darkness.

Chapter Twenty Seven

Hogtied was the phrase that came to mind, when Liv became conscious. She tried to wiggle parts of her body without success. Instead of physically moving them, this time, she concentrated on moving the soft material away from her body. Success! It took all her concentration and she noticed, once she got an arm freed, that her skin wasn't glittering white anymore. It was a dull, moldy gray. Nasty. Her other arm was similarly devoid of the energy she'd been using so freely in Iceland. So, not Iceland any more.

She tried filling her little finger with Light. The finger turned dark gray and Liv stopped. She watched the little finger but the remaining Light didn't fill it up or even it out. Ah, Nigbor, what had he concocted this time?

The soft stuff moved back towards her as she concentrated on her finger, like the stuff was alive. Maybe it just sought out her energy. She heard or felt something digging at the gray material. An animal? Would she have to deal with that once she escaped this?

Liv worked on making space. She held her hands in front of her and pushed. When that showed some movement, she put her back on one wall and her hands and feet on the other to push. The wall in front of her began to thin and she struggled to get more leverage.

A tiny tear opened and the air whooshed in. If she'd needed to breathe, it would have been most welcome, but she was in control of herself this time. In the dim light, Liv examined her skin. Her finger still looked gray and lifeless. She was pushed forward from behind and stumbled. Something latched onto her lower leg. Sharp teeth dug into her flesh and then she was hit.

When her brother shot her with a BB gun when they were pre-teens, the sharp bright pain was similar. The agony shot up her leg with each passing moment as if the creatures were injecting poison. The creature was the size of a basketball and gray like everything else in this world. Liv created a sword with the last of her energy and hacked at it. The pieces scurried away out of sight and Liv took the pause to put some Light into her damaged limbs and finger. The finger remained gray and lifeless, hard to move. The gashes on her legs remained unhealed and raw. The redness was vibrant against her white skin.

She wasn't healing. In fact, she was being drained of energy. She needed to get back to Iceland as soon as possible. Plus, if she was here, where was Nigbor and what was he doing?

She didn't gather her energy this time, but blew it out of her like a shot from a gun. The portal screamed open and she slammed into the gym like a ball from a pitching machine. Liv hit the floor and tried to cushion her head as she fell. Her head bounced once on the hard gym floor, and her vision narrowed to a thin tunnel of light. Her whole body cramped in agony, and Liv curled into a small ball, trying to relax her muscles. She laid on the floor for a moment, collecting her thoughts.

What was the point of Nigbor putting her in different realms? Was it to find a realm that could hold her? Liv felt like she got stronger with each escape. She gained more confidence for sure.

Liv was sore in every cell of her being except her little finger that was still gray. She felt nothing in her finger and it wouldn't bend, but she'd escaped and pumped her fist in the air. The pain lanced through her shoulder from where she'd landed.

"Made it!" Liv laid on the floor and wondered where the Esbats were. She was sure she'd left them here. Of course, she had no idea how much time had passed. Minutes? Hours? Days?

Liv was grateful Nigbor didn't understand how much that would destroy her life to be missing for any length of time. Her sisters-in-law would no doubt try to have her declared missing. The Lake House seemed like a far away dream from the gym floor. Liv got up, checked the kitchen and then used her senses to reach out.

She pulled up, gasping for air and clutched her hand. It hurt like she imagined acid would feel, coursing through it.

Had the realm damaged her and would she be able to repair herself? This was not an easy journey. She'd never had a lot of pain as a kid, only what her brothers dished out. She tried sending a slender filament of Light into her hand, ignoring the damaged finger. She moved slowly and wrapped the finger gently in a cocoon of Light. Liv brought in more Light, slowly and was able to fix her shoulder and the ragged edges like scrapes from throwing herself through the portal. Her head still pounded and nothing seemed to fix that. Standing up felt like someone had her head in a vise and was squeezing.

Liv walked gingerly to the kitchen and looked around. Debris littered the counter and she swept everything into the bin.

Liv went out into the clear twilight. Nigbor was sitting on a rock, waiting for her.

"Where are the Esbats?" She sat on another large chunk of lava, facing him.

"What do you care?" Nigbor scratched his head. It was not a human scratch but more like that of a dog, fast and powerful.

"Not sure I do. I just wondered." They were a habit, like smoking, she supposed. Were they enemies or allies? Better to pretend she didn't care about them.

"Maybe they're being burned alive, like the witches of your world."

"That's old history."

"They just think they are being burned. Hurts the same, but doesn't leave damage. Still effective. Maybe you'd like your family to join them? How about the children?" He peered at her to see if she betrayed any emotion.

"Whatever. Since starting to turn crystalline, I really haven't had any strong feelings of regret or outrage. Why do you think that is? I used to be so emotional but now? Nothing. I don't have any strong ties to the Elves so that's a dead end."

"The Elves have to go, surely you see that now that you have some perspective," said Nigbor.

Liv was consumed with wondering whether the Esbats were burning alive or thought they were. They might have to suffer a little, or a lot in the meantime, but for the greater good, she had to ignore the threat. Her family had to be spared at any cost.

"No, I don't see it. I'm an Elf, remember. Explain why the Elves have to go again?"

"They upset the balance. They don't die. If they get bored, they fade. It isn't right. It isn't fair and it upsets the balance of the universe. I'm here to fix that. That's why the Elf Warrior never wins. You can't. It screws up the balance."

"But on earth, everyone dies," she said.

"Yes, your world or your former world is in balance."

"How did the Elves get an Elf Warrior?" Nothing lived forever. Why should the Elves?

"I'm like the Elf Shepherd. I keep it all in balance. You're the black sheep giving me problems, but I eventually will overcome you. The Elves have to be contained. When they bleed over to your world, your former world, the balance is off and can bring dangerous violence to Earth. They don't start the mayhem, but their appearance triggers it somehow."

"It would be nice to talk this over with someone. Someone else," Liv said.

"Say no more." Nigbor waved a hand and the Esbats appeared in a circle around him. Liv, without thought, put a knife in each Esbat's hand and the women struggled forward with their teeth barred and chopped at Nigbor. Their walk was unsteady but their red-rimmed eyes glared with hate. Liv kept the knives intact but diverted a portion of her power to open random portals. As the women hacked off pieces, she kicked a piece of Nigbor into it. It didn't matter where they were going as long as they were separated. The sound they made as the parts hit the floor made Liv gag. Wet thuds of meat dripped long tendrils of gray fluid.

When the last piece slid off into another realm, there was an eerie silence punctuated by weeping. Liv wasn't sure she wanted to know if the Esbats had been tortured. And she surely didn't want them to know she'd appeared callous as part of a strategy to save the children of her family.

"Is everyone OK?" Was the best she could manage.

"It was horrible. I don't want to talk about it," said Bea. Her reluctance to discuss it, kept the others silent. Banya wept.

"I'm not sure if he's gone for good. We have to come up with another strategy to imprison him somewhere. I think this will hold him off for a while, but he'll be back. So, let's get something to drink and work on some ideas."

"I got nothing. Maybe check your book?" Gale asked. Her eyes glittered with interest and Liv pursed her lips, suddenly wary of the group.

"Kitchen, everyone?" Asked Liv. The ladies reconvened in the kitchen and Banya left the group but Liv could hear her retching in the nearby locker room. Liv glanced around at them and noticed they were smudged around the edges, like their aura was damaged. Minerva had more than all the rest, but Liv was used to her looking half in Nigbor's influence. Now, it looked like the whole bunch was under his influence.

Liv had been going to suggest she try to heal them, but now, she didn't bother asking. They were Nigbor's and she could only use them to give her hints on how to trap him. Their acquiescence to cutting him to pieces signified to her that it was a temporary solution at best.

Chapter Twenty Eight

Liv left the room and found a corner of the gym where she could observe the room and part of what was happening in the kitchen. She concentrated and sent out a request to the book but knew it wouldn't go anywhere with her attention divided.

Gale approached. Her red rimmed eyes and the smudges under her eyes belied her alliance with Nigbor. She knelt next to Liv. "He wants the amulet. Just give it to him and this can all be over. I want to go home," she said. "This was just a lark for me. I'm not much of a religious person and the tour sounded like a hoot. We were going to see the Witch museum and the Elves' Hidden Valley. I was going to have some awesome pictures and start a travel blog. Now what am I going to write about? Demon Possession in a Far Land? Anyway, he just wants the amulet. Do you have it?"

"Amulet? What does it look like?" Liv wanted to avoid any cutting it out of her while she slept scenario.

Gale frowned. "He didn't tell me. I think he thought you'd know."

"That's just great," said Liv. "What does this amulet do?"

"Beats me," said Gale and patted her knee as she got up. Gale hissed, "You have it. He can feel it. You must give it to me."

"Move or I'll blast you with some Light. I'm betting you don't heal up that well, do you?" Liv stood and faced her nose to nose. Or nose to the top of Gale's head, since Liv was so much taller. She felt the Light bubble up with her rising anger. Gale backed away, running a bit when she felt safer, back to the kitchen.

So, somehow Gale could sense the amulet. It helped Liv focus her questions for the book. The amulet became activated when Liv felt danger or anger. Interesting. What else could the amulet do for her?

Liv concentrated and then pictured her amulet. Her shoulder grew warm and comforting. She opened the book and dragged over a chair. A part of her remained on watch in the gym so no one could ambush her but most of her was engrossed in the story the book told of the history of the amulet. The pages showed her the earliest days.

The stone was a sink. It could strip off the magical auras of others. She just had to visualize it correctly. It didn't seem like it killed the one using the magic or the one the magic was used against, so that was good. They just weren't magical anymore or until they regenerated, if they had that power. Liv paused a moment and thought about Nigbor. She could use this. Maybe she could strip the aura off of him

Liv had been sucking the Light from the auroras and lightning, but she could take the magic from others too. It was much harder to drag it out of the atmosphere. Liv was kicking herself that she'd taken the hard road. Damn Anthor. If he had just trained her like he was supposed to, none of this might have happened.

Why had the dwarvish creature given her the amulet if it was so valuable? She sent the question out and waited.

The answer materialized on the page. The creature was required to give a gift for someone saving it and the amulet may have been the only thing of value it had. Perhaps he had thrown it in anger, not realizing the wonderful thing he had given away. Was it so wonderful though?

Liv wondered if she'd been happier not being the Elf Warrior. This was certainly more interesting than your basic trip to Iceland. When she was young, she'd been convinced that magic didn't exist. After seeing a fairy in her mother's garden, her family had mocked her relentlessly for years. She finally put it from her. How could there be magic if she was the only one who could see it or use it?

Liv sighed. Banya made her way over to Liv. She didn't look burned at all. Had she regenerated herself? Neat trick, if it was true.

"Can I be over here by you? Gale is acting strange and her eyes are all glittery."

"You seem like you didn't fare so poorly in Nigbor's realm."

"Nigbor? I never knew his name. I wove a protection spell. It's about the only spell I have that really works. And, obviously, it only partially worked. He's too powerful."

"Good for you," Liv said. She was itching to draw the magic out of them all but instead walked to the center of the room and pictured her amulet, she set it spinning and reached her hands out to Gale. Liv imagined drawing the magic out of Gale like spinning wool into thread.

Gale screamed and writhed until she fell on the floor. A loud pop like a huge firework being lit and the air moved in and out of the room. Liv's eardrum vibrated and she held onto the spinning thread image until she had pulled everything out of Gale. An arm was attached to the last bit of smut and made a squelching noise when Liv pulled it out. It wasn't Gale's arm. Had she killed her? Gale lay inert on the floor, an explosion of ash around her. The wet arm flopped and found its fingers, moved them in a blur and ran upright out of the room. Creepy as a nightmare on a bad day.

Liv went to Gale and kneeled to take a pulse. Gale's eyes fluttered and opened. They were hugely dilated, but she sat up on her own, leaning over to retch.

"You OK?" Liv asked, surprised that she cared at all. But she did care, now that Gale was released from the dark smut of Nigbor. "What do you remember? Anything that could help me beat him?"

"He reminded me of some of my friends who really get obsessed about some guy and they don't even really know him. He's like that, but with you. He wants whatever you have or represent or something. He is convinced the Elves need to be wiped out but I don't know why. Sorry, that's about it." Her face was pale and her eyes weren't as shiny as they had been.

"Thanks, that's actually very helpful. He presents as a real person, but he really is almost a shadow of a person, not totally fleshed out fully."

"And he is really easy to goad, so maybe you can force him into a mistake," said Gale.

"Can you do any magic? I pulled out Nigbor's smut but I'm not sure I left you any of the good magic."

"No, I think you took everything. I'm a little sad about that," said Gale.

"Maybe I can give you back some, but I'd rather wait until after this mess is over. I'm not sure I can, but I'll try."

"Thanks," said Gale.

"Do you know anything about an arm inside you?"

"An arm? No. Ick."

"The last thing I pulled out was an arm. It was severed neatly. It got up on its fingers and ran off."

"That is disgusting."

"Yeah, I just stood here and gaped at it. Maybe I should have cut it up or something."

"I thought you put all the parts in different realms."

"I thought I did. Maybe Nigbor put access points in the Esbats. I think I need to find them and try it again."

"Wait, I cut an arm when I was fighting Nigbor, I think. It's pretty hazy. Maybe that's why it connected to me specifically."

Liv looked around. "I think it's time to find the other Esbats and see what's inside them."

"Do you have a plan when a leg or some other piece jumps out?"

"Hm, not really." Liv thought about what she could do to finally entrap Nigbor. "It doesn't seem like anything would work. He needs to be somewhere where his negative energy constantly has to be replenished so he can't gather enough to free himself."

"So what you need is a place where there isn't any Dark energy, only Light?"

"Like the Elf Realm," said Liv. "Boy, that idea is not going to go over well. They didn't welcome me when I washed myself in their pristine river. They acted like I defiled it or something."

"So are you afraid you're going to lose your union card if you do it? They haven't exactly been kind to you," Gale pointed out.

"I was never asked if I wanted to be this Elf Warrior. It would serve them right to deal with their own problems."

A lower torso and two legs ran across the gym and pushed out the side door.

"After them!" yelled Liv.

She and Gale charged through the side door, but didn't see the legs when she got there. "Fast," said Gale.

Liv examined the ground but the hard lava didn't pick up any impressions. They both searched the horizon but without success. Liv was about to go back inside when something pulled inside of her. She fought it, leaning back on her heels and yelling but it pulled inexorably at her midsection. Smut dragged out of her, ripping at her and trying to take other, vital things with it as it left her body. Liv put both hands on the stream and focused Light on the disgusting stream of uck. It was impossible to grip, like slime or oil but she thought she slowed it down.

When it seemed over, Liv sighed but then something pushed out of her and she fell to the floor in agony as it tore out of her. The hole it ripped was as big as a bowling bowl. Nigbor's head hit the floor and rolled like a lop-sided playground ball.

Liv's eyes closed and was grateful the pain stopped when the head appeared. Pieces of her guts lay in a puddle around her abdomen hole and she gritted her teeth and slid them back in. She healed the hole and was able to sit up with discomfort. She must have been the one who cut the head off. Either that or Nigbor chose random people to store his bits in. Like Gale, she couldn't remember what she'd done in the previous fight. He must have taken the memory with him when he reclaimed his 'parts'.

Gale came bounding back. "Man, that was intense. I didn't really process it when it happened to me but when I saw it happen to you, that was awful. Are you OK?"

"I'm a little queasy but seeing you gives me encouragement that I'll recover." Liv stood up and rolled her shoulders and twisted at the trunk. She winced at the pulling discomfort.

"I saw where they were going! The parts. They're in a little cave not far from here. I know the head didn't see me. I'm not sure if the rest can see or not."

"I'm not in the shape to fight anything," Liv shook her head, noting that even that hurt.

"Couldn't you send part of him to the Elf Realm?"

"Possibly," Liv focused her inner Light and tried to draw Light from the atmosphere. The magnetosphere as well as the ionosphere could provide her with energy but she hadn't tried to tap into them yet. So far, she'd used lightning and the aurora and fire but those were only available occasionally.

She felt the power of the ionosphere pressing upon her. Liv tightened her focus. She reached up with a thin tendril and touched the ionosphere. It neither recoiled nor drew her in. It was powerful and served more masters than just Liv. She skimmed off a layer of energy like a ribbon and prepared to bring it with her.

Something smacked her like a board. It snapped her concentration and she lost the ribbon of power she'd work so hard to get. Liv opened her eyes and an arm with an upper torso attached ran past her on its fingers. He must have hit her with his torso as he ran past.

Liv made a noise deep in her throat that might have been a growl and scrambled up after the torso. As she walked, she went up and retrieved the ribbon of energy that her consciousness had separated from the ionosphere. She rounded the corner, gaining on the arm-torso combination.

By the time they reached the cave, Nigbor's head was yelling instructions. Liv formed the ribbon into a whip and cracked it at the biggest piece. The running torso tripped and a line appeared on his back and sizzled where Liv's whip had struck it.

Liv reformed the Light into a net and captured the torso. She pushed the torso into the Elf Realm. Although she sealed the opening, she heard the beginning of Nigbor screaming, whether in pain or anger, she couldn't tell.

The remaining ionosphere wrapped around her like a cloak. Some of it healed her dead finger and the rest concentrated on repairing her damaged abdomen. She took a moment to regroup and make sure she had Light stored and had fixed all her wounds.

"Time to find the rest of the Esbats." Liv took a deep breath.

"Where did you send him?" Asked Gale.

"Elf Realm. They might just toss him back, I don't know."

They walked into the gym and found the other Esbats collapsed in various stages of agony. Liv healed what she could, feeling their thin layer of magic slide off them like peeling a hot sweet potato.

Minerva was the last and Liv wondered if curing her was worth taking her magic. She went ahead anyway, using the remaining ionosphere energy. Minerva screamed and scratched at her skin but Liv finally wrenched the soot and magic out of her. Minerva collapsed on her side, sobbing.

"It's all gone. You took my magic," she said.

"I had to as part of the healing. Nigbor left you all with a gaping hole, like he did me. You might have died without the healing. I can't control taking the magic with it. It just happens." It was sad that some of them were crying but she had healed them. Their small magic had caused nothing but harm and mischief.

Something began to sizzle in the middle of the gym. Liv sighed, would it never end? She wasn't tired, despite not having slept. She was more weary than anything.

The sizzle spread into a circle and parts of Nigbor fell out of the portal. Liv watched, fascinated, as the torso-arm attached to the lower torso-legs. The last thing to pop out was the head, and Nigbor was definitely not happy.

He stomped over to where Liv stood. "Not appreciated." Liv saw the crimson seams heal on his body as she watched. Instead of his usual immaculate appearance, he was covered in soot. He brushed at it until he finally just waved his hands and it was gone.

"Do you even realize how aggravating the Elves are to non-Elves?"

"I was there. I polluted their water when I washed my hands," Liv said.

"See? So you know. Why would you send me there? That's just cruel. I didn't send you anywhere like that."

"How about the suffocating realm? Is that what you would term as 'nice'?"

"Hrmph!" Nigbor made a noise in his throat of disgust and walked over to look at the weepy Esbats. "And you ruined them! There isn't a speck of magic to work with. You did what you accuse me of doing: taking all the magic out of the world. Maybe you're the one everyone needs protection from, not me." He turned and left the gym, fading into the night.

The Esbats turned their eyes to Liv and she felt their acrimony. She wondered if they'd rather stay in the smokey realm, wrapped around their precious little bit of magic. She walked to the kitchen and filled up a cup of coffee and went out into the dark twilight. What was left? She didn't have any allies with the Esbats bereft of magic. The Elves were certainly unhappy with her. Her family was out. The people of Iceland still believed. How could she rally them to her side though, and what could they do to help capture Nigbor?

Liv came to no conclusions and wondered if she should go back into the gym or not. What was the point? The door crashed open and the Esbats came out with what looked like whatever they could find in the kitchen to use as a weapon. Since it was a school kitchen the Weapons of Mass Destruction included a spatula, a big fork, a metal serving spoon and tongs.

They looked deadly serious. "Let's think this through," Liv said. She got up and put the table-sized rock in between them.

"He offered us our magic back," said Gale.

"You know he'll do it, but you'll end up looking like Minerva did. And you'll be enslaved to Nigbor. " The semicircle stopped closing in on her. "Do you want to be evil?"

"We just want our powers back," said Bea.

"Understood, but you misused your powers. There's a cost for that," said Liv. "Are you going to beat me to death with stainless steel serving utensils? Go back inside."

They hesitated, exchanging looks. Liv tried to look bored, but she really didn't want to have a beat down with these women. She had no doubt her training with her brothers would hold her in good stead. She could slug it out with the best of them and be proud. Liv just didn't feel like it though. She turned her back on them and walked away. She waited to feel the stainless steel spoon bouncing off her head, but it didn't come.

Liv kept walking back towards the building in Grindvik where she'd found the other coffee maker. She'd rather be alone than have to watch her back constantly. She needed to study the book without interruption. During the entire walk over the crunchy lava, Liv thought about how to trap Nigbor. He'd gotten out of the Elves' realm or they threw him out. Next time she saw him, she'd goad him into telling her.

She reached the building and was relieved it was still unlocked. People would be heading back soon now that the eruption danger was over. She found another coffee maker in another part of the office and brewed herself a strong pot. There was a comfortable couch and she said an affirmation before opening the book. How was she going to fight Nigbor? He was impossible to kill and now she had aggravated him on top of everything.

The book showed some kind of history of Nigbor. At least the stick figure looked like him. As she watched him fight various Elf Warriors, he got darker and darker like he was gathering evil into him. Liv ran a hand over her amulet tattoo. It tingled, whatever that meant.

Liv put the book away and laid her head down. When she woke, it was twilight. Must have missed the four hours of daylight. Lucky her.

Liv warmed up a cup of coffee and looked out the panoramic windows of the second floor. Why didn't her office have a window? It wasn't fair. She brought in big bucks to the educational community through her grants. None of that money came to her. Just enough salary to keep her hanging onto the ancestral home.

Outrage blew through her. The Lake House wasn't the sanctuary she envisioned. She needed a different job. Especially now that she could add Elf Warrior to her resume.

What was appropriate? Soldier of Fortune? She wasn't sure her powers of Light would work if she used them for money.

As she looked out the window, the top of an enormous head came into view out of the rocks on the curving road. Liv shook her head to clear it. The troll had to be at least thirteen feet high with a brown scarf around her head. Maybe Liv did need to be committed. Deep therapy at the least. The troll's hair was black and scraggly down past her shoulders and she dragged her head from one side to the other as if looking for something. A dark brown skirt that looked homespun and a loose gray shirt secured with a cloth belt completed the look. She wore dark leather boots, worn at the toes. The troll dragged a burlap sack behind her on the ground.

"What in the hairy hell?" Asked Liv. The troll stopped in front of the building and Liv was eye to enormous eye with the thing. It smiled a gap-toothed smile at Liv and shook the empty bag. Liv forced a smile and waved. The troll growled at her, a low tone that walked down Liv's spine like a spider. Then the thing plodded on toward the town. Liv shook as she watched the figure walk down the road. The ground vibrated under her heavy steps.

Liv remembered the legend from the tourbook. The Christmas visit of Gryla The Troll Queen. It didn't even feel odd for her, as she watched the Troll Queen from Icelandic fairy tales make her way to town. Gryla was used to frighten little children and had been outlawed in the 18th century by Iceland's Parliament due to her frightening children so badly. Gryla devoured naughty children and had an insatiable appetite. After parliament outlawed Gryla, naughty children got rotten potatoes in their shoes instead.

Liv waited in the shadows at the window. Could the Thirteen Lads be far behind? The Thirteen Lads were Gryla's sons. They came down from the mountain cave they lived in and tormented children during Yule. They were foul and disgusting with names like Door Slammer and Pot Licker.

She felt the pounding of their feet before she saw them coming down from the mountain.

They were foul creatures, each one vile in its own way. Merry Christmas to one and all. She pressed back into the shadows while they moved past to the city.

Liv waited a few minutes to make sure they were on their way. That they were on the hunt, meant it must be close to Christmas or Yule, whatever they called it. Not every night you see Gryla the Troll

Queen and her Thirteen Lads under the twilight. They were an old magic.

Liv finished her coffee and pulled out the book again while she refilled the cup. Fireworks launched over the city celebrating Christmas Eve and Liv admired their beauty and uncomplicated life cycle. The half hour display was incredible. Liv had never been one for the Fourth of July but in the cold still air, with snow just starting to ramp up, it was spectacular.

Sparkles appeared in the air over the road. Liv sighed and returned the book to her inside pocket. She shotgunned the coffee, cracked her neck and went out to meet Nigbor. Great timing.

Chapter Twenty Nine

But, the sparkling wasn't Nigbor, after all. It was the huge, vicious Yule Cat. Its fur was full black and it was as big as a two-story house. She could see the jagged white teeth and red tongue. Liv grabbed a scarf off the closet hook as she went out. The Yule Cat hunted those without new clothes and devoured them. The huge beast licked his paws and sniffed at the scarf as Liv came out of the building. Liv had thought to make friends but there was blood on the cat's fur, dried and matted. Its tail jerked a couple of times and it hissed at something only it could see.

Then, Nigbor walked out of a portal next to it. He started when he saw the Cat. Liv had to admit, Nigbor looked good. His face was repaired, and his draped clothing hung the way it had when she'd seen him the first time. He definitely had his swagger back. A wicked gleam in his beautiful hazel eyes and a quirky smile was on his lips.

Liv felt that same magnetic pull that she'd felt for him when she thought he was just a fairy or some other magical being hanging around. She almost smiled when she saw him. This version of Nigbor embodied her ideal man: tall, slim with that sarcastic wit and dark eyes and was probably something he had pulled from her subconsciousness. Before, she had seen his demon form around the edges but now it was just the man she saw.

"I'm sorry this has to end now, Liv." He swept his long leather jacket behind him like a cape. Snow began to fall harder and Liv stood stunned as she watched a demon and the Yule Cat. What had her life come to? The cat cleaned his paws, its rough black fur dotted with snowflakes. It ignored them both until Nigbor swung his coat behind him.

The Yule Cat reached out a paw the size of a large tree trunk and batted at the coat. Nigbor ignored the giant and took a step towards Liv. His long coat moved behind him in the stiff breeze and the cat hooked the hem of it with a claw and spun Nigbor around to face him.

Anger suffused Nigbor's face and he gathered a mass of Dark energy into a ball of dense smoke and threw it at the beast. When it hit the black fur, sparks flashed and the cat screamed at him. Faster than she could follow, the Yule Cat bapped Nigbor on the head five times, rapid fire.

Nigbor reeled back, Liv forgotten, and regrounded himself as he faced the feline. Both his hands gathered darkness and filled with smoke and sparks. The cat stood on all fours and grew exponentially by fluffing his fur till he was enormous. He growled deep in his throat and it rumbled through Liv's chest. Her legs shook and she took a couple of steps back, clearing the field for Nigbor and the cat.

Maybe the cat could do what Liv could not: defeat Nigbor. The cat's ears pinned back tight to its head and it screamed at Nigbor. The attack, when it came, was faster than the eye could follow and only Liv's enhanced vision allowed her to see it. Whirling paws with sharp claws on them swept over Nigbor and flashing teeth hit him a dozen or more times. Liv was transfixed by the fierceness of the attack. Bits of smoke and sparks exploded from the nexus of the fight.

They broke from each other to assess damage. The cat had dark smudges in his fur and Nigbor had chunks missing out of his body and he stumbled as if dizzy. The Yule Troll Queen, Gryla, appeared from the gloom behind the Yule Cat and reached over the Cat to pluck Nigbor off the ground. He only had time to kick his legs in outrage before she thrust him into her grimy burlap bag. The last Liv saw, his arms and legs were moving wildly in an effort to escape but Gryla didn't make any notice of his struggles.

The Yule Cat sat licking his fur. Liv turned to run but found herself dragged into the air above the cat. The Cat's beautiful and terrible eyes watched her with disinterest as Gryka threw her into the bag.

Chapter Thirty

The smell in the sack was sickening. Blood and ruined flesh combined with the smell of loosened, terrified bowels. The silence in the pile under Liv was deafening and bespoke of broken bodies and blood. The fall into the bag seemed farther than the ten feet it looked like from the outside. Looking up from where she lay, it looked almost a hundred feet. Liv lay on a pile of bodies, perhaps hundreds of unfortunate souls.

"Get off me," Nigbor shoved her and Liv slid down the slick side of the mound of bodies. Liv grimaced. Her shoulder where she'd been pushed by Nigbor was wet and stained with blood, vomit and who knew what else. Nigbor balanced on the stack of bodies and worked his hands to open a portal, but nothing was gaining traction inside the burlap.

Parts of him were missing and Liv could see through him to the burlap sack behind him. Why had the Troll Queen taken her? She was Light personified. Except that she was fighting or at least getting ready to fight Nigbor.

Liv watched Nigbor struggle to get some magic working. She should do the same. She sat up and felt the stickiness trying to keep her down. It made her struggle harder to get up. Once up, she felt for the Light. Nothing. What could she do without magic?

The jostling of the Troll Queen as she walked was nauseating to Liv. Nigbor's movements became more desperate and she heard him muttering in strange languages like he was swearing. Finally, his hands fell limp next to his thighs.

"You! This is your fault." Nigbor struggled over the mound of bodies towards Liv. She dodged him easily but still he pursued her.

"Stop," Liv told him. "This isn't helping us get out." The bottom of the bag opened into darkness. They fell and Liv was hit by bodies falling behind her. Liv landed on her left hip. Agony lanced up from her buttock to her back. She could see various bodies and parts of bodies in the blackness. Liquid cascaded onto them like a waterfall. Liv could smell it was some kind of animal broth. They were going to be a stew for the Troll Queen and the Yule lads. Well, not if Liv could help it. She pulled and pulled the atmosphere but still couldn't generate any Light.

She dug inside herself and accessed the Light she had stored for just such an emergency. Something was wrong. Liv couldn't access it. More broth cascaded onto her head and she saw Nigbor skirting the sides of the cauldron to avoid getting hit. Liv gave up as she realized there was no escape. The broth began to warm and Liv added her tears to the liquid as she stood waiting for death either by drowning or being eaten.

A slap knocked her back to reality. "Snap out of it. Some Elf Warrior you turned out to be." Nigbor wound up to hit her again but Liv held up a hand for him to stop.

"Point taken. Any ideas?"

"We can't access our magic. The Troll Queen has older, stronger magic, so let's see if we can work together to get out of here. Put your foot in my hand and I'll hoist you up. Maybe you can reach the lip." He pointed up and Liv saw the edge of the pot seemed within their reach.

A giant spoon carved out of wood plunged down between them and stirred the warming mess. Liv locked eyes with Nigbor and they both jumped for the handle as it was drawn out of the pot. She lost her grip and slid down to the bowl part of the spoon, her boots dangling over the stew. Nigbor had claws instead of his hands so his grip was secure. When she slid off the spoon, she almost landed in the fire but was able to swing to the counter and scramble behind a jar of seasonings. Nigbor dropped lightly to his feet behind the next jar over.

While the Troll Queen's back was turned, Nigbor moved so he was behind the same jar as Liv.

"Our next mission is to get outside and see if we can open a portal. Agreed?" Asked Nigbor.

"I'm at a complete loss. This magic is a little too much for me."

"The window is open. We'll fit through." Nigbor led the way across the counter and Liv followed him. At the end of the counter, a window was cracked to let the heat out or the smell, one of the two. They were able to crawl out. Liv inhaled the fresh air. The cave was part of a string of smaller caves within the major cave. The openings dotted the path. Only two had lights in them and Liv couldn't look at them without shaking. She and Nigbor climbed down the rough rocks from the window to the floor.

"We have to get out of here by the morning, or we'll be trapped in this cave for a year," Nigbor told her.

"Crap, the tour book glossed over that part of the legend." Liv followed the contour of the cave until she saw light. She began to run but Nigbor pulled her back by the back of her coat. The light flickered and shaking started under Liv's feet. The Thirteen Yule Lads plodded past them, rocks shaking as they moved. They didn't go to Gryla's house but went down the tunnel to another cave close by. The smell as they passed was horrific and Liv struggled not to gag.

The giant Yule Cat sauntered by next and both Liv and Nigbor squeezed back into a crevice. It went into Gryla's house and they both heaved a sigh of relief.

"Now," Nigbor said, "And don't run."

Liv tried to walk but the terror of all she'd seen threatened to overwhelm her. Her heart pounded and her legs shook. Little mewling noises came out of her despite Nigbor squeezing her hand with some urgency.

Nigbor pulled her around the entrance of the outer cave into the light. Liv would have plunged on blindly. There was a narrow lip in front of the cave that allowed entrance and Liv would have flung herself over it. She wasn't thinking straight. Panic made her jump at every noise and movement.

"It's OK, we're out. One step at a time." Nigbor looked over the edge carefully and didn't like what he saw.

Liv tried to gather the Light but couldn't focus enough to stop shaking.

"Together," Nigbor said and took her hands. He moved their hands together in a mirror image of each other.

Liv relaxed enough to help him open the portal and they stepped through together.

They lay on the fresh snow near the gym and watched more fireworks flash against the dark sky.

"Merry Yule," Liv said.

"Not the way I thought we'd end today," said Nigbor.

"I can't believe any of that happened."

"Said the magical Elf Warrior."

"Yes, but I know I'm still me inside. Gryla the Troll Queen and the rest are all legends." She struggled to sit up. "And I know the Elf Warrior is a legend too. I just can't process the world I live in now. Up until two weeks ago, I would have argued to the death denying magic existed. Now, I'm trapped inside an Icelandic fairy tale."

Nigbor stood up and moved to pull her up from her seated position but recoiled.

"You know, you can use your magic to clean yourself. You smell nauseating." His face wrinkled up in a grimace.

Liv tried. There wasn't anything there, magic wise. "Sorry, I can't seem to do it right now."

"Unbelievable. Go take a shower and clean your clothes. I can't deal with this new, apathetic Liv. I'll come back later and destroy you," he told her. When she didn't react other than to shrug her shoulders, he added, "Maybe I'll torture the witch women."

"They were never nice to me anyway."

"Maybe I'll do your family next."

"They aren't really my family."

"I'll destroy magic from this world forever."

"I'm ok with that. The magic I've seen is so gross: the Troll Queen, her sons, and that nightmare of a cat. The world will be better off without them."

"Go take a shower. Get your head in the game," Nigbor gave her a little shove towards the building and then wiped his hands on his pants.

Liv sighed and walked through the deep snow to the gymnasium. Maybe the key to defeating Nigbor was to just not care.

She took off her clothes and shoved them into the washer to cycle. She wrapped herself in a small blanket and started the shower to warm the water. It heated quickly and Liv stood under the water, letting it run over her. Chunks of guck fell off her and Liv gagged. She found some soap and used it on her hair as well as her body. If she never felt any magic again, she'd be happy.

Liv laid down and waited for her clothes to finish drying. Once the dryer stopped, she got dressed again even though her clothes were still damp. She wrapped herself in the blanket and laid down on the cot that was probably used by sick kids. Liv could sense that Nigbor came and looked at her twice. She was drawn up into the fetal position facing the wall, and wouldn't open her eyes to look at him.

The last time he visited her, he kicked the cot frame. She ignored him.

Chapter Thirty One

"This won't do," said the Maiden, plucking the spindle.

"I think they broke her," said the Mother, winding the string.

"She's not strong enough," said the Crone.

"She doesn't *understand* the bracelet," insisted the Maiden.

"We have to take some responsibility for that, don't you think?" Said the Mother.

"She is a magical creature, isn't she? We shouldn't have to explain every little nuance to

her," said the Crone.

"She's newly magical. Just a babe." The Mother reached out and touched Liv on the wrist where the bracelet had been.

The bracelet under Liv's skin glowed and spun. The three Norns joined hands and made a circle around Liv. The glow spread up Liv's arm and chest and then activated the amulet. Together, the two talismans filled Liv with Light.

She opened her eyes and smiled at the three women. "I'm sorry I'm not the Elf Warrior you had in mind. I'm just not strong enough."

"It's all right, dear. We can give you back your old life if that's what you want," said the Mother.

"Really? Before all this happened? Before the magic?"

"All you have to do is ask," said the Maiden.

"I'm ready to go," Liv said. "I never asked for this."

"You can't...." began the Crone.

"Hush," interrupted the Mother.

Liv felt golden swirls diving through her body. Darkness closed in and when Liv could see again, she was in her office back in the States. She still wore her traveling clothes and she sat behind her small desk. Everything felt claustrophobic. There was no window and Liv longed to see the weather. The walls were close enough to touch on three sides if she spread her arms out, evidence of her office's former life as a supply closet. It was Christmas morning here so the office was empty.

Liv walked out the office door and her front yard appeared around her. The Lake House was imposing and cold when she walked in. Liv looked at the thermostat and saw the heat was off. She tried moving the dial a couple of times but realized the furnace had probably given up in her absence.

Liv bought a Christmas tree before she left, thinking there would be a family gathering. The needles were dried out from lack of water and an entire branch dropped its needles like a burst of rain. Boxes of ornaments sat around the tree and Liv could see where a mouse had been at the foam wrapping around the ornaments.

Liv sat at her enormous oak kitchen table in the predawn darkness. Liv flipped the switch for the lights and something snapped. Sounded like a circuit breaker flipped. She grabbed a flashlight and made her way down to what she always thought of as the creepy basement. The house was old enough that the basement was large round fieldstones formed into walls with a gravel floor. The basement had terrified her as a child and it was doing a number on her tonight as well.

Liv pulled out the fuse and replaced it with a new one from the shelf. She flipped the switch and hoped it worked. She went upstairs and the kitchen light was on. Liv smiled and set up the coffee maker. It was good to be home.

Or was it? Liv felt strangely disconnected from this time and this place. In Iceland, magic was everywhere and she could reach out and touch it. She was a part of the fabric of the land, the entire ecosystem welcomed her.

Here at the Lake House and her job, nothing reached out to connect with her. She was alone and felt the grave loss of that connectivity. She pulled her phone out of her inside pocket and checked her email.

James had written.

Dear Liv, We ended up going to Acapulco when the Lake House wasn't available and made our way to the beach. You should be thankful you aren't here. It is very rainy with the hurricane building out in the Atlantic and we hope to get out before it hits. The rain is warm and gentle right now so we were still able to go into the ocean and use the pool. We should have saved our money and come to the Lake House but of course, no one will admit this but me. Everyone agrees we need to have a family meeting to talk about the Lake House after this vacation. Translation: the sisters in law want to sell it and pressure you into splitting the profits with them. Fair warning! Love you James.

Should she do as they asked? It wasn't going to make them think any more kindly about her. She always rolled over and played dead to keep the family peace. Liv debated writing back to him but what would she write? Liv settled on writing 'Thanks for the heads-up,'and sent it before she made any apologies or explained how she was feeling with her family arrayed against her. She knew that James would fade before the will of the sisters in laws, everyone did. He was on her side but, like her, passive enough to just go along with the stronger personalities.

What was she doing here? Liv didn't belong here, wasn't comfortable, and would never go back to sitting in a windowless office supporting a house that had endless needs. Where would she put her sword? Liv began to giggle and then laugh. She sent off several emails. It was much easier to cut the ties to her old life than she thought it would be.

"I'm ready to come back to my destiny," Liv said out loud. Nothing happened. Was she stuck here in this depressing reality? She drank her coffee and waited. She found a bottle of whiskey and poured herself a shot. After a while, she took all the photo albums and piled them on the table. Then, she dragged the tree out onto the back porch and hefted it over the rail into the woods. The lake shimmered beyond the trees, catching the sun as it rose.

Even if the Norns didn't take her back to Iceland, she was changing her life for good. No more taking one for the team. Now, she knew there was magic in the world and that it was worth fighting for. All those years taking abuse and ridicule because she had seen a fairy in the garden. She should have stood her ground but how do you tell a youngster to ignore the very real voices around her and listen to the voices in her head?

She wished there had been a book about the adventures of a girl who meets an elf, when she was younger. It would have really helped her to have a heroine to look up to.

Liv put a hand on her upper chest and felt for where the amulet had been. Nothing. She remembered the bracelet the Three had given her but that skin was smooth too. Just in case, she checked her hand for the sigil Anthor had given her. Nothing. Liv took down the garlands and swept up the pine needles. There were tons of family photos in beautiful frames around the fireplace and she put them in a box next to the photo albums.

Liv walked through all the rooms and found there wasn't anything she much cared to keep. She packed a couple of changes of clothing into a backpack. The rest of the things in her room, she boxed. She did the same with each bedroom and labeled each box. The library caused her the most heartache. Many of these books she had used to learn how to read. None of them had much value other than sentimental, so she left them.

The kitchen had a huge coffee machine but Liv just looked at it with longing. Wouldn't fit in her pack. Liv touched the ancient metal cookie cutters she'd thought to use with her nephews and nieces. Someone else could have those memories.

It was dark by the time Liv finished boxing up personal things and moving them to the garage. Someone else could fight over the tools and the jet skis. Next, she went through all the house paperwork. It was already in almost perfect shape since Liv had been through it once after gaining ownership. She prided herself on her meticulous organization of paperwork, whether it was home or work.

Was there anything else she needed to do? Her plan was to head back to Iceland and see if she could connect with her magic again. She knew it was there, somewhere in the atmosphere or other charged ions. She had to find it.

Liv looked around and liked how decluttered the house looked. Although it was massive, it looked somehow more spacious and calm. Liv went up to bed, happy to have a plan in place.

Chapter Thirty Two

Her dreams were golden and swirling and Liv enjoyed the peace that came with them. There was a nauseating lurch at the end, but when she opened her eyes, she knew she was back in Iceland. She felt her chest, hand and wrist for her amulets and they were there. Her phone and the Magic book were in her long coat. Best of all, she drew the Light into her. The magic would do her bidding, she only had to decide how to use it. What had she learned from the past two weeks that could help her with the Nigbor problem?

True, he had helped her when she really needed it, but he was helping himself too. He represented the darkness and the presence of evil. He was the kind of evil that lured with its reasonableness. It caressed rather than clobbered. It misled rather than outright deceived. The type of evil that made you feel like the choice was yours, but was obvious.

The horror of the Yule Troll Queen and her Lads was receding in her memory. It was no longer something she could taste and feel. She would remember everything but it wouldn't make her shake with chills in the night, she hoped.

The Three Norns were gone, but she wanted to thank them. They reminded her who she was and how she'd changed. She knew magic existed and that the world needed it. More, she needed it. Her destiny. She was back in the gym outside Grindvik. She could smell coffee.

First, coffee. Then, Liv would figure out how to take care of Nigbor. The best success she'd had was when the witches helped her cut him up. There was a full pot brewed in the kitchen of the gymnasium. She sipped and felt the warmth of the coffee fill her up. She didn't trust the Esbats. She didn't even know where they were at this point. They had traded loyalties too many times for her comfort. The last time she butted heads with them, she had stripped them of their magic. Could she even restore their link to magic? Iffy, at best. But, who could she else could she trust?

Anthor was out galaxy hopping or whatever. The Elves were not reliable partners either. She couldn't bear to even think of making a liaison with the Yule Troll Queen and the Yule Lads. The thought of it made her gag. They ate people! The Yule Cat was likewise an inappropriate ally, not to mention the communication issue. They belonged to an older magic.

Who else was there? Liv went down her short Christmas card list. Her family didn't believe in magic, they'd proved that to her over and over again and drummed the belief out of her. More importantly, her family didn't believe in her. No help there.

Liv opened the book with a new question: a plan was stirring in the back of her mind.

The drawings that appeared on the page were populated with a cast of hundreds, maybe thousands. The aurora danced above them in the stars.

Who were the people in her book? Where should she find them?

Were these people her new allies? She concentrated on each figure and scanned their faces. There must have been a hundred figures on the page. They appeared and disappeared every time she refocused. Where were all these souls?

She opened her phone and saw James had written a long, passionate letter about her family and their plans. Liv wrote to James.

Dear James, I have the glimmerings of a plan of my own forming in my consciousness. I'll put it in motion and let you know as soon as I get some final results. Love Liv

She checked her other emails and sent curt replies and instructions to the pertinent ones. A realtor and a lawyer would be her new Lake House team. That pot could simmer a while longer while she worked out the details of her plan for Nigbor.

Liv felt calm as she stored her phone in her coat and touched the book again for luck. She never would have admitted to luck before this trip but now it was a treasured ally in her life. She would need its full cooperation for this crazy plan to work.

Liv would let her problem bubble in her consciousness for a while. Not too long, in case Nigbor made a move, but she knew the answer was within her somewhere. Liv stored the book in her jacket.

A knock at the door startled her. The metal door of the gym opened a moment later, Jin and Jane came in. They looked like Santa and Mrs. Claus with their red noses and pink cheeks. They wore thick, cable knit sweaters and dark pants with their hiking boots. Little knit hats perched on their white hair.

"How are you, my dear?" Asked Jane.

"Fine. What are you two doing out here?" Liv asked.

"Why, we thought you might like to celebrate Yule with us! No one should celebrate alone. We're going into town. You should come with us," said Jin. They came over and each of them took one of her elbows and walked her out into the night.

The nearest town was Grindavik. Liv could see the lights of the city as they left the gymnasium. Most of the people of the city were probably back after evacuating for the eruption, plus it was Christmas Eve. People wanted to be home for the holidays, except her stupid family.

It didn't matter if her family tried to rule her incompetent or took over the Lake House. If the plan here bore fruit, the situation at home was trivial and would resolve on its own.

The more she considered it, the more the picture showed to her in the book made sense. Liv just had to make it happen. Liv's eyes adjusted to the darkness. Huge flakes floated past her, forming large clumps that stuck everywhere.

Liv reveled in the cold clear air. She saw the large footprints and drag marks where the Yule Troll Queen and her Lads had passed. The snow was attempting to erase any evidence, like they were never there but Liv knew they had been there. She saw where the Yule cat sat in the snow and the light marks of its paws. The trio of Jin, Jane and Liv followed their path.

As they neared the town, the bright Yule lights bounced off the snowflakes and gave a kaleidoscope effect. When Liv got to the town square, she looked around for a sign she was on the right track, but saw nothing. Liv connected to the Magic, filled herself with it until her skin glowed. She accessed the plasma above the snow, pulling it down to her and then spreading it out around the square and to the homes. Now that Liv well and truly believed in Magic, nothing could stand in her way.

The homes lit up and people streamed out to join her. They all had long white candles. As they joined the circle, they lit the tapers.

All ages, bundled up, and Liv felt their commitment to the Elves and to Magic as if there was a motor running deep within her, revving faster and faster.

The snow stopped and the skies cleared. A brilliant aurora danced overhead and someone handed Liv a taper and lit it for her. A boy with a soaring soprano voice started singing. At first, Liv didn't recognize the tune because it was in Icelandic, but then, it came to her. The song appeared in her brain, fully formed and translated. This one was about the vicious Yule Cat. After encountering it in person, Liv found fresh meaning in the words that marched through her. The next song was about Yule night and the magic it brought to the land.

The singing brought more people from their homes, tapers were lit and the town square filled. The aurora grew brighter and stretched down to touch the lit candles. It filled Liv's body with energy and the hand that held her taper appeared to be alabaster white with crystals glittering along her arm's length.

Nigbor burst into the dark sky to the side of the gathering. He sputtered, with sparks flying from all sides of his portal before it dissolved. He hovered in the air above the candles.

"Haven't you learned anything? I help you out and you are ready to stab me in the back at the first opportunity. If you'd join me, we could stop all this foolishness."

"I appreciate the help," said Liv, "But you knew it couldn't end in the Yule Troll Queen's cave. It would have put our finale on hold for years until I could find my way out. Every Yule, I would get a chance to escape when the portal opened. You're far too impatient to wait so long."

"Have it your way. You can't beat me. You aren't strong enough."

Liv smiled and gestured around her. "This time I have help." The circle had grown. The candles held back the night.

Nigbor spread his arms like they were wings and the Esbats came hissing out of the black cloud around him. They floated in a loose circle, their faces contorted in rage.

They hardly looked human anymore, Liv thought, burned skin with glowing red eyes, hair dry and broken and clothing, dark and cracked in spots. Their mouths were open as if screaming but no sound was heard other than the hissing from the portal. Was it her imagination, or were their teeth sharp? Their hands were reaching out, claw-like. Liv had no intention of letting them touch her. They had gone back to Nigbor, lured by the promise of magic.

Liv spread her arms wide and gathered the Magic from the atmosphere. The aurora sparkled and vibrated as Liv activated its power.

Nigbor pulled the Esbats into his hands and wove them into a cage of darkness around Liv. His slim fingers moved in an intricate ballet as the cage formed. Bony fingers from the Esbats reached out from the walls of the cage and their faces looked out in agony where they had been incorporated into the bars of the cage.

The flickering candles twinkled at her through the openings in the web, although the openings were quickly being covered. Liv could barely see the people in the square anymore, but she knew they were still there singing. Liv pulled the plasma from them and tried to break the cage. It burned her hands where she touched it so she tried kicking the walls. The cage barely moved. Liv tried to pull the Light to her but it was more and more difficult.

The black cage began to constrict. When it touched her arms, Liv's heart beat an irregular tattoo and sweat gathered on her brow. The bars were stronger than steel but warm, like blood. They stuck to her and she shivered. Then, they started to burn her. She struggled against the darkness and the tendons in her arms stood out with her effort. Inch by tortuous inch, she forced the darkness back until she had room to think in the cage. But she could not banish the cage. She settled herself and cleared her mind. How to get out of this trap?

The people of the village sang and Liv sang with them, even as the cage renewed its effort to squeeze her and she couldn't hear them anymore. These people believed in magic. Liv reached out and instead of taking their Light, she connected with their belief. The faces of the witches disappeared from the bars first and then the fingers. Liv was able to batter her way out of the cage as it became more brittle.

Liv stepped out of the shattered cage and Nigbor growled. He wrapped himself in his cloak and looked more like a demon and less like a handsome man. His facade slipped off like silk on glass. People in the crowd gasped and some ran for their homes.

The people with children hustled their children home and Liv couldn't blame them one bit. The ones who stayed sang louder to make up for the ones who had left. Pieces of the cage grabbed at her legs and Liv braced herself against the pull. She noticed the people who had gone home turned on every light in their home. She saw them standing in the front windows singing. Strength surged through her but she needed more to fight Nigbor.

And a plan. Liv also needed a plan. She concentrated on what she remembered from the book. What she needed was more bodies, more power, but from where?

The amulet began to burn in her chest. Nigbor opened his arms like dark wings. Liv could feel him taking in energy. Whatever he was planning, was not for her benefit.

"Give it up, Liv. I'm going to suck the magic from this world and destroy the Elves in one final purge and you're not strong enough to stop me." He flexed and small red sparks jumped in the atmosphere. Nigbor was clearly enjoying this too much.

No, he was right that she wasn't strong enough by herself but was she really by herself? Liv gazed at the people around her in the square. They were singing forcefully and smiling. It made Liv smile. Her people. Her tribe. Every one of them believed in magic. Every one of them was counting on her to lead them. She saw the van driver, Galen, and the elderly couple, Jin and Jane, and the innkeeper and his daughter. Other faces flashed past and she didn't have names for them all.

Liv opened herself to them, became the center of their wheel. If they wanted magic and Elves in their world, they had to fight along with her. The miasma of magic swirled around her, and Liv opened a portal behind the rows of houses, out of Nigbor's line of sight.

Chapter Thirty Three

Light poured out of it and she saw Elves standing and watching. Her eyes narrowed and she beckoned with her fingers.

"Your world too. Help me fight for it." She said.

The Elves, pale and slender, hesitated but finally one breached the threshold and others followed. They entered the world with quick light steps and moved softly like a breeze through the trees to stand behind the humans. The humans saw them bolster their ranks and Liv felt power surge through her. Her chest amulet burned. Her bracelet whirled. Anthor's talisman sizzled as power flowed through it.

Nigbor clenched his fists and struggled against her, his face a mask of rage. His power was overwhelming and seemed to have no end and no source. She held onto her coalition of humans and Elves, stretched out, ready to break.

Nigbor hammered her and Liv bent under the assault. Her connection with the Elves and humans, shredded like torn spider silk.

Her last act, before she was completely overwhelmed, was to open a new portal and call out for help. At first, there was no reply, but then a huge, dark figure with golden eyes and a twitching tail slid through. The Yule Cat was followed by the Yule Troll Queen and her seven sons. The ground shook under their steps and both humans and Elves cowered. Nigbor faltered as the Troll Queen's eyes found him. The Yule Cat trotted to him through crowds that melted away before him and Nigbor turned to face it.

His attack on Liv ended as he gathered himself for the new threat. Liv gasped a breath and strengthened her circle of Elves and humans.

The cat smacked Nigbor once and then twice, faster than the eye could follow. Nigbor wobbled and Liv saw his power fluctuate. Liv sent out her idea and the Troll Queen moved forward. Her seamed face didn't show any recognition to Liv, but she opened her burlap bag. Would her bag hold Nigbor?

The Yule Cat continued his assault on Nigbor, knocking him from side to side. Nigbor's power had no effect on the feline. The Cat grabbed Nigbor in its mouth and shook him. His magic crumbled around him and Gryla scooped Nigbor into the rough bag. Gryla tied the bag with a dirty ribbon of leather and slung it over her shoulder. A cheer went up and Gryla, the Troll Queen, seemed surprised.

Comet Hyakutake, named for the amateur astronomer who found it in 1996 was rocketing out of its perihelion and back towards the sun. The comet's tail consisted of gas and dust that trailed hundreds of millions of kilometers behind. It had a plasma tail of ionized gas and a dust trail of small solid particles. It sparkled in the Yule sky.

Liv gathered her coalition of the Trolls, Elves and humans to help her launch Nigbor and the sack to the comet. Its bluish green appearance was notable as was its period of 70,000 years.

Magic opened for Liv and she affixed the bag into the ionized stream behind the comet and watched as Nigbor began his next cycle around the sun. She hoped the ionization would keep Nigbor put for a while. Liv thought she heard a scream of rage, but it could have been the noise of the comet crackling as it went past the sun.

Liv released the powers that had been loaned to her to secure Nigbor on the comet. She was unsure when the gourds of home-brewed liquor appeared, only that they seemed to be in everyone's hands. And then the dancing began under the flickering aurora.

She danced with Elves and humans and even took a turn with one of Gryla's sons. The Elves took their leave as the sky lightened. Gryla, the Troll Queen, the Yule Cat and Gryla's sons faded back through the thick foliage and disappeared into their portal. As dawn touched the horizon, the dancing and drinking finished. It was Christmas morning and people drifted back to their homes.

"I'll take you to the airport," Galen, the van driver yelled at Liv out the window. She got in the van and a million questions surfaced. "Not to worry. Everything is taken care of." He grinned at her. Liv started when Mr. and Mrs. Volk got on and took their customary seats. Galen didn't kick them off, so Liv trusted everything would work out.

Liv dozed in the seat while the driver sped through the darkness. He drove her past the main entrance to the airport and turned into a gated entry at the far end of the concourse. The gate slid back after the guard identified the driver and they drove through. Liv noticed the gate closed after them.

He pulled up to a private hangar and parked. Liv got out, followed by the Volks. They waited while a plane was towed out of the hangar.

"See? No problem with customs or your sword or book," Galen said.

"You're my pilot too? This is really a full service outfit." She turned to the Volks, "And you guys!"

"We're part of your team," said Jane, getting on the plane.

"There's coffee and sandwiches on board, even a bunk if you want to sleep," said Jin as Liv boarded.

Liv got on the plane and found they were the only passengers. The plane was luxurious with loungers and dim lighting. She ate a sandwich, drank some coffee and relaxed. The plane started moving. The Volks settled into two facing seats in the back. Liv got up and banged on the cabin door.

It opened and she was relieved there were two crewmen. Always a wise thing.

"Where are we going?" She asked.

"Greenland first for gas. Then, I don't know. I haven't received instructions yet."

"I'm sure it will all work out," said Liv.

"Always does," he answered.

Liv pulled out her phone and started through her emails.

Back home, the siblings had been allowed to pick up whatever photos and things they wanted from the Lake House, while the lawyer supervised. The cleaners had been to the Lake House, the stager had done her magic and baked cookies to make it smell nice or whatever they did. The Lake House had sold for over the asking price and the money was in her account.

The next email was from her sister in law. It was signed by her brother but it was in all capital letters so she knew the true author was her sister in law. The rant went on and hit the highs and lows of Liv's underhandedness. Somehow, she had the impression that Liv had to ask her permission to sell the Lake House, although they had been happy enough to dump it on her with all the repairs it needed. After paying off all the debtors, Liv still had an excellent balance, none of which any of her siblings would ever see.

She was polite but referred them to her lawyer for any issues they had. Liv was through being a people pleaser.

Her letter of resignation from her job elicited a heartfelt plea and a promise of a salary increase to return but Liv politely declined.

She had a higher calling now. Liv wasn't sure where her next destination was after Greenland or who she was meant to help, but she knew she wasn't going back to the Lake House or her job. New adventures awaited.

Next, she opened James' email.

Dear Liv,

You've stirred up a hornet's nest. It's hard for me to hide my smile, little sis. The sister in laws are plotting but I think you've outsmarted them. Are you coming back at all? Sounds like Iceland changed you. What will you do now?

Dear James,

I think Iceland did change me but in a positive way. Probably not coming back for now. I think I'll travel. I'll keep you updated. Love Liv

Liv had more coffee and dozed for a while. She woke up when they were landing in Greenland. As the co pilot got out to refuel them, the pilot came back and grabbed a sandwich.

"Looks like we're headed for Africa after this. Ever been?" Asked Galen.

"No. Any idea what's going on there?"

"Some bad witch doctor is enslaving his people to work in a cobalt mine."

"But I'm the Elf Warrior, not the Witch doctor fixer."

"He came out of a portal. We don't know a lot about him. I'll send you what we have to your email."

"Elf Warrior, at your service."

"Elf Warrior may be too specific a term for your new job description," Galen said. "Don't get me wrong, it fit your first mission. A more accurate name would probably be Balancer. When things are out of balance, you correct the balance for the universe."

"Balancer is actually better than Elf Warrior," Liv said. "Am I an Elf, though?"

Gaven shrugged. "Part Elf, part human, part celestial being, like Anthor. Your type balances the forces in the realms. What do you say? You in?"

Liv stared out the window. It looked cold and bleak. The airport was just a strip of pavement cleared of snow between mountains. Sharp outcroppings of rock dotted the landscape. Did she want to pop around the world and into the different realms, however many there were, and be a Balancer?

Or would she rather go back to her job in a closet with no window and a family who were wildly unsupportive?

It wasn't even close. Liv poured herself another cup of the excellent coffee.

Lime Jello with Horseradish
Ingredients
1 (6 oz.) pack lime gelatin
1 tsp salt
2 cups water
2 cups cold water
1 1/2 cups cucumbers, peeled and diced
3 tablespoons horseradish (or more if you want it spicier)
1/2 teaspoon grated onion
2 tablespoons vinegar
1 1/2 cups diced or crushed drained canned pineapple (you cannot use fresh pineapple with gelatins. The bromelain enzyme in fresh pineapple will keep the gelatin from bonding.)
Method

In a bowl, dissolve lime jello and salt in 2 cups of hot water (don't use boiling water, just regular hot water). Add 2 cups cold water. Chill until slightly thickened - the consistency of egg whites, about 30 minutes.

In a separate bowl mix cucumber, horseradish, grated onion, and vinegar. Fold pineapple and cucumber mixture into jello. Pour into a jello mold and chill for several hours (about 6) until gelatin sets.

To remove jello from its mold, fill up a basin half-way with hot water. Lower the jello mold into the hot water, metal side down, until the water comes up almost to the edge of the mold. Keep it there 5 seconds and remove. Place a plate on top of the jello mold and turn upside down. The jello salad should just slide out.

(Lest you think this is a joke LH)

Don't miss out!

Visit the website below and you can sign up to receive emails whenever Dixie Jo Jarchow publishes a new book. There's no charge and no obligation.

https://books2read.com/r/B-A-PEUS-SFGQD

BOOKS 2 READ

Connecting independent readers to independent writers.

Also by Dixie Jo Jarchow

The Hunt for Mel's Gold
Hades' Redemption
Huntress Moon
The Gingerbread Man
Walking In the Graveyard
Crossroads Magic

Watch for more at dixiejojarchow.com.

About the Author

Dixie Jo Jarchow writes in Black Wolf, WI with her husband and her two fearsome hounds.

Read more at www.dixiejojarchow.com.